THE
# RUINING

# THE
# RUINING

## ANNA COLLOMORE

Palmer Public Library   DISCARD
655 S. Valley Way
Palmer, AK  99645

razOr
bill

An Imprint of Penguin Group (USA) Inc.

The Ruining

RAZORBILL

Published by the Penguin Group
Penguin Young Readers Group
345 Hudson Street, New York, New York 10014, U.S.A.
Penguin Group (USA) Inc., 375 Hudson Street, New York, New York 10014, U.S.A.
Penguin Group (Canada), 90 Eglinton Avenue East, Suite 700, Toronto,
Ontario, Canada M4P 2Y3 (a division of Pearson Penguin Canada Inc.)
Penguin Books Ltd, 80 Strand, London WC2R 0RL, England
Penguin Ireland, 25 St Stephen's Green, Dublin 2, Ireland
(a division of Penguin Books Ltd)
Penguin Group (Australia), 250 Camberwell Road, Camberwell,
Victoria 3124, Australia (a division of Pearson Australia Group Pty Ltd)
Penguin Books India Pvt Ltd, 11 Community Centre, Panchsheel Park,
New Delhi – 110 017, India
Penguin Group (NZ), 67 Apollo Drive, Rosedale, Auckland 0632, New Zealand
(a division of Pearson New Zealand Ltd)
Penguin Books (South Africa) (Pty) Ltd, 24 Sturdee Avenue, Rosebank,
Johannesburg 2196, South Africa

Penguin Books Ltd, Registered Offices: 80 Strand, London WC2R 0RL, England

10 9 8 7 6 5 4 3 2 1

Copyright © 2013 Anna Collomore

ISBN 978-1-59514-470-6

Library of Congress Cataloging-in-Publication Data is available

Printed in the United States of America

All rights reserved. No part of this book may be reproduced, scanned, or distributed in any printed or electronic form without permission. Please do not participate in or encourage piracy of copyrighted materials in violation of the author's rights. Purchase only authorized editions.

The publisher does not have any control over and does not assume any responsibility for author or third-party websites or their content.

For the Happy Bunch of Cousins:
beautiful, brilliant, fearless women
who are a little bit crazy and a
lot lovable.

# CHAPTER ONE

**I'D NEVER BEEN TO CALIFORNIA.** For the first eighteen years of my life, it was some other girl who watched the sun rise over the hilltops of San Francisco, dipped her toes in the Pacific Ocean, and ate raspberry frosted cupcakes from Cups and Cakes on a pier at Fisherman's Wharf. It was always some other girl, and I'd grown used to that. Then one day it was me. I knew from the photos the Cohens sent (in e-mails and letters, every other day for a whole month before I arrived) that San Francisco would be hilly; that my new neighborhood would overlook a vast expanse of water with a concrete playground rising up beyond; that the sun would be perpetually brilliant. But I didn't feel it, and so I was unprepared for its essence: the thing that seeps into your bones only after you've been inside a place and felt it surround you. I'd imagined all these things, but nothing can ever prepare you for a place—the way it comes alive—except being there.

The day I got my letter from San Francisco State University, my stepfather had been sitting on the sofa we'd picked up at the Salvation Army a year before. He was smoking inside the house, even though my mother constantly begged him not to. The sofa itself had been beat up already, but within a month of purchase it was sunken in at the middle and stained with Dean's sweat residue. The tips of Dean's fingers were always dark from nicotine, and I was glad I hadn't bothered showing him the letter—hadn't let him hold it in his grimy palms. I hadn't wanted his filth to ruin it. Dean's front teeth had brown spots on them. It made me sick.

The smoke had begun to feel oppressive, and Dean's focus had already turned back to the TV. I crossed the short expanse from the living room to the kitchen to the tiny patch of faded green-and-yellow linoleum that marked our foyer. I let the screen door settle in place behind me as the cheap, rusted outer door slammed hard against the side of our dilapidated home. I hated it there.

It was gray outside, and if I hadn't spent my entire life in Detroit, I'd have assumed all of Dean's cigarettes had leaked their charred air out the window and settled onto the surfaces of the city. But Detroit was nearly always like that: everything was different shades of gray no matter where you looked. The grass, the pavement, the buildings—but also the animals and the people. Like if you looked closer, the word *hopeless* would be scrawled all over everything, just under all the tattooed and graffitied exteriors.

California, though, was the opposite of Detroit. California was golden to Detroit's gray. I'd always known I needed to be there, ever since I saw it in *Little Miss Sunshine* when I was in middle school. And when I'd found the Cohens' ad on the SFSU virtual billboard—"New to Marin County/Fam of 4 Needs Nanny"—I knew I had to be there. We could be new together, the Cohens and me. Dean and my mother didn't know anything about the Cohens, of course. It was my secret—my ticket to a new life—and I needed it to stay that way.

I needed a clean break from my reality.

*First day in our new home—soon to be yours, too!* Someone—probably Libby Cohen—had written it on the back of one of the pictures in a delicate script. The photo itself showed all the Cohens smiling happily in front of an enormous yellow home with white trim and two balconies. Walker Cohen had one arm wrapped around his wife's waist, and baby Jackson nestled in the crook of his other arm. Walker was tanned and handsome, no older than thirty-five. Libby was gorgeous: radiant, slim, and young-looking. She wore a solid green shift dress and looked incredibly put together, her blonde hair swept up in a loose bun off the nape of her neck and a tasteful gold necklace circling her throat. She was utterly different from the women in Detroit. She was one of the most beautiful women I'd ever seen.

Zoe, the three-year-old, stood off to the side, a little gap separating her from Libby. It looked like she'd been caught off guard when the photo was taken; as a result, part of her arm was blurred where she'd been reaching toward her mother, maybe to hold her hand. Her body was angled to the side, but even in profile I could tell she was adorable. She had rich, chocolate-colored hair the same hue as her father's, and it fell down her back in ringlets that maybe she wouldn't grow out of, if they were still there at three. She was wearing a little white dress with a bib top and polka dots. Her eyes were wide and her expression grave. I remember wondering briefly why they hadn't taken another shot, one with Zoe looking at the camera, but that thought was quickly eclipsed by my excitement. Their life—it looked perfect. It was the kind of life I'd always wanted, and the knowledge that I was about to become a part of it still felt too much like a miracle.

That photo was the one I slipped into the back pocket of my cutoffs the day I left Detroit. It had gotten more than a little wrinkly because my palms were sweating from nerves, and I kept taking it out to look at it again and again while I was packing up all my last-minute stuff.

My room in Dean's house was barely big enough to hold my twin bed and a dresser. I couldn't even close the door because the dresser stuck out halfway into the threshold, so I was perpetually covering myself up, talking in a hushed voice on the phone, plugging my ears with cotton when I got sick of hearing Dean's gravelly, hacking laughter and my mom's half-dead voice. I'd never had any privacy, and as a result I'd developed those complexes and maybe some others I wasn't even aware of. I had to make a point of reminding myself not to act mousy when I wasn't at home.

I didn't expect my mom to remember I was going, really, so it was a surprise when she dragged herself out of bed that day and leaned in my doorway an hour before I was supposed to meet the cab, her thin frame looking like maybe it couldn't stay upright for long. I couldn't help stiffening. Lately it had become my natural response around her.

"Hey, sweetheart," she said. Her voice was thick and congested, and her red-rimmed eyes were only half open.

"Hey, Mama."

"Weren't you gonna give me a proper goodbye?"

My mother's eyes were already filling with tears, but her face was strangely inert. We all knew I wanted to get out. But I hadn't confronted the reality of it or let myself feel guilty until then. I was, in a sense, abandoning her to this freak she'd decided to link her life with. I wrapped my arms around her small frame and held her close.

"I love you, Mama," I whispered, feeling the brittle ribs of her back under my fingertips. "I really, really love you." She didn't say anything at first, just let me embrace her while she stood limply folded in my arms. Then she said something I couldn't make out, so I pulled back and leaned my ear toward her lips.

"Don't you worry," she was saying, repeating it over and over in her thin, wren-like voice. "Don't you worry about her."

"Who, Mama? Who are you talking about?"

"She's okay now, you hear? God's taking care of her and

it's time you let her go. So don't you worry no more out in California, okay, baby?" I felt the tears sliding down my cheeks, their damp marking my mother's thin cotton shirtdress. She was talking about Lissa. I buried my face in the space between her neck and shoulder, so I wouldn't have to see Dean sneering at us. My mother had never said anything before to absolve me of my sister's death.

"But what about you?" It was something that had been in the back of my mind since the day I'd vowed to leave. She hadn't exactly been the best mother, but she'd never done me any harm. And now both of her girls would be gone.

"I already had my chance," she whispered close to my ear, so Dean couldn't hear. "This is yours. Get out of here and don't come back."

She pulled away from me, straightening up and squaring her shoulders, looking more resolute than I'd seen her in years. "Don't come back, you hear?" she said loudly, provoking more sneers from Dean. Then she shuffled across the dingy living room in her nightgown, heading back toward her bedroom, the physical manifestation of her own dead-end future.

"I won't," I whispered quietly, unsure of whether she could hear me or not.

My mother, I think, was pretty once. Or at least she was in the one picture I have of her from when we were little. It was a day on the lake, and her long hair was wild and windswept, grazing the side of her face lightly as she looked out at me and Lissa playing in the water. She'd looked contented then. But now the things that once made her pretty were gone: her broad smile, the light in her eyes, all signs of health and vitality. It must be impossible to stay pretty, though, after you watch one of your babies die.

I couldn't take it anymore; it was as if the things I'd grown used to living with were magnified all of a sudden: Dean's sour, cigarette-tinged odor; the perpetual ticking of the broken grandfather clock in the corner, a monstrosity that took up way too much room in our cramped quarters; the ring of congealed grease that lined the stove no matter how frequently I scrubbed. I threw the rest of my things in my duffel in five minutes flat, swept my long hair up in a ponytail, and was out the door. I waited on the curb until my cab showed up twenty minutes later. And on the plane, as I stared out the window watching the city of Detroit recede, I wasn't sure if I'd see my mother again. The reality of my life in Detroit, a reality I'd spent almost every day wishing to escape from, was gone. Disappeared, like I'd never been a part of it at all. And in order to leave it in the past, I couldn't let myself worry about leaving my mother behind. She'd made her own decisions, and for years I'd had to live within a situation I'd had no choice in creating. Now, I was heading toward a new family. In California, I would reinvent myself. I would finally have the life I deserved.

# CHAPTER TWO

"ANNIE!"

Libby rushed toward me as I exited the US Airways terminal, somehow looking graceful despite her towering, five-inch heels. She was even more gorgeous than in the pictures, her blonde hair so shiny it practically sparkled, her figure curvy yet somehow tinier in the waist than I'd ever been, even in my gangly preteen years. She wore green, strappy snakeskin stilettos with a simple white T-shirt tucked into a black chiffon A-line skirt. Enormous white-rimmed sunglasses took up half her face. The other half was radiant: dewy skin and lips the perfect shade of pink. Her toned arms suggested hours spent at the gym, or maybe she just hit the genetics jackpot. And she looked youthful, too—it was almost impossible to believe she had two children, one of them already three years old.

"Hi, Mrs. Cohen." I offered my hand but she ignored it altogether, leaning in to give me a kiss on the cheek.

"It's Libby, darling. God, doesn't 'Mrs. Cohen' make me seem *old!* Just call me Libby, okay? You are just exactly the same as your pictures," she told me in her oddly lofty language, without pausing for breath. "I'd know you anywhere. Gorgeous, darling. You're just lovely. Come on now, the car's waiting out past baggage, I *told* Walker to pay for short-term parking but he does this ridiculous thing where he circles around and around and it's just insanity, so embarrassing, but he's set in his ways. You know how men can be," she said with a wink. "Oh, but your bags! Of course! What number is the claim?"

"This is everything," I said, nodding toward the green duffle I'd taken as my carry-on. Libby pushed her glasses down slightly on the bridge of her nose and peered at it strangely.

"You can't be serious. You're living with us an entire year and this is all you brought?"

"Light packer, I guess." I could feel the heat traveling from my cheeks to my ears and forehead; the truth was, this was pretty much everything I owned. I had the sudden, crazed thought that maybe all this was too good to be true. Maybe once the Cohens realized what I came from, they wouldn't let me within a mile of their perfect lives.

"The best way to be," Libby declared. "The smartest lady doesn't carry any baggage, I always say. She knows how to leave it in the past. Now come on," she called out, already speeding ahead of me toward the passenger pick-up. "We wouldn't want Walker to have to put in an extra lap."

A black Range Rover was just pulling up to the curb as the sliding doors opened before us. The horn tooted twice short and once long, and for a second I thought I saw a look of irritation cross Libby's face before she broke into a wide smile. Walker hopped out of the driver's seat and made his way around the back of the car, looking sheepish. He had on a checked button-down with jeans and flip-flops, but he pulled the look off almost as if he'd stepped out of a Levi's ad. Tanned, muscular, athletic-looking—it was hard to tell which half of the Cohen duo was more attractive.

"Don't yell at me about the horn," he began. "It was all Zoe. Little lady doesn't know when to stop. She climbed out of the car seat herself. Pretty smart though, you gotta admit."

"Pretty *annoying*," Libby responded lightly. "Not to mention dangerous. We've got to kid-proof her kiddy-proof seat a little more, I guess."

"Sorry, babe." Walker leaned in toward Libby and gave her a passionate kiss, as though they'd been separated for days and not a mere twenty minutes.

"Walker, this is Annie," Libby told him, breaking free of his embrace. "Grab her bag, will you?"

"Yes, ma'am," he replied, winking in my direction. I got the feeling Walker had grown up in the South; from his mannerisms to his rugged appearance, Texas or even Kentucky would have made sense. He looked like one of those guys who'd never been worried in his life—who'd negotiated every age with the kind of playful confidence that eluded me. Libby hopped into the front passenger seat as Walker reached for my duffle. Despite myself,

I felt a little nervous and awkward. It was the way I always got around attractive guys. *Get yourself together, Annie,* I told myself. *You're working for the guy.* Besides, he was probably at least fifteen years older than me. The fact that he looked kind of like a younger Hugh Jackman was irrelevant.

"This is it?" Walker asked of my bag. His admiring look implied that maybe Libby wasn't as light a packer as she'd claimed to be.

"Yeah, um . . ."

"Let's go, Walk," shouted Libby through the window. "Zoe's getting cranky."

"So says the queen." Walker sighed in mock exasperation. "Between you and me, Annie," he said as he tossed my duffel in the back seat, "I could not be happier that you're here." He turned his eyes skyward. "I just want my wife back," he proclaimed dramatically.

"Very funny," came Libby's voice from the front. "We're holding up the line, Walk!"

"Sally forth, then," he said in a faux British accent, making me laugh. His good-natured personality was actually a little overwhelming, like a puppy's. I could see why Libby wouldn't think he was quite as hilarious after a few years of this. "Your chariot, madam?" Walker stepped aside and opened the door wider for me to climb in.

And there, awaiting me inside a vehicle that seemed cavernous compared to the other cars I'd ridden in, waited the sweetest little angel I'd ever seen. She was buckled into her car seat, sucking on a *Dora* sippy cup, peering at me from under long, upswept lashes. Her chestnut-colored waves stuck a little to her car seat from static, and her toddler feet were encased in little lacy socks and Mary Janes. My heart expanded a little just looking at her, and for a second I forgot about Libby's perfection and Walker's exhausting buoyancy.

"You must be Zoe," I told her, extending my hand. "I'm Annie. I've been so excited to meet you."

"My mom and dad alweady told me your name," she said with this weirdly precise elocution, a kind of adorable thing coming from the mouth of a three-year-old.

"That wasn't very polite, Zoe," said Libby. "Please apologize to Annie."

"Go easy on her, babe," said Walker. "She's only three."

"It's okay, really," I started.

"No, Annie, Zoe really needs to learn better manners," Libby interrupted. "Actually, it's something I hope you'll help us work on. Walker, you know how important it is for Zoe to be more polite. Yet she's still doing things like what she did a moment ago with the horn."

"Daddy told me I could honk the hown," protested Zoe, popping her sippy cup out of her mouth momentarily.

"Traitor," said Walker, making me laugh.

"Daddy did not tell you to force your entire body weight onto the horn until it qualified as noise pollution," Libby responded. I glanced toward Walker but he'd already zoned out, leaning forward to adjust the radio dial. Libby looked pointedly at Zoe.

"Apologize to Annie," she said again.

"I'm sowwy, Annie," Zoe said in a serious voice, looking worried. "It's nice to meet you." Her excessive formality blended with her tiny, high-pitched voice and that bit of a lisp was the sweetest thing I'd ever heard.

"Nice to meet you, too," I told her. "Shake?" Zoe extended her hand and I took it in mine, noticing Libby watching us through the rearview mirror. Zoe's hand was warm, sticky, and small. In it—and in her eyes, which evaluated me carefully as I smiled at her—was something like trust. I felt a sudden, desperate urge to please Libby, to do everything right, to be the most exemplary nanny the Cohen family had ever had. To make this sweet little girl love me as much as I knew I would love her.

"Where's the baby?" I wondered aloud, as Zoe popped the sippy cup back in her mouth, humming around it.

"Jackson's at the house," Libby said. "He was napping when we left, and I didn't want to disturb him, so I left him in his pack-n-play."

"Alone?" The word slipped out before I could stop myself. I'd let my guard down, transfixed by the cityscape that slipped past my window in a blur. But leaving a baby alone for even a couple of minutes felt insanely irresponsible. Bad things happened to kids when you didn't watch them. Bad things you couldn't ever take back. I felt a shudder worm its way from the base of my spine to my neck.

"Of course not," Libby responded in an even tone, flipping down the vanity mirror to check her lipstick. She removed her sunglasses and applied another coat of mascara to her long lashes, and it was only then that I saw just how young she looked. "He's with the baby nurse. Today's her last day. Good thinking, though," she said, flashing me a broad smile. "That's why we need you so badly. There's no way Walk and I could manage both the kids ourselves. Zoe, quiet, please." Zoe had removed the sippy cup from her mouth and her humming had, as a result, gotten a little louder.

"What are you singing, Zo? What's the pretty song?" It sounded familiar, but I couldn't place it. Zoe ignored me and kept on singing, kicking the back of her mother's seat in rhythm. We idled at a light, and I watched as a man wearing a tie-dyed shirt passed us on a bicycle, the basket up front holding a small dog. Maybe I'd get a bike, eventually. It would be such a fun way to explore the city.

"Zoe," Walker warned, looking concernedly at Libby. "Stop kicking Mommy's seat, okay?" He turned the volume on the radio up even louder, his fingers drumming a nervous—no, *energetic*—beat on the steering wheel.

"CWADLE AND ALL!" shouted Zoe grandly, making me jump. I glanced her way and there she sat, smiling at me, arms outstretched. Apparently that had been the finale to what I now recognized as "Rockabye Baby." It didn't seem like this was the first time she'd graced her parents with a performance. I heard Libby sigh from the front.

"Sorry, Annie. Zoe's had this little tune in her head for months, and we're getting kind of sick of it, but that's kids for you. It's giving her mom a headache, though," Walker said pointedly from the front. Sure enough, Libby had slid her sunglasses back on and was resting her head against the windowpane.

But I was barely listening, because what towered in front of me was so much more majestic than in the pictures they'd sent me.

The house was enormous. It was more like an estate or a castle. It was like something I'd seen in a BBC *Masterpiece Theatre* version of *Pride and Prejudice*, all angles and stories and covered in landscaping so it had the illusion of extending on forever. Then we pulled into a massive four-car garage, and Walker killed the engine.

"I'll get the kids and bring Annie's things in. Libs, why don't you give her the tour?"

"Come on," Libby said, leading me out of the garage. "We'll start with the back. Your first impression needs to be the best one."

It was easy to see that the house was positioned over a hill, but I hadn't been able to see beyond the winding road that led higher and higher up the slope, nor had I been paying much attention to the scenery. So when Libby led me along a small brick path to the left of the garage, the last thing I expected to see was water spreading out in all directions.

We were standing on a terrace that overlooked San Francisco Bay. Herons circled the coast in search of their next meal. The mid-afternoon sun was hitting the ripples in the water just right, making them look like a million tiny gems. The blue of the water had a crystalline quality, so pure and vivid that it merged with the blue of the sky. It was extraordinary.

"Welcome to Belvedere Island, Annie," said Libby in a reverent tone. "The most beautiful place on earth."

# CHAPTER THREE

**ZOE NESTLED DEEPER** into the crook of my arm. I was flipping through my course catalog—orientation was in three days and I wanted to be prepared—while distractedly reading aloud from Zoe's book of Aesop's fables. She was saying some of the lines along with me, obviously enjoying herself every time she beat me to the end of a sentence.

"Why don't you tell *me* the story if you know it so well?" I asked, poking her in the ribs. She giggled and shrieked a little, burrowing under the afghan in the extravagant second-floor "family" room, aka Zoe's personal sitting room, because no one really used the second floor but her, and now me. My mind began to wander as Zoe's little voice danced patterns around the room. It had been a whirlwind twenty-four hours, and I felt caught in a haze of something that felt strangely close to happiness. I'd felt this way only once before: when a friend in middle school invited me to spend the Christmas holiday with her family. Everything was so perfect at her house—such a wonderful chaos—that I'd been content to just curl up and watch it all unfold in front of me. The stacks of gifts, the laughter, the shimmering white lights on the windows, the candy ornaments hanging from a real holly tree. It was hard to explain; even though I wasn't really a part of it, I was happy just to be a spectator, to bathe in the warmth that emanated from it as though its happy energy could make me happy too, if I absorbed it all up inside me. Then, of course, I'd had to go home to Dean and my mother and Lissa, whom I'd felt guilty for leaving in the first place.

But now, Zoe's voice was swirling around me as I nestled deeper into the green-and-blue pattern of the antique loveseat in her sitting room, and I had something more: the knowledge that this time, I didn't have to leave. The catalog in my lap was just proof of it—now I was looking forward, watching the minutes spread out in front of me instead of clinging to them desperately as I felt them slip away. It was wonderful to have a future that was wide open. The funny thing was, it was hard to feel comfortable inside this newfound happiness. I sat there with Zoe, with the distinct feeling that I didn't deserve this— miracles didn't happen to people like me, especially after what happened with Lissa. I had this weird, disconcerting feeling of waiting for the other shoe to drop. *How could I make it last? How could I make myself believe I deserved my new chance?* The only thing to do, I decided, was to work myself to death, being the best nanny I could be. I would make everyone else believe I deserved it, until *I* believed I deserved it. That was the plan.

The sitting room was perfect. The whole house was; there was more to look at and take in than I possibly could on my first day, and it occurred to me that maybe I'd be discovering things—ivory ashtrays and blown-glass lamps and first-edition Mark Twains—for months before I knew the place in and out. I'd never seen anything like it, except in magazines and movies. It was funny how the discordance of it somehow worked as though it had been meticulously planned, even though Libby told me much of their décor was just odds and ends they'd picked up on their honeymoon and other trips. Only Zoe's room was strangely minimalist in comparison, with a little twin bed covered in blue pillows, a rocking chair in the corner, a bookcase, and a dresser with a couple of porcelain dolls lined on top. "She's too little, still," Libby had told me offhandedly. "God knows I'm worried enough about her breaking the valuables in the rest of this place. Believe me, Annie, I know what I'm doing." And so my tiny girl had her books and her Falafel, a stuffed pig whose fur was grimy from her fingers and teeth. Zoe had a nervous habit of chewing on Falafel's fur, it seemed. But what was there to be nervous about on Belvedere Island? If there'd ever been an Eden, it had looked like this.

Architecture. Art History. Beginning Photography. Eastern Religious Theory. I flipped through the book as I felt my eyelids growing heavy. Zoe had already nodded off against my side, her thumb in her mouth and her arm clamped tightly around Falafel. What area of study was perfect for the reinvented me?

That was the thing about leaving a family that doesn't care; you get to start over completely.

"What about interior design?" Libby's musical voice may as well have been a scythe for how easily it jolted me awake. "Dozing on the job, Annie?" she asked as I started, the rhetorical question dancing through the space between us as lightly as the silk duster she wore over her nightgown. "Not a great start, I'd say."

"I'm so sorry," I managed to stammer out, feeling warmth spread across my cheeks toward my ears. I'd always blushed easily, not just when I was embarrassed—when I was *anything*: worried, anxious, angry, whatever. It took just about nothing for my face to burn and my ears to throb with the heat of my emotions, which were often frighteningly powerful.

"Oh, I'm only kidding," she said with a laugh. "You've had a nutty day. It's hard getting used to the energy levels of a three-year-old. Mind if I sit?" I shook my head, and she settled in next to me, propping her moccasin-encased feet on the immaculate, glass-topped coffee table in front of us. Her relaxed manner surprised me; but then, I wasn't used to relaxing in settings as nice as this one.

"Well, it's even harder with the baby," I said carefully. "Why don't you let me watch him more often? I'm sure you could use a rest."

"No, no," she said with a wave of her hand, drawing a long sip from the glass of wine. "He's easy, really. He sleeps most of the time. Plus, I love having his cute little face nearby. Sometimes I just want to squeeze him, you know?"

"Yeah." I smiled then, glancing back down at the catalog in an effort to hide my reaction. Libby's friendliness was filling me with this weird, giddy feeling, and I was a little embarrassed by how she was affecting me. I wanted her to like me; it was how it had been when I was a kid, desperate to make friends at school.

"You have the cutest kids," I said, casting a glance at Zoe. "She's such a little sweetheart, all curled up like that." I laughed. "And I can't get over Falafel. How did she come up with that name?"

"Oh, that was all her dad," Libby said, rolling her eyes a little. "He's just basically a ten-year-old in an adult body. All guys are. Forever. I don't know, I think he was just goofing around with Zoe, suggesting names like 'String Bean' or something, and Falafel stuck."

"Or 'Fluffel,'" I said. "I wonder if that'll change when her lisp goes away."

"Probably not. And hey, it's cute, so whatever."

"I really like how you guys seem so laidback with the kids," I commented. "It's just like . . ." I trailed off, searching for the right words.

"What?" she prodded.

"Sorry," I said, shaking my head. "Not to sound sentimental, but it's exactly how I want to be someday. It's nice to see that it's a real thing for some people."

"So," Libby started carefully, "I guess that means that's not how it was for your parents." I shook my head; I wasn't about to tell her my sordid family history. As cool as she seemed to be, she wouldn't think of me the same way if she knew everything.

"I know a little about you," she mentioned gently. "I know it couldn't have been easy, growing up in inner-city Detroit, going to that high school. . . ." My head shot up. I hadn't told her anything about my school. How did she know? But her eyes held mine kindly.

"We had to do a little background check," she said. "Just the basics. It's customary, you know. You were going to be living with us, looking after our children . . ."

"So what did you find out?" My heart squeezed tightly, shriveling up into something hard. Libby peered at me as though surprised I'd ask.

"Nothing," she said. "At least, nothing much. Just that your school was kind of rough, but you still managed to pull off a near-perfect academic record. Nothing to be worried about, I'd say." She smiled a little, tugging at the corner of my sweatshirt. "If anything, I was impressed."

"Thanks," I mumbled.

"Can I be honest with you?" she asked then.

"Sure." Zoe cozied herself into me some more, eliminating any inch of space that might have existed between us. Her closeness reminded me of Lissa, whose affection had always been unchecked despite Dean's bullishness and our mother's dazed, half-aware ministrations.

"I'm sensing that you're a little shy about your background, but there's nothing to worry about. If you think we're going to judge you because you didn't come from money, you're totally wrong. And you might be surprised to know that we're not so different, you and I."

"Indeed," I told her wryly. "I *am* surprised to hear that."

"Oh, stop," she said. "Is it because I'm so ensconced in this life of luxury? Trust me, you'll get used to it too. It doesn't take long. When I was growing up, though, I lived in a double-wide. I worked two jobs to put myself through school. That's why I liked you. I felt right away like we might have a lot in common." I met her gaze and was surprised to find that her eyes projected total openness and honesty. No one had ever shown an interest in my life or assumed I had any particular worth. *I* hadn't even assumed these things. And now here was Libby, telling me that she and I were a lot alike. Which meant that maybe this life of hers wasn't so far from my grasp.

But there was one way we differed: I'd never feel comfortable with this much money. I'd never get used to feeling safe, like disaster wasn't just around the corner, like I was just always barely escaping poverty and sadness. I'd never stop looking over my shoulder. How could I? Lissa had been the only source of unbridled joy in my life, and then she was gone. All because of a stupid above-ground pool that Dean insisted on putting in, and a stupid gate that he'd never bothered to fix. *And stupid you*, a voice whispered from somewhere deep inside my head. *Stupid you, who should have kept a better eye on her.* The truth was, I was the world's least qualified person to watch Libby and Walker's kids. The last time a child was in my care, she had died. Sure, Mama had been home. But Lissa was always my responsibility first: that was the unspoken rule.

"Hey," Libby said softly, jolting me away from my ruminating. "Let's talk about something else. God, the first time we really get a chance to get to know each other, and I've already made you cry." She handed me a tissue from the box on the table. I dabbed at my eyes. I hadn't even noticed that I'd been crying, but sure enough, the tears were just beginning to spill over.

"I know!" she exclaimed excitedly, leaping up from the sofa. "How about you tuck in Sleeping Beauty, and I'll grab a fresh glass of wine . . . and one for you. And then we'll go do a little spring cleaning." A glass of wine sounded okay, but cleaning wasn't exactly what I felt like doing just then. My head was foggy, and my body felt like a truck had backed into it.

"Okay," I said. "Sure. If you don't mind me drinking while I'm on the job. And underage," I added, because it felt like the responsible thing to say.

"You're in college," Libby said. "I think a glass of wine from time to time isn't going to cause you any permanent damage. I'm not suggesting you get raging drunk," she said mock-sternly, "but a glass here and there to loosen you up while you're *not* on the job is fine. And by the way, you're not on the job."

"Okay?"

"What, you actually thought I'd make you clean the house at ten P.M.? Give me a little credit, Annie, I'm not a total witch. I'm talking about cleaning out my closet! It's been ages since I got rid of stuff. We're about the same size, right?"

"Um—"

"What are you, a four?"

"Six," I corrected her.

"Okay, well, maybe some of my stuff will be a little small." She was careful to mask disapproval. Libby was probably a size two at most. She had an annoyingly petite body to go along with all the other perfect things in her life. "But I have some billowy styles that would look just lovely on you. And don't take this the wrong way, but your wardrobe could use a makeover. Which is totally understandable," she clarified, glancing at my old Levi's and Detroit Lions hoodie. "I didn't learn how to dress myself until I was about twenty-two. And anyway, you can't believe what they say. Looking good does take money. At least a little of it."

I felt embarrassed for about a second, until I realized that she was right. It wasn't that big of a deal that I dressed somewhat slovenly. Most kids my age did. And now she was offering me the chance at her castoffs, which would probably make me the best-dressed girl at SFSU. Castoffs from Libby, moreover, would probably be the nicest clothes I'd ever be able to afford. Despite myself, I found that realization somewhat thrilling. I had never been above taking an interest in fashion; I just could never really indulge it before.

While Libby went down to the wine cooler to refill her glass and pour me one—they had a temperature-controlled cupboard as big as a refrigerator just for storing wine—I threw my course catalog in the Whole Foods tote I'd found bunched up in a ball under the kitchen sink. I hoped she might possibly have some old bags to pawn off on me, too.

**AN HOUR LATER,** I was officially intoxicated. Not just from the wine—from the whole experience. I sat on the floor of Libby's "closet," which was actually an entire unused room devoted to storing her clothing. She'd had custom-made shelves installed, and it struck me as odd that the room was even bigger than Zoe's nursery. One entire wall was lined with shoe cubbies all the way up to the ceiling, which must have been ten feet high, if not higher. It was dizzying. There were at least a hundred pairs of shoes, some of them by designers I'd heard of but never seen up close—Kate Spade, Jimmy Choo, Manolo Blahnik—and a bunch of the red-soled kind that I knew signified wealth. Then there were some by designers I'd never heard of at all. Those ones had Italian- and Spanish-sounding names and high-number sizes like 39. Also, I was pretty sure Libby wasn't a member of PETA. Half her shoes and handbags appeared to be snakeskin, and the section of fur coats in the far right corner had to be real. Libby wasn't the type to wear anything synthetic.

"So, any idea what you're going to major in? Here, try this." She flung a white silk peasant top my way.

"Not really," I sighed. "I mean, I've always been kind of interested in art. But I'm pretty bad at it, so I guess that's just a fantasy."

"There are lots of types of art," Libby remarked offhandedly, her head buried in a long row of color-coded sundresses. "I'm assuming you're talking about fine art—painting and drawing and sculpture and all that? Did you know there are actually some types of art that generate profit?" She dropped an armful of designer dresses on the floor with the sort of care one might give to a moldy orange.

"Um . . ." I racked my brain for a tactful thing to say. "No?"

"Being young and idealistic is all well and good," she remarked, "but you'll be leagues ahead of everyone else at school if you operate on the fact—and it *is* a fact—that you can't build a life on dreams. You need money. I realized that early on, and look where I am now," she said sagely. "Believe me, I was just like you at one point."

"I doubt it," I mumbled, annoyed despite myself. There was no way Libby—who looked barely out of college herself—had ever had it as tough as she'd been claiming. She looked like she was born in the satin she was wearing. Even if I won the lottery, I'd never move among luxury with the confidence she did. I'd always feel like an impostor. Also, it just felt *wrong,* this extravagance. I couldn't help thinking what my family could have done with the value of two pairs of Libby's expensive shoes. Not that I was complaining, now that she'd decided I could be the recipient of her hand-me-downs.

"Listen," she said in a serious tone. "Don't doubt *anything* I say. I believe in being frank, and I'll always be frank with you—if you screw up, if you deserve praise, or if you've got a chip on your shoulder like you do now. Oh yes, I did," she said in response to my startled look. "I called you out on it. There's nothing I'll tell you that's false. I promise. And I'm telling you now that I'm not like my daughter." She rolled her eyes with what seemed like a hint of bitterness.

"She won't ever know what it's like to worry about anything other than her own emotions. All her basic needs will always be met. All her wants will always be met, if she just extends herself ever so slightly. She'll never know what it's like to truly worry, to wonder whether she'll make it until tomorrow or the day after." Libby placed her wine glass on one of the shelves and turned to me quickly, the silk sash on her dressing gown unraveling as she did. She knelt down and clutched both my hands in hers, and it was so unexpected that I couldn't do anything, couldn't react at all other than to let myself fall into the intensity of her gaze. "But I have, Annie. I've been there." She paused, as if deciding whether she wanted to continue.

"I was adopted," she said finally, choking out the words from between twisted lips, like they tasted bad. "I was the daughter of a drug addict. Apparently it's a miracle I turned out normal," she told me, laughing bitterly. "Do you know what drugs do to a baby? Anyway, I was adopted into a middle-class family that later became poor. Hence the trailer. And there you have it. Suffering all around."

"I'm so sorry," I said, my throat constricting. By now Libby had settled herself on the plush carpeting beside me.

"Honestly," Libby told me, "I'm not. It may sound corny, but it made me tougher. It taught me how to fight for the things I want. And besides, even if we were poor, my parents were loving. But anyway, the point is, you shouldn't worry about your past. It's who you are now that matters."

*But who was I now? I was still the girl who let her little sister drown.* And Libby deserved to know the truth.

"I had *way* too much wine," she said. "I'm usually not such a blabbermouth. Here, try these things on before I pass out altogether." She gestured toward an enormous mound of clothing that took up most of the floor.

"Are you sure?" I asked.

"Absolutely! It'll be good to see these things get some use. Lord knows I don't need them. Go ahead, try them." I stood up, stumbling awkwardly. I was feeling a little tipsy too—I wasn't used to drinking. I hardly ever had. I grabbed as many of the items as I could hold and stood there awkwardly.

"What are you doing?" she asked.

"Is there . . . is there a bathroom I could use?"

At this, Libby burst out laughing. "Oh come *on,*" she said between fits. "Seriously? We're both girls. Plus, the bathroom is in such a state. Molly doesn't come 'til next week—she's the cleaning lady. Just try them on. I promise I won't try anything." She held up her hands in a gesture of mock surrender. My cheeks flamed, and she dissolved in giggles again. There was something about it, though, that I liked. I hadn't had many close girlfriends in high school. I had been part of a group, but sort of on the fringes. With Dean and my mom, I'd never felt comfortable enough to invite anyone over.

I pulled off my shirt and slipped the first article of clothing, a breezy blue sundress with a paisley print, over my head.

I could feel Libby's eyes on me, intent. I slipped my jeans off from under my dress. There was an extra wide, full-length mirror on one end of the room. It had a dark wood frame and was propped up by a bronze stand. I stared at my reflection, framed by the polished wood. I looked pretty in the dress. I could tell. It was a wraparound style that clung just right to my chest and cinched my waist with a tie, making it look smaller than ever.

Libby stood and came up behind me, tugging at the dress's waist. She reached toward my head, and I cringed, but she was just going for the black elastic that held my hair in a messy bun. She pulled it out and my hair tumbled down my back in a mess of unruly waves. "Beautiful," she said, meeting my eyes in the mirror. "If it weren't for our hair, we could be sisters." I laughed at that; Libby was far prettier and more glamorous than I was. I tried to ignore the tingling moving up my spine and over my shoulders. *This is it,* I heard the voice inside me say. *This must be how it feels to be close to someone.* What had come naturally to other girls but never to me—at least ever since Lissa died— was happening now.

"It's a little tight," I said, blushing. I was being so awkward; I was never this awkward. But I was tired, and tipsy. In the mirror, the clock hanging from the opposite wall read midnight.

"Baby fat," Libby said with a smile. "Nothing to worry about. I can show you how to shed a few pounds quickly." I smiled back uncomfortably. I'd never thought of myself as overweight. Libby yawned, a big sigh that made her look more vulnerable than I'd seen her.

"I'd better let you get some rest," I told her. "I can try on the others tomorrow."

"Okay," she agreed. "Here, why don't you just take them to your room? You can throw out whatever doesn't fit."

"Is there a donation center nearby? Maybe I can just do that."

"Sure," Libby said carelessly. "Whatever. We'll look one up in the morning." It was odd, the way she'd so easily forgotten how it felt not to have enough. How something cute from the thrift store could be enough to light up a whole afternoon.

Libby turned from the closet room, waiting to flick off the overhead light until I'd gathered up all the clothes. She didn't offer to help. *But why would she?* I chastised myself. She was being so generous. And I was being critical. Too critical. *Just because she knew a little more about me than I felt comfortable with?* I took a deep breath and followed her into the hall.

Libby turned to me, a strange expression on her face. "Is everything okay, Annie?" I had to tell her about Lissa.

"There's something you should know," I said to her.

"Okay." She waited. We'd reached the end of the hall that led out of the master wing; it was now or never. "Whatever it is, I'm sure it's fine."

"I had a sister," I said finally, my words spilling out in a rush. "She died."

"Yes, I know."

"How could you know?" Her words stung me. I felt a cold panic sweep over me; my legs were suddenly weak. "What do you know?"

"Annie, relax." Libby's voice was all honey, warm and soothing. "Lissa's obituary popped up during an Internet search, when I was researching you. It was right there; it wasn't that hard to find. I'm so sorry," she told me, pulling me into a hug. She wrapped her arms around me, and she felt strong and protective in a motherly way I hadn't felt in a long time. "I didn't want to bring it up, because I know how difficult it must be for you."

"But you don't know everything," I said into her shoulder, struggling out of her grasp.

"Then what?" She looked at me expectantly, her eyes bright and concerned.

"It was my fault," I whispered. I'd never said the words out loud. "She asked me to come play with her, and I brushed her off. I wanted to keep reading. And then fifteen minutes later, she was dead. If I'd gone, it never would have happened."

"It's not your fault," Libby said. I nodded, swallowing hard. I couldn't cry. I couldn't make Libby think I was weak or unstable or anything other than capable. I couldn't ruin the best thing I had.

"No," she said, more sharply then. She tilted my chin up, forcing me to look directly at her. "It is *not* your fault. And if I think you're thinking otherwise, I'm going to be very angry. Self-pity is a vice, Annie. It will only weigh you down." I blinked. I'd never expected this reaction. It was something like anger, but not the kind I was expecting. I was weak and drained. My whole body felt limp and feverish. All of a sudden I craved sleep with every ounce of me.

"Don't you see how wonderful this is for you, Annie?" Libby asked, her hands still resting on my shoulders. As the kindness in her voice wrapped itself around me, I felt my panic subside, little by little. I felt the blood returning to my brain, my vision clearing. I registered her face, perfect even in its concern, in my line of vision. She gently placed one palm on my cheek. "Walk and I know all your worst things," she said, "but we still thought you'd be a great fit for our family. That should be a relief to you. You have nothing to hide."

"I want to leave all that behind me," I managed finally. "That stuff—I didn't want to bring it here." I felt tears welling up in my eyes despite my efforts to keep them in. I didn't want to cry—I was making such a mess of things, such a horrible mess on only my second day. I couldn't trust myself for even twenty-four hours not to screw things up.

"And you will," Libby said firmly. "We are very discreet, Walker and I. You can trust us with your secrets. We would never say anything about your family—about what happened to Lissa"—she paused—"to anyone. So quit crying, darling. This is a very good thing."

"Okay." I nodded, wiping my eyes with the sleeve of my hoodie.

"You don't wear crying very well," she noted critically. "Some girls look all vulnerable and sweet when they're crying, but you look pretty horrendous." I choke-laughed into my sleeve, blotting at my eyes.

"Good thing Zoe's out cold," I said through my sniffling. "Wouldn't want to freak her out."

"No, definitely not," Libby said with a smile, tightening her sash. "Now go ahead, you've got to get some sleep! We both do. By the way, did you finish picking your classes yet?"

"Nope." I shook my head. "I'll have to get up a little early tomorrow to do it."

"No way. Let's get it done now. We can do it quickly if we work together. Where's the catalog?"

"It's in my room," I told her.

"Great. Let's get moving then. So what do you think of interior design?" She followed me down the hallway until we reached my room, settling herself on the white comforter that covered my elevated bed frame. I brought the catalog up beside her, and she rifled through it until she found what she wanted. She tapped at a black and white course description with her pointer finger. "That's what I studied, and I loved it. You know I run my own business, right?"

"Yes, from home. You mentioned that in your letters."

"Well, if you'd researched us as well as we researched you," Libby said with a grin, "you'd know that my business is incredibly lucrative. Plus super fun. I basically read *House Beautiful* every day and dillydally on my sketchpad. I mean, okay, there's a lot more to it than that. But it's pretty great. And talk about the *perfect* career with kids. Not that you're there yet, but someday," she said with a conspiratorial grin. "I could definitely mentor you, if you wanted. That would be huge on job apps later on."

"I'd love that," I told her, genuinely touched. "I really would."

"Okay then, sign up for your freshman requirements and

any interior design courses that leave you free in the late afternoons and evenings; remember, I need you here. It'll be fun!" she said happily, a glint in her eye. "I've never had a protégée. Makes me seem pretty important, right?" I laughed at this—it was fun to see Libby let down her perfect veneer. She was sitting rumpled and cross-legged atop my bed, her hair falling messily from its knot on her neck. I imagined she didn't let herself relax very often. It felt good to be let in so early.

"Thanks, Libby," I said carefully. "I really don't know how to thank you. For all of this." I gestured toward the pile of clothes that completely covered the arm chair in the corner of my bedroom.

"Don't mention it," she said. "Every now and then, you need someone to believe in you. I had someone like that when I was your age. She saved my life. She gave me opportunities. . . ." Libby trailed off then, her face darkening. "Otherwise you wilt. I'm not going to watch you wilt, okay? Not under my roof."

I couldn't help it then; I leaned in and hugged her, gripping her awkwardly over our cross-legged perches.

"All right, all right, I'm outta here," she laughed. "It's got to be one o'clock by now." And then she swept out of the room grandly, as if I hadn't just been snotting all over her shoulder. As if she hadn't just told me that the biggest secret of my life, the thing that had weighed on me every day for four years, was forgivable. Something about what she'd said had made me feel lighter. And that was the best gift I'd ever received.

# CHAPTER
# FOUR

**THERE WAS A PARTY** my first night at SFSU. "Disorientation" is what they called it, a joking play on the seven-hour freshman orientation we'd had that morning. Normally my weekends would be spent working for the Cohens, but Walker had convinced Libby that I needed a night off to "assimilate."

"What about assimilating *here?*" she'd asked a little petulantly, but Walk just smiled a little and kissed her on the forehead, and she let it drop. I was grateful for Walker's laidback attitude. I was grateful for the way he wrapped his arms around Libby until her type-A tenseness visibly melted away, shedding itself under her husband's salve. I thanked him inside my head every single time he did it, because it meant more for me than just a night off with my would-be college friends; it was a promise that these relationships, these happy couplings, *did* exist and might exist for me.

So there were Libby and Walker, nested up in domestic happiness, and there I was, setting off toward the first party of my college career.

"Be careful," Walk had said when he dropped me off near Main Circle. "Just make sure you take a taxi home, no crashing on campus, okay? We need you in the morning by ten." I nodded and waved as I stepped out of the car, wiggling the fingers in my right hand in a semiflirtatious manner that surprised even me. I heard a long whistle behind me as he pulled away, and I turned to meet the sparkling eyes of a girl I vaguely recognized from that morning—she'd smiled broadly at me from near the coffee booth outside the enormous seminar room where orientation had been held.

"Who's *that?*" she asked admiringly, tapping one red patent leather–clad toe on the sidewalk. "You sweatin' him?" The girl was wearing a black sequined tube top with tight jeans and the patent red heels. She had big gold hoops in her ears, and she wore her blonde hair flipped out at the ends. Her arms were thin and muscular where they folded across her chest, and her shoulders were thrust back confidently. She made me feel simultaneously admiring and painfully drab from where I stood, wearing a simple black tank dress and flip-flops.

"Um, no, I just live with him."

"Even better," she said, whistling. "They don't make 'em like that anymore, not where I'm from."

"Where's that?" I asked shyly. I found the energy she exuded, which seemed to me all hot pink and gold, a little intimidating.

"Kentucky," she said, pronouncing it like "Kin-tuckee,"

emphasis on the *kin*. "I'm Morgan. You're that girl who's into skating, right? I loooove figure skating. Did a little myself 'til I got into gymnastics." Just then a group of guys in baseball caps and jeans walked by with beer cans in hand. One of them turned and gave Morgan a long stare from head to toe. She grinned at him, and I folded my arms beneath my chest more protectively.

It was true; we'd had to introduce ourselves at freshmen orientation, and for some reason the fact I'd chosen to share was my childhood obsession with figure skating. I'd wanted to be Katya Gordeeva; I'd wanted to have a tragic love story that paralleled hers. But I'd never actually been on the ice, other than in my daydreams. I guess it had been easier than sharing real facts. It was part of my reinvention.

"I haven't skated in a while," I told Morgan. "It was more of a thing I did when I was little."

"What's your name again?" she asked distractedly as we began walking side by side toward the apartment complex where Dis-O was being held.

"Annie," I told her.

"How cute," she grinned. "As in, Little Orphan?"

"Not too far off." Maybe she sensed my reluctance to talk, or maybe she was hyped up on the energy of the place, but she pulled out a little leather flask, monogrammed with what looked like her initials, and detached from it two small cups. She poured clear liquid into one and passed it my way, filling the second as I took it. I sniffed the little cup; it smelled like nail polish remover and all the things it burns. It smelled like my mother's breath in the midafternoon.

"Vodka," Morgan confirmed for me. "Gordon's. Cheap 'n' easy. Only thing I had in my suitcase. Cheers!" We clinked shots and took them. I felt the alcohol searing my throat and felt my muscles tighten against it and worried for a second that I'd throw up. For all my mom's habits, I'd never tasted much alcohol myself, other than beer. *But this is what college kids do*, I told myself as we took a second shot, and then a third, and then walked into a narrow alleyway lined on one side with a fence and on the other with brightly lit apartments, each packed with SFSU students who were dancing on tables, drinking beer upside down from kegs, sipping out of red plastic cups.

"*That's* what I've been looking forward to," Morgan yelled, gesturing to a group of shirtless guys in the corner, their six-packs marked with different letters of the Greek alphabet. "They didn't grow 'em like that in Kentucky," she told me.

They hadn't grown them like that in Detroit, either. The guys I'd grown up with were city-hardened, backward-cap-wearing, jean-slouching types. They were the kind who idolized Eminem and Proof. Not that I minded; there was something about a bad boy that I found appealing.

Thinking about Detroit guys naturally provoked thoughts of Daniel, the only guy I'd ever dated kind of seriously. Daniel could have been my boyfriend, but about four months in, I didn't want him to be. I did and I didn't: I wanted him to kiss me in the front seat of his car, his tongue tasting like Lucky Strikes. I wanted him to cradle my face in his hands and look straight into my eyes the way he did when he was trying to make a point he was especially passionate about. I wanted to walk the ten blocks to his house after school and crawl under his sheets for the brief hour we had alone until his mom got home from work.

But then about four months in, he wanted to come to my place, to learn more about me, to hear about Lissa, to meet my mom and Dean. And it all came crashing down. It had been a fantasy until then: bringing him into my life would never have worked. So I broke it off and wandered through the halls for the last few months of school pretending like I didn't see him, like I hadn't once blanked on an American History speech midline just because his ice-blue eyes had locked on mine.

"Come *on,*" Morgan said impatiently, tugging me through the crowd on an outdoor patio. She was weaving expertly across the garden area, her tiny frame easily dodging elbows and drinks. She paused and held out her hand for me, and I took it. I felt heady and light and a million times more confident with Morgan's hand tugging mine along and her magic potion working its way through my blood and into my brain. The chaos was alarming; it was beautiful. Morgan and I shouldered our way into an apartment, and it seemed like the eyes of a dozen guys turned *our* way, not just hers. It seemed like the first step in my metamorphosis.

Morgan screamed something over the music. I smiled as though I knew what she was saying—it didn't matter that I didn't, because in that moment I would have agreed to anything she suggested. We finally found a little open spot near the kitchen, a place to stand without being knocked around. A tall, broad-shouldered guy with pink in his eyes where there should have been white came up to us, handing us each a red cup by way of a greeting.

"Thanks," I managed, sipping from the top of the cup after Morgan did the same.

"Sure. You ladies freshmen?" But he was looking only at Morgan as he said it, inching his way closer to hear her response. I watched as he leaned his ear toward hers, then moved his hand to the small of her back. She curved close as if she were his partner in some instinctual, choreographed mating dance. I drank my beer, warmish and watery and flat, casting my eyes around the room in an effort to give Morgan space with her new guy. How was I going to make friends? Everyone else looked like they knew what they were doing—like they'd grown up knowing how to walk into a room full of strangers and own it. I wanted to go home. I shocked myself by thinking of the Cohens' like that—*home*—so easily. I wanted to curl up on the sofa next to Zoe, cradle little Jackson in my arms, laugh with Libby as she recounted tales of her own misguided, awkward youth, the days before she blossomed.

I tried looking at everyone around me from an anthropological perspective. I tried turning them all into monkeys, to see if my old trick from high school would still work, and it did. They had all turned into primitive creatures in heat. The girls were all dressed in practically nothing, bending their bodies to the music in an effort to entice the boys, who stared and stalked and approached and claimed. It was that easy and that weird, and I wasn't sure if I was going to like the college party scene. Morgan and her guy had long since slipped away, and

I was starting to feel exhausted and dizzy and invisible, thirty seconds away from calling a cab, when I felt a hand on my own back.

"You need more?" the guy asked, gesturing to my cup. I was so relieved someone had acknowledged my existence that I felt myself smiling eagerly. *Pathetic*, I told myself, feeling the familiar flush spread toward my hairline. But at the same time, it was nice to be noticed, and the guy in question was objectively hot. He was easily six feet tall and muscular. His broad shoulders tapered into a narrow frame, and his orange T-shirt showed off tanned muscles as he worked the pump at the keg. He glanced over at me as if confirming that I hadn't left. I shot him a smile that I hoped was flirtatious and not just completely awkward, and he grinned back, revealing a square jaw and a dimple in his right cheek. He motioned for me to come his way, so I followed him into the filthy, linoleum-tiled kitchen.

"Want to head upstairs?" he shouted. I felt myself blushing harder. "Just to talk! I promise!" he laughed, noticing my discomfort.

"How can I be so sure?" I teased lightly. "You don't strike me as very trustworthy."

"I'm horribly offended." He raised a hand to his chest dramatically. "I'll give you a chance to make it up to me. Upstairs."

"Ok, now I *definitely* don't feel safe." I laughed, but I didn't resist when he took my hand in his broader, rougher one and led me up the stairs to a little bedroom on the left side of the hall. He knocked twice and then pulled me in, shutting the door gently behind him.

I perched on the edge of the bed and tried not to focus on the pillows, on his body next to me, or on the dizziness that was beginning to feel way heavier than a buzz. The walls were lined with pictures of Charlie Brown.

"What's with the *Peanuts* obsession?" I wondered aloud. "There's, like, eight posters of Charlie Brown in here."

"Three of Woodstock," he corrected. "And the obsession is born from a long and accursed history with the name 'Charles Brown.'"

"This is your room?"

"Guilty. And now that you've insulted me twice in five minutes, I think it's time for your penance."

He leaned toward me and kissed me, wrapping his arms around my waist and pulling me close. He wasn't a bad kisser, and I supposed in any other situation I would have enjoyed it, but all I could focus on was the taste of his tongue (pizza?). It was prodding and insistent and a little aggressive, not to mention a little awkward with all the Charlie Browns and Woodstocks staring down at us. There was a flash of silver from his bedside table. . . .

I pushed him away.

"Is that a necklace?"

"Where?"

"Right there," I said, pointing toward the little nightstand.

"Yeah," he admitted, pulling me close again. I locked my elbows against his chest.

"Wait, like a girl's necklace?"

"Yeah, my girlfriend's," he said. "I mean, whatever, my ex-girlfriend's. She's kind of a bitch."

Things weren't adding up in my head. The clock on his bedside, the one that had illuminated the pieces of silver that were carelessly tossed as though the owner were totally confident she'd be back to claim them—as though she did this all the time—read two A.M.

"I should probably go."

"Don't be lame." His warm breath tickled the side of my face. "It's a rite of passage. All the freshman girls hook up at Dis-O. And I'm kind of a good catch," he informed me. "Did you know I'm a senior? I mean, look at me." He craned his neck in order to admire himself in the full-length mirror that adorned the back of his bedroom door. Sensing my opportunity, I struggled to my feet.

"I have to work in the morning," I said, feeling strangely guilty, "and it's going to take forever to get a cab. . . ."

"But you're so pretty," the guy slurred, sensing his mistake. "You know why I like you?" He ran his hands from my hips to the waist of my dress. "You're not, like, stick-thin. That's why I like you." I jerked away from him and moved toward the door. The backhanded compliment stung. The whole night was a mess. I needed to get out of there. But I felt so, so dizzy. I wasn't entirely sure I could make it home.

"What are you, a lez?" he wanted to know.

"No." I yanked open the door, my face flaming from intense anger and my body trembling, partly with nerves and partly with drunkenness. "But I would rather chop off my ovaries than mess around with you."

"Whatever," he shouted after me as I moved down the stairs. "You're missing out on the hottest lay of your life!"

I wanted to throw up.

So I did—all over the backyard, which was blessedly emptying out.

I glanced around for Morgan for a few minutes before realizing she wasn't worried about me, so what was the point of worrying about her? She'd only been my friend for a total of twenty minutes anyway. She was probably following through on the apparent "freshman rite of passage" even as I stumbled around looking for her.

The cab took forty-five minutes to come. I fell asleep on the curb with my arms resting on my knees and my head resting on my arms. I woke to the sound of the horn blaring less than a foot in front of me.

When we finally pulled onto Belvedere Island, the sun was beginning to peak over the horizon in a brilliant display of early-morning yellows. I had to be up to babysit in only a few hours. I decided to sneak in the back way rather than through the front. I'd make less noise that way, and the back door, which led out onto the terrace and the pool, was furthest from the master bedroom. Walker and Libby weren't my parents, but I wasn't sure how they'd feel about me stumbling into their house reeking of cigarettes and booze. I felt a weird sense of role reversal as I realized now that my mom wasn't around, I'd started *acting* like my mom. I shook off the uncomfortable feeling that accompanied that thought and slipped my shoes off, opening the gate as quietly as possible.

I followed the long path to the pool, feeling the tiniest bit revived by the sunrise despite my raging headache. It really was beautiful; the house sat on a hill overlooking the bay, and the reflection of the sun on the water was the loveliest thing I'd ever seen. Returning to the Cohens' was beginning to wash away my night of hell.

Leaning out over the guardrail next to the pool, I sensed movement from my periphery. I turned just in time to notice a sandy-haired guy on the second-story deck of the house next door, which sat atop a hill and hovered just over the Cohens' estate. Most of the mansions in Belvedere were hidden behind artful landscaping, but the house next door was the exception. It was set a little higher on the hill and towered above the Cohens' place like a watchdog. From my vantage point on the deck, I could easily see the neighbors' more elevated, multi-level decks beyond the property.

The neighbor guy was wearing a T-shirt and boxers, like he'd just rolled out of bed. His back faced me, and I saw him struggling with the latch on a sliding door before slipping back inside. Then he turned, and I ducked quickly. But my knee crashed into the grill in the process, causing it to clang loudly against the side of the iron fence. Several grill utensils fell off the side tray, clattering to the pool deck. "*Shit*," I muttered. I knelt behind the grill, my heart thumping. My knee hurt like hell. And he had probably seen me.

Okay, he had definitely seen me. Anyone would have seen me.

I sat there awkwardly, my back against the grill, clutching my aching knee. I'd definitely have a bruise from this one. My instinct was to run back inside and hide in my room, but I was afraid to move in case he was still looking out toward the Cohens'. Maybe he'd think I had already slipped back inside. I was just beginning to relax again when I heard a door open and close next door, and a set of footsteps jogging up the walkway toward the pool gate. I barely had time to register what was happening before he was standing by the gate to our pool area, grinning at me.

"Hey," he said. "Taking a rest?"

"Um . . . yes?" I could feel my cheeks heating up. This was one of the absolute worst, most awkward nights-slash-mornings. Ever.

"Are you okay?" His voice was loud this time—loud enough to wake the house.

"Shhh!" I jogged over to the gate and opened it a crack. "I'm fine! Stop yelling. It's barely six o'clock!"

"Sorry," he said in a loud whisper. "I just . . . I was getting up for a run, and I swear I thought I saw you fall. But now I suspect otherwise." His eyes were wide and sincere, but I detected a tiny smile worming its way onto the corners of his mouth. Despite myself, I thought he was cute. He was so athletic and rugged. Not at all my type. He didn't look like he knew what a wallet chain even was. Like he'd never been near ill-fitting pants. Yet there was something about him that I found unmistakably appealing. I, on the other hand, probably reeked of booze and sweat and other unappealing odors. And if he couldn't smell me, at the minimum he could see the damage the night had done to my face. It was not my loveliest moment. I wiped the edges of my eyelids in a futile attempt at removing mascara smudges. Realizing I was fighting a losing battle, I squared my shoulders and pretended to be confident.

"Of course I was," I said, crossing my arms over my chest. "I mean, I did. Why else would I have been sitting down? I don't, like, hang out by the pool in the wee hours of the morning. I slid on some water," I continued, failing at my resolve to play it cool. "But I'm fine. I swear." I watched his eyes slide over toward the dry wooden surface lining the terrace, then back to my face.

"Yeah," he said, like he didn't believe me. "Okay."

"Thanks for checking on me, though."

"It's my neighborly duty," he told me. "Much like a friendly watchdog, I prowl the neighborhood seeking to help the less nimble-footed among us."

"Well," I said lamely. "Here I am! Safe and sound. So you can go lurk around someone else's backyard now."

"Sure thing," he said. "Ciao. Maybe I'll see you around . . . if you don't see me first." Then he grinned wickedly and walked back to his house, hands shoved casually in the cargo shorts he must have pulled on just before dashing to my rescue. When he had almost reached his front door, he turned back.

"Hey," he shouted across our yards. I looked at him from where I stood by the glass sliding doors that led to the Cohens' living room. I could just make out his frame beyond the iron fence that surrounded the pool. I used one hand to shield my eyes against the torturous sun, which seemed designed to make my head explode.

"I'm Owen," he yelled.

"Okay," I said more to myself than to him. He stood there, waiting expectantly. I waved to let him know I'd heard him, but he didn't turn to leave.

"What about you?" he shouted.

"What?" I walked closer to the fence in hopes that my voice would carry away from the Cohens' house.

"What about you?" he yelled again. "What's your name?"

"It's Annie," I said loudly.

"What?"

*Oh my god.* He was relentless.

"Annie!" I yelled. "It's Annie, okay?" Only then did he turn, laughing, and disappear through his front door. With all the remaining dignity I possessed, I crossed the deck and opened the sliding glass door that led to the living room. Then I padded up to my bedroom, where I promptly fell asleep.

**THE REST OF THE DAY** passed me by in the sort of fog only a sleepless night of drinking can bring. For a few hours after my brief nap, I felt extra-alert, sharp, and incredibly exuberant, as if the alcohol hadn't fully left my system. I was a whirlwind: straightening up the kitchen, organizing Zoe's closet, playing finger paints and making a bird house with Zoe for the backyard. Then later, I fell into an awful slump that couldn't be cured even by splitting a box of macaroni and cheese with my little charge, who ate about half a serving to my three and a half. All I wanted was to go back to sleep. I'd never been so tired in my life, and Zoe could wear anyone out on the best of days. I hadn't thought about how to balance a normal college social life plus homework and babysitting. It quite honestly hadn't occurred to me that I might have one, since I'd spent most of my high school career working and taking care of my mom after school. I'd thought my job here would be a breeze after my life in Detroit.

Suddenly I felt ripe for new opportunities . . . exhilarating opportunities. One in particular came in the form of the guy next door. I'd never known an Owen. What kind of a name was Owen, anyway? It didn't sound quite as pretentious as Libby and Walker, and it didn't speak of old money like something along the lines of Alistair or Blake. These were the thoughts that went through my head that afternoon, as Libby tucked herself away in her curtained office and Zoe and I entertained ourselves around the house. I had a desperate urge to go outside, to see if I could sneak another peek of Rescue Owen, or Watchdog Owen, as I'd been calling him in my head all day. But I put a lid on it. I didn't want to seem overeager. And besides, I had all year to get to know him.

And then I had a stroke of brilliance. I had the perfect excuse to talk to him. It was so obvious—I had to thank him for checking on me. I mean, I couldn't just not thank him, because that would be rude. Or so I told myself. While Zoe was affixing hair extensions to her Miss Kimmi doll later that afternoon,

I thought about what I would say. (I also thought about why someone had created a doll that encouraged such vapid behavior in children.) While I fixed her afternoon snack (sliced bananas, no peanut butter because of her peanut allergy), I thought about what I'd wear. This was a totally foreign concern, but it was funny how having more clothing had done that to me. But worse, my mind was elsewhere when I should have been paying attention to Zoe.

And then she said it.

Zoe mostly babbled in that transitional way kids do when they're no longer babies but only just barely. Her manners of the first day had dissolved into the kind of speech I imagined she felt more comfortable with. She said things like "hold you" when she wanted to be held—probably a result of hearing "Want me to hold you?" from her parents—and "I'm hungwy." She was adorable, but she wasn't the most stimulating conversationalist. But then, just as I was putting her down for her nap, she wrinkled her whole forehead together into one worry line and began vigorously sucking her thumb.

"What?" I asked, looking down at her; but she only tucked her dark head into her chest and shook it back and forth, pursing her lips into a scowl.

"What, Monkey? What's the matter?"

"You'we in twouble," she informed me.

"What do you mean, Zo? Why am I in trouble?"

"You woke up Mommy, and now she's mad at you." A glimmer of panic pierced my chest.

"How do you know?" I asked, careful to keep my voice

neutral. Zoe pulled her thumb back out of her mouth in order to speak. It made a loud popping sound as it slid out of her mouth.

"She mad," she said. Then she shoved her thumb back in.

"I know, sweetie," I said carefully, trying not to get annoyed. "But what did she tell you?" Instead of answering, Zoe just turned over on her side and grabbed Falafel. "Zoes?" I asked one more time. But she shook her head vehemently, as if she was just as mad at me as her mother was. I felt myself getting frustrated, but she was only a toddler. It made sense that she wouldn't understand.

So instead of trying again, I tucked the striped cashmere throw that usually decorated the foot of her bed around her shoulders, which were clenched up tightly next to her neck. She seemed like such a tense little girl. Like she lacked all of the carefree innocence other kids enjoyed. So unusual for a child of three. Usually it terrified kids to see a grownup upset, but apparently this wasn't the case with Zoe. In order to get the scoop, I'd have to go to the source.

All of a sudden, it made a lot of sense why Libby had been avoiding me all day.

Taking the back stairs two at a time (the house had three separate staircases connecting its two main floors, a fact that never stopped seeming incredible), I made my way down to Libby's office. It was a sunny little room with roughhewn floors they'd apparently had shipped in from Walker's grandfather's old ranch house. Floor-to-ceiling windows lined the back portion and looked out over the San Francisco Bay, and French

doors separated it from the myriad of rooms that made up the
rest of the ground floor. A sky-blue patterned area rug covered
the bulk of the floor, and the windows displayed white curtains
with delicate lace embroidery. A large mahogany desk sat in
the center of room. On its surface was an ornate coffee mug
decorated with the letter *L*, several stacks of paper, and a laptop. The effect was professional but serene.

Libby sat cross-legged at the opposite end of the room,
rifling through a book of fabric samples and tacking some onto
the bulletin board behind her every so often. The baby was in
his vibrating chair beside her, sound asleep. For the first time,
it struck me that Jackson hadn't been mentioned at all when
Libby had debriefed me on my responsibilities when I first
arrived. It seemed like I'd rarely be looking after him—only if
Libby and Walker went out. Zoe, on the other hand, had been
with me all day—Libby hadn't checked in on her once. Nor
had I ever seen Libby tuck her in or serve her a meal. But, I
reasoned, she probably kept the baby close because of feed-
ings and stuff.

Libby's hair was swept up in a messy ponytail, and she
wore jeans and a simple white button-down. On her, it looked
totally chic. Her feet were bare, her toenails painted a deep
purple. I stood there, admiring everything for several minutes
before I caught myself. Was it creepy to stare like that? Maybe.
But Libby was everything I wanted to be; I couldn't help admiring her. It made me all the more nervous that she was angry
with me for getting in so late, for making so much noise in the
yard with Owen.

I was going to have to get over being starstruck, though, if I ever wanted to earn her respect. Being timid and wide-eyed wouldn't exactly bolster my credibility. And she was taking a huge chance on me, that much was clear. I'd have to figure out how to hold on to her respect. I took a deep breath and knocked twice before poking my head in. Libby smiled by way of a greeting.

"Hey," I said. "I just wanted to let you know that Zoe's down for her nap. And I also wanted to apologize." I clasped my hands in front of me and took a breath; I suddenly felt unsteady.

"Apologize?" Libby said with what sounded like genuine confusion. "Whatever for?"

"For coming in so late," I said. "And for talking so loudly with Owen. I guess I woke you up? Zoe mentioned that you were unhappy." Libby chuckled then, continuing to flip through her book of samples.

"I don't have a lot of time right now, Annie," she said. "But you shouldn't take Zoe so seriously. We heard you, and then we fell right back to sleep. And quite honestly it's not up to me to keep an eye on you. If you're going to go out late, I'll just expect you won't let it interfere with your job."

"Okay," I said. "I understand. I'm really sorry for waking you, though; it won't happen again."

Finally Libby looked up and sighed. She gave me a tired smile. "I remember what it was like to be in college," she told me. "I'm not exactly naive. But I do want you to remember that you have a job to manage. I can't have you being tired, or smelling like booze, or flirting with the kid next door when you're on the job."

"Oh, I wasn't—"

"You weren't flirting? I've seen Owen, Annie. If I weren't way too old for him and married already, I'd have a serious crush. Attractive *and* a do-gooder. He's an EMT, you know. Just as a volunteer gig. Walker told me. Look, he seems like a nice kid. Just keep it to a minimum, okay? I don't want to have to worry about you getting into some sort of messy romance with our neighbor's son. Though I must say I'm relieved you're interested in boys your own age." I turned cold. It was such a weird thing to say, and it wasn't without venom.

"What do you mean?"

"I see the way you look up to Walker," Libby said matter-of-factly. "I'm not angry. But I don't want to see you developing some sort of puppy crush on my husband and winding up with a broken heart." My cheeks were flaming; I could feel it. Even my ears were throbbing. It had occurred to me that Walker was cute, but this felt like it was coming out of nowhere.

"I don't have a crush on Mr. Cohen," I said carefully, hoping my voice sounded firm and not shaky.

"Honey, I'd be offended if you didn't. It's totally normal. He's a handsome man. Besides, I know that you know better than to act on it. I'm not worried; I'm just glad to see that you're noticing the neighbor." Since it seemed like defending myself would be futile and I was too flustered to do it in a way that would sound remotely convincing, I redirected the conversation.

"Mind if I drop by the neighbors' house really quick? I kind of do want to thank Owen." Libby raised one eyebrow, and my face began its predictable heating routine in response. "I fell," I explained. "And he came to check on me. That's how we met."

"Oh dear," she said. "Are you okay?"

"I'm fine."

"He's pretty cute, Owen," she commented again, making a note on her computer.

"Um, I guess so," I said, confused. Why did she keep pressing it?

"Don't be absurd, Nanny, just say it. He's cute. You'd have to be blind not to notice." Her voice was oddly flat, almost as if I'd done something to make her angry. And had she called me "Nanny"? Or had I misheard that?

"He is pretty cute," I agreed. She didn't look up, but her face softened a notch.

"I'm afraid it'll have to wait. You can't leave the house while you're on the job."

"Oh," I stammered, taken aback. "I guess I thought since you were here . . ." I trailed off as she whipped her head up and trained her eyes on mine.

"Yes?" she said coldly. "What is it you thought? *I* thought I made myself clear when I said your hours today would be ten to seven. Let me clarify. Ten to seven means you're here with Zoe at all times during that period. You don't leave her side. And you don't leave this house. Unless of course I ask you to. But you will never leave this house without my permission when you're on the job. Is that easier to understand?"

"Yes," I forced out. She seemed really angry; I wondered if she actually thought I had a crush on her husband. Maybe this imagined scenario was affecting her more than she'd let on. There was no other explanation for her sudden brusqueness.

"I'm sure Owen can wait. Though your eagerness is sweet."

"Okay." I was blushing intensely by then. It was all I could do not to run away from her. Instead, I made myself square my shoulders and take measured steps out of the room.

"Oh, and Nanny," she called after me, just as I'd reached the hall and begun to shut the door behind me, "I noticed that the hinge on your door was broken, so I had the whole thing removed while you were playing with Zoe upstairs. So don't be shocked when you see that it's missing. We'll fix it as soon as possible, but it could be a while. The wood's very old and we'll have to custom-make a new hinge. I hope that doesn't bother you. You still have your bathroom for privacy, of course, and that end of the hall is basically empty anyway."

"It's not a problem," I assured her quickly. "I don't mind at all."

But I did mind. I minded a lot. Being able to close a door behind me at night meant more to me than Libby could realize. It was something I'd been looking forward to, something that had allowed me to sleep better the past couple of weeks than I ever had before. And there it was again, that title, *Nanny*, rather than the use of my name. But "and Annie" could have just blended together, or something, to sound like "Nanny." *I'm being paranoid*, I told myself over and over. It was the lack of sleep combined with the scare that was making me take a pessimistic view of everything.

I took the long way back up to Zoe's room, and as I passed my own room I couldn't help noticing how large the gap left by the missing door was. It seemed to swallow up the space, as if my life were some sort of museum exhibit, *Life of the Typical Teenage Nanny.* You could see the whole room easily from the hallway now, and I couldn't escape the feeling of dread and revulsion this sudden lack of privacy triggered within me. Some people are more private than others. For some, privacy is everything. It is dignity. It is contentedness. It is the only way to stay sane.

# CHAPTER FIVE

**THE SUN FLOODED** across the room, shocking me awake.

"Get up get up getupgetup!" Zoe's voice, which normally made me laugh, may as well have been a bullhorn. She jumped on top of my bed, her knee colliding painfully with my elbow.

"Zoe! Get *off*," I shouted, flipping over to face her. Libby was standing in the doorframe watching us. Ah, the empty doorframe. That explained why I hadn't heard them come in. I couldn't fight off the involuntary shudder I experienced every time I felt my space being invaded.

"Oh," she said. "I thought you'd like to be greeted by Zoe. You two seem to be bonding so quickly. But I suppose I should have used the intercom." I shook my head violently to clear away the lingering fog of sleep. Right. They had an intercom for communicating, because the house was so vast. So far I'd only been on the receiving end of that, because something innate prevented me from wanting to communicate over a device while in the same house with the person I wanted to talk to.

"I'm sorry, did I miss my alarm?" I glanced toward the clock on the wall, but it read eight o'clock. I still had well over an hour to sleep.

"No, no," Libby assured me. "It's just that we—"

"We going to the beach!" shouted Zoe exuberantly.

"Yes," Libby said. "It's unseasonably warm today, so Walker suggested it might be nice. Never mind the work that goes into cleaning them up after they've gotten all sandy, but you know Walker." She sighed melodramatically. "He gets these ideas . . ."

"Oh," I said. "The beach sounds nice." I kept my voice even, because from the sound of it, a day at the beach may as well have been on par with licking the bathroom floor. But the truth was, I was thrilled by the prospect of a day at the beach. I hadn't seen any of San Francisco since I'd arrived a week before. I'd hoped to explore a little before school started, but I'd been so busy looking after Zoe that I hadn't had a day off yet. That was supposed to be tomorrow, Sunday. Maybe then I'd finally stop by Owen's house.

"So get Zoe dressed and put yourself together, too. We're just going to Stinson, but some of those people can be snobs, so I suggest you borrow a suit from me and wear one of the tunics I gave you. We'll be going out to eat afterward. On us, don't worry," Libby clarified, before I even had time to register the plan. I tried not to bristle at that; she was just looking out for me. "Walker's already packing up the car, and I've thrown together a picnic lunch. Let's try to be ready to leave in twenty minutes. I'll bring that suit up in a minute." I nodded, watching as she turned and headed back in the direction of the staircase that led to the kitchen.

"I wanna weaw my yellow suit with the polka dots," Zoe informed me seriously.

"Okay," I said. "Just a second." But she was already dashing back toward her room, excited about the prospect of one last beach day before the onset of fall. By the time I caught up with her, Zoe had already found the polka-dotted suit in her dresser and was pulling the bottoms over her pajama shorts.

"One sec, little girl," I said, grabbing her under the armpits and hoisting her onto her bed. "First, I believe somebody needs a swimmer's diaper." Zoe frowned petulantly and I laughed. "Don't smile," I told her. "Yep, that's it. No smiling allowed." The corners of her mouth started to tremble and turn up a little. "No smiling, Monkey," I told her in a deep, serious voice. Finally she caved, her giggles tumbling through the air the same way her curls tumbled over her shoulders: perfect, beautiful, full.

I managed to locate a Little Swimmer diaper, which wasn't difficult given how sparsely decorated the room was compared to the rest of the house. With a bit of effort, I helped her pull it on. The swimsuit was a two-piece number in yellow and white dots with a frilly skirt. I selected a pair of yellow jelly shoes to round out the look. I carefully fastened a Hello Kitty barrette into her hair. Then I stepped back to admire my handiwork. *Yep,* I told myself. *Pretty darned adorable.* Zoes was the cutest kid.

Then I felt the usual pang, the one associated with Lissa.

The kind that was always followed by a sick lurch before I realized what my body was reacting to. It was funny, the way my guilt provoked a physical reaction. *Or, you know, not funny at all*, I thought.

I snapped out of my gloom and walked Zoe back down to my room. A plain red one-piece lay folded on my bed. I escaped to the bathroom and slipped it on, leaving the door open a crack so I could see Zoe playing with the phone Libby had given me a day ago. So far it had only one number in it. But it was a smartphone, the fancy kind with all sorts of apps already loaded. Libby's old one, I'd guessed. Zoe seemed more skilled with it than I was.

I took a second to admire myself in the mirror. With the addition of Libby's semi-sheer tunic, I looked almost cute. I swept my hair up into a messy ponytail and grabbed a book—a collection of Poe stories I'd had to purchase for my Gothic Lit class—just in case. Zoe trotted down the stairs, singing softly.

"Finally," Libby said as we rounded the corner. "Hurry up now, just head out to the garage. The baby's already in the car, and Walker's getting impatient."

Walker looked anything but that as we piled into the car. He grinned broadly at me and reached over to honk Zoe's nose, causing her to break out in another fit of giggles. Zoe was happier than I'd yet seen her.

"Guess what I'm gonna do, sweet pea?" Walker asked, glancing back at Zoe.

"What?"

"Well, why don't you take a look in the back and you'll

see." Zoe and I peered into the hatch, where an inflatable raft rested.

"Zoes, it's a shark!" I told her. She looked at me doubtfully. I could understand her skepticism; it looked more like a tent all deflated like that.

"That's right, babycakes! I'm gonna take you out on those waves in your shark boat, so you can scare off the other fishies and have the ocean all to yourself!"

"Don't be ridiculous, Walker." Libby had just opened the passenger door, armed with a picnic basket. "The water's going to be way too cold for that."

"You never know, Libs," he replied, refusing to be put off. "These heat waves, they can get under your skin"—he reached back and ticked Zoe under her knee—"and make you crave an icy dip."

"I suppose," Libby allowed.

"Libby does not like the beach," Walker informed me seriously. "Which is why we're heading there today. I'm determined to convert her."

"I don't understand why we can't just stick to the pool," she argued. "Pools are the perfect compromise. No sand, no wind, water for you to play in with the kids . . . no jellyfish, no stingrays . . . we could even go to the club if you want a change of pace."

"I have news for you, little lady," said Walker, his Texas accent suddenly thicker. "Stinson Beach ain't got no stingrays." Libby sighed dramatically, as if annoyed, but she was clearly trying to hide a smile. They were cute together, Libby and

Walker. They worked. They gave me hope in romantic relationships. I looked at Libby, staring out the window; at Zoe,
sucking her thumb from her car seat; and at wide-eyed little
Jackson beside her. And I looked at Walker's tanned, muscular
forearms gripping the wheel; the way he fidgeted, playing with
his bottom lip with the fingers of his left hand while he drove;
the light shadow of stubble that covered his jaw. I didn't want
Walker, not the way Libby had suggested. I wasn't some sort
of college kid with a crush. Walker was very attractive, but that
wasn't it. I realized in that moment that more than anything, I
wanted to *be* Libby. I wanted all of it: her entire life.

**A FEW HOURS LATER,** my arms were sore and I felt like I'd
run a marathon. I'd never swum in the ocean before, and so I
hadn't been prepared to brace myself against the cold, or for
how battered I'd feel by the waves. Walker and I were out with
Zoe, tugging her along in the shark raft as promised. Libby was
right: it hadn't been a good idea. But I'd already entertained
Zoe with a sandcastle for far longer than her attention span
normally allowed. And so finally we'd caved. Zoe was having a
blast, but even Walker looked like he might collapse.

"Does she ever come in?" I called to Walker over the crashing of the waves. He gave me a questioning look.

"Who, Libs?" he asked. I nodded. "Nah, she likes to do
her sunbathing right over there. She thinks the ocean's dirty
and all." I glanced toward Libby, who was enjoying the setup
Walker had created for her out of a beach blanket, an umbrella,
and a foldable lounge chair. It looked like she was sipping

on something, maybe a beer, while she flipped through her magazine. She looked so glamorous sitting there, in her sunglasses and her big floppy hat and her blue-striped bandeau bikini. As I stood there with sodden strands of hair sticking to my cheeks, I felt as if twenty lifetimes, and not twenty yards, separated us.

"Watcha thinking?" Walker called out. I turned back to him, the violence of the waves, and ruddy-cheeked Zoe. Maybe there was more than one way to have it all.

"This is so much fun," I shouted, my mouth widening into a grin. "It's my first time, you know."

"Your first time at the beach?" Walker looked at me in disbelief. "But you're . . ." He clamped his mouth shut, as if he'd thought better of whatever he was about to say. Then he got a devilish gleam in his eye and let go of Zoe's raft for a second, reaching out toward me. My heart quickened as he moved toward me, narrowing the gap between us. I kept my hand on Zoe's raft, anchoring her.

"Daddy!" she cried. "Daddy, Daddy, Daddy!" But his eyes were trained on mine, and they didn't flicker away for even an instant. I was aware of Libby watching us from somewhere close to the shore, but I didn't care. It was as if I'd lost all control.

And then he dove under the water and grabbed my legs, and before I knew what was happening, he was pushing me up, up, higher than the water until he let go and I soared. For a moment, I flew. It was a brief feeling of delirious freedom. And then I hit the water, its icy fingers dragging me down, pushing me back and forth against the sand until I lost all sense of direction and hoped only that it might let me go before I drowned.

And then it was over; he was helping me to my feet. I coughed, choking up water and phlegm. I blinked the salt out of my eyes, which were burning furiously.

"Why did you do that?" I shouted, shaking in fury. I'd been certain I was going to die. Walker looked at me with concern. Zoe looked back between the two of us, her big eyes wide.

"Initiation," Walker told me, his voice abashed. "I'm sorry; I didn't realize you'd be so scared."

"I think we should go in," I told him. "Zoe's looking pink." I was just saying it as an excuse, but when I looked at her more closely, Zoe *did* look pink. More like red, actually. My little goose was frying. And then it occurred to me that I hadn't put any sunscreen on her.

"Zoe, did Mommy give you sunscreen?" I asked her.

"Mmm-mm," she said, shaking her head.

"Oh god."

"It's fine," Walker assured me. "She doesn't look that bad."

"I bad, Daddy," she said, sensing his concern and my panic. Her eyes began to tear up.

"Shh, you're fine, sweet pea," he told her. But I was already beginning to drag her back to shore. I prayed that her burn wasn't as awful as it looked in this light. But as it turned out, it was worse. Once we got in the shade, it became evident that Zoe was going to be in a lot of pain later on.

"I can't believe you didn't put any sunscreen on her!"

Libby's voice was shrill, more furious than I'd ever heard it. "How could you be so careless?"

"I'm so sorry," I stammered.

"Sorry? Do you even know what sun exposure does to baby skin? It should have been the *first* thing you thought of!"

"She didn't know, Libs," said Walker, trying to soothe her. "You're her mother. She probably just thought—"

"And *you're* her father!" Libby said coldly.

"What about Jackson, should we put some on him? Even in the shade . . ."

"I already did that!" Her fury was almost more terrifying because it was controlled. She wasn't losing it, the way I'd seen my mother lose it with Dean back when he first moved in. She was completely calm.

I stepped away as they spoke in low voices, reaching for my bag. I'd packed a T-shirt for myself, and I pulled it out and over Zoe's head to cover her exposed skin. She was crying softly, bothered by her parents' fighting.

"Hush," I whispered. "It's going to be okay." It struck me that Libby hadn't so much as glanced at Zoe's skin yet, but I guessed she would once we packed up and got into the car. Besides, the burn hadn't fully manifested itself. It probably would be much brighter and more painful by evening.

I settled on the opposite end of the blanket and pulled Zoe into my lap, reading to her from my book. I glanced over after a minute, and it appeared that Walker was apologizing profusely. Finally, he reached over and squeezed Libby's hand,

and she offered him her cheek for a kiss. I couldn't help feeling grateful that Walker had absorbed the brunt of her anger.

"How's my butterbean?" he asked as he approached.

"Good, Daddy. Annie's weading me a stowy."

"Is that so?" He glanced down at the book in my hand. "'The Pit and the Pendulum?'" he asked. "Don't you think she's a little young for that?"

"I was giving her the abridged, G-rated version," I said. "I'm really sorry about the sunscreen. I should have thought of it."

Walker sighed. "You probably should have," he agreed. "But so should I. And so should Libby," he added. "I don't know why she'd do Jack's sunscreen and not Zoe's."

"Zoe is Annie's responsibility, Walker," Libby called. "And by the way, I can hear you."

"Have I told you how gorgeous my wife is?" Walker asked, reacting quickly. "I'd say she's the most beautiful woman on the planet, really, if I had to put money on it. . . ."

"Oh please," Libby said. "Nice try. Come on, let's pack up and get out of here. We can eat our lunch by the pool at home, like civilized people."

"Yes, ma'am," Walker agreed. "Come on, troops. You heard the woman. Let's load up."

"You know I hate it when you call me 'woman,' Walk."

"Noted." But he was smiling again. They both were. I clasped Zoe's hand in mine, and we headed for the car, a beach bag slung over my shoulder and Falafel, none the worse for wear, cradled under her chin.

# CHAPTER SIX

**OWEN'S FACE LIT UP WHEN HE**—thankfully *not* one of his parents—answered the door. It had nearly killed me not to visit him sooner, but I wanted to show Libby where my priorities lay (with them) and refute her suspicion (that I had a crush on Owen) even if it was true (it was). But now it was Sunday, my day off, and I could spend it however I wanted.

"You either have the world's worst manners, or it took you a hell of a long time to recover from your fall." His face broke into the cutest closed-lipped smile I'd ever seen on a guy. A toothpick hung out of one corner of his mouth, and he was a little sweaty, but not unattractively so. Quite the opposite. I'd caught him unawares, and yet he looked even better than the last time I'd seen him. I sighed inwardly. It wasn't fair—I'd spent a half hour selecting the perfect outfit from my meager wardrobe, a balance between subtly alluring and effortlessly casual. And the perfect makeup: lip gloss and a swipe of mascara.

"Actually, I happen to be the epitome of mannerly," I informed him, trying to sound both cuter and more confident than I felt. "So polished are my manners that I even brought you a gift." I pulled a plastic container from behind my back. Zoe and I had labored over its contents all morning. Owen looked through the side of the container and, seeing only a brown mass, pried its corner open and sniffed skeptically.

"If you're trying to poison me," he said, "it's not going to work. My stomach's built like an armory."

"I would never. Apparently I need you too much."

"So what is it?"

"Invite me in, and I'll tell you." Owen stepped aside and assumed the affected half bow of a butler. I couldn't believe how bold I was being; it was totally unlike me. But that's the funny thing about reinventing yourself: you can be any way you want to be at any given moment. I felt hopeful but without any confidence. I guess I didn't truly expect things with Owen to go anywhere. I still felt too much like the old me, no matter what sort of masks I put on in the meantime. It would take more than a new home, family, and school to really change that. But for a while I could be satisfied with playing pretend.

Owen led me through the foyer and into the kitchen. The house seemed to be composed of a lot of tiny rooms, rather than an open expanse of just a few large rooms, like Libby and Walker's. And from the looks of two of the rooms we passed on the way to the kitchen—a family room and din-ing area, maybe?—these small rooms were far homier and less formal than anywhere at the Cohens'. My brief glimpse told me that they were chaotic but lovely, filled with objects that didn't make any sense individually but formed some sort of discordant harmony when all lumped together. The dining area was colorful and bright, lined with windows that overlooked the bay and decorated with Japanese vases and vintage Euro-style furniture in shades of green and blue. There was a gate up in the kitchen, the childproof kind, blocking the room off from the rest of the house. Owen disassembled it, blocking my line of vision. As soon as it was down and I was free to peek around the corner, I saw her.

"Annie, meet Izzy," Owen said. "Isabella, Annie is our neigh-bor. Say a polite hello." An enormous dog about the size of a small pony barked twice in response, her tail wagging expec-tantly. "'Say hello' was one of the first commands we taught her," Owen explained. "That and 'Pee outside.'"

"Hi, Izzy." I knelt down and stroked the dog's head and belly. Her rough tongue lapped at my palm in response. "What breed is she?"

"She's a Rhodesian Ridgeback," he said. "Izzy here won Best in Group at Westminster back in her day."

"And how old is she now?"

"Pushing ten. She was two back in her glory days." He turned to the dog, grabbing her around the muzzle so he could address her directly: "I'm only saying this for our guest's ben-efit, Iz. You know I find you more glorious every single day."

I laughed, helping myself to a stool by the large granite island that graced the center of the room. On it rested a plate with a half-eaten bagel. And on the bagel rested a substance that closely resembled cat puke.

"*What* is that?" I asked him, not attempting to hide the horror in my voice. "Please tell me it's something for the dog."

"Don't be ridiculous," Owen replied. "Izzy has far better taste than that. I'm the only one in the family who eats sardines out of the can."

"You're disgusting."

"You brought me a container full of brown slop as a thank-you gift," he reminded me, raising the sardine-covered bagel to his mouth. He bit off a huge hunk. "Mmmmmmm," he said through his chewing, his voice slightly muffled. "Delicious."

"You're disgusting," I repeated, and this time I actually meant it. "And Zoe slaved away at that slop, I'll have you know. It's dirt pudding, and it's delicious. Extra cookie crumbs, and I already picked out all the worms."

"The worms are my favorite part!"

"The worms are no one's favorite part. They're a terrible idea. It's like someone had an extra bushel of gummy worms they needed to get rid of."

"I like the worms."

"Take it up with Zoe," I told him. "They're probably at the bottom of her stomach by now." We stared at each other for a second, an awkward silence descending. I leaned over to pet Izzy so I'd have something to do with my hands. Owen cleared his throat.

"So how are you liking it over there?" he finally asked.

"It's great," I replied. "Really great. The Cohens have been super welcoming."

"Yeah?"

"Yeah. Why do you sound surprised?"

"No reason, really." Owen looked mildly uncomfortable. "I just . . . we don't know them very well. I think my mom swung by a few times to invite them to dinner, but they seem to prefer to hang out by themselves."

"Well, Libby did just have a baby," I heard myself saying defensively. "And they just moved here, so I'm sure they're still settling in." That last part was a blatant lie—their house was fully set up and their belongings unpacked like they'd been there for years.

"It's cool," Owen said, raising both palms in the air in a gesture of innocence. "I didn't realize you were so close to them. How do you know them, anyway?"

"We met online at the beginning of the summer," I mumbled. "I answered their ad."

"So . . . you don't actually *know* them," Owen stated. "You sort of Internet-dated them."

"I've been living there for two weeks now," I told him. "I think that's enough time to get a sense of anyone. I guess I trust my instincts. Libby just kind of . . . gets me. I can't explain it. And besides, you're hardly one to talk. You're my age and you're still living at home."

"I'm probably older than you. I'm twenty."

"Case in point."

"Touché."

I laughed. Owen was fun to talk to; he didn't seem to take anything too seriously. My budding crush, which had originally been based on superficial things like looks combined with scenario (being "saved" by a handsome EMT was a meet-cute too good to waste), was full-fledged now that I liked his personality, too.

"Can I have a glass of water?" I asked. "I'm feeling parched from all this verbal sparring."

"Yes . . . if you'll also join me for a milkshake." I felt myself blush—*was he asking me on a date?* Then Owen gestured toward the blender, already half-full of ice cream, chocolate syrup, and milk. Not a date. Right here, right now. I ducked my head down, hoping he didn't notice my face's rapid transition to a vivid shade of pink.

Owen brought down a glass from the cupboard above the island and filled it with water at the sink. Then he dropped two more enormous scoops of ice cream into the blender and squeezed chocolate syrup on top, sighing melodramatically as it oozed slowly from the bottle.

"You'd think they'd have developed a better way of dispensing it by now," he remarked.

"I think it's all about portion control. You're not supposed to use half the bottle every time."

"Once you try it, you won't be complaining."

He was right. It was awesome. Somehow he'd perfected

the ratio of milk to ice cream so the end result was thick, like something from a restaurant, rather than runny, the way home-made milkshakes usually were. It was heavenly.

"Yum," I told him. "Thanks for making it."

"It's my favorite thing to cook," he said.

"Oh yeah? What else is in your culinary repertoire?"

"Sardine bagels. S'mores. Grilled cheese on the Foreman."

"An impressive range."

"I've never actually utilized the oven or stove," he remarked in between slurps. "I find them superfluous."

"I think your overwhelming talent has probably surpassed them," I said. He laughed in the way only confident people do, loudly and with his head tossed back.

"So what's your greatest fear?" he asked, when he finally caught his breath.

"Oh god," I groaned.

"What?"

"Nothing." I shook my head. "It's nothing, really." I didn't want to say what was on my mind for fear of offending him.

"You're a nihilist?"

"Very funny." I scowled.

"Then what?"

"I just really, really hate these kinds of questions."

"What kind? The curious kind? The kind that show an interest in who you are?"

"YES! Exactly. The getting-to-know-you ones. The only lamer question is, 'What kind of music do you listen to?'"

"Actually," he said offhandedly, "it wasn't really about

getting to know you. Had you allowed me to explain myself before jumping to conclusions, you might have learned that I was asking for different reasons, reasons that directly contribute to your well-being."

"Okay, what? Why did you want to know? And it's bats, by the way."

He raised his eyebrows, grinning a little. "We'll get back to *that* in a second. But that's a relief. I'm just really glad it's not spiders, like the rest of the female population."

"Why?" I asked. "And by the way, that is such a stereotype."

"I only asked because there is a massive tarantula right outside the patio window, and I didn't want you to freak out if you turned around and saw it." I jumped and whirled around, making a strange squeal-grunt noise that I hadn't thought I was capable of producing. The spider's hairy leg and half its body were lazily feeling around on the glass in the upper left-hand corner of the door.

"Huh," he said. "It'll be interesting to see what you get like around bats." He came around from behind the counter to stand next to me. "God, it's been so long since I've seen one of these. Pretty sick, right?"

"Definitely," I told him. "And not in the way that you mean it, either." I could feel the heat from his body touching the heat from mine, our two heats meeting somewhere in the middle and sizzling together to form electric circuitry I hoped he could feel, too.

If he felt it, he clearly didn't find it as fascinating as the fist-sized spider in the window. "I used to have one of those," he remarked. "Before I got Izzy. His name was Chad." I glanced at him out of the corner of my eye. He appeared to be dead serious.

"Go on," I encouraged. Owen moved closer to the window, his eyes locked on the furry arachnid. Izzy nuzzled close to me, her snout wetting my kneecap as if to commiserate.

"Yeah," he told me. "That was back when I was ten. It was how I wound up with Izzy, actually. I begged my parents for a dog for years, and my mom always said, 'No dog, but you can have any pet that lives in a cage.' I thought that was sort of insensitive of her, given that living things of any kind shouldn't be caged, but I went ahead and picked out my consolation pet."

"Chad," I said.

"Chad," he agreed.

"So Chad, being revolting, shed a favorable light on dogs?"

"Not exactly," he said, tapping the window a few times until the spider scuttled away, hopefully not toward the Cohens' house. "My mom put up with it for a while. Everything was totally fine. She just wouldn't come into my bedroom. Which worked, because then I didn't have to clean it. But then I started feeling bad for Chad, so I set him free outside. And then the next day, he came back. My mom found him on the front stoop, where he was eating a mouse."

"Oh my god." I shuddered. "That's so gross."

"I thought it was good of Chad and kind of catlike, but my mom was freaked out. So that was the end of that."

"How could you be sure it was him and not some random

other tarantula? Apparently they're abundant in these parts," I said, nodding toward the door. I pulled out a bar stool behind me and took a seat, sucking up the remains of my milkshake while I listened. I liked hearing Owen tell stories. He was so open and easy to talk to. Plus, he was kind of a weirdo, like me.

"Yeah, well . . ." He trailed off, looking uncomfortable.

"What?" I asked, sensing my chance to pry out an embarrassing nugget of information.

"Nothing," he mumbled.

"Seriously," I told him, "you can't do that. Not after your nihilist comment."

"Fine," he sighed, obviously reluctant to tell me. "Chad had an identifying feature. I had spray-painted him gold."

I choked, snorting milkshake up my nose. I coughed several times before I was able to talk again. I hadn't been expecting that. "Jesus," I said. "How did he live through that experience? And *why* did your parents allow you to have contact with any living thing ever again?"

"The spray paint was nontoxic," he said defensively. "It was just that kind kids use on their hair at Halloween. It wasn't a big deal."

"Right," I said, unable to control my laughter.

"Forget it. I never should have told you."

"Izzy, you're just lucky to be alive, aren't you?" I said in my most obnoxious baby voice, scratching Izzy under the chin. "Aren't you, girl?"

"All right, all right," he said, rolling his eyes. "It's all soooo hilarious. Now let's talk bats."

"Just tell me you're not easily grossed out," I warned him.

"I've got a stomach of steel." I tried not to picture what his stomach of steel might look like . . . or feel like. . . .

"Okay, well," I said after I'd cleared my head. "When I was nine, my mom shut a bat in the closet door. She beheaded it."

"Jesus," Owen said. "How did that happen?"

"She opened the door, the bat squeaked and started to fly, she freaked out, slammed the door, and the bat wasn't fast enough. It was really sad. Not to mention gruesome."

"I bet," he said, nodding. "So the image of a halved bat has haunted you ever since."

"I literally don't see bats the same way. They're just disconnected heads and bodies."

"I get it," he said. "I one hundred percent get it. I don't even think this warrants further discussion."

"You asked," I reminded him.

"And now I totally wish I hadn't," he said. We smiled at each other, and this time he was the first to duck his head. It was one of those moments when, if we'd been dating, we would have curled up together or kissed or something. But we weren't, so instead there was awkward space and silence between us.

"Well," I said, clearing my throat and pushing back from the stool. "I guess it's time for me to return to my duties."

"Be off with ye, scullery maid," he said drily.

"Shut up." I turned to the door as another uncomfortable silence fell. If I didn't leave right that minute, what had been a fun hour together was in danger of spiraling downward very quickly. But I couldn't help dragging my feet. It was the best time I'd had since I'd moved to Marin County. Unable to delay further, I gave Izzy a scratch behind the ears and headed for the door with Owen trailing behind me silently.

"So, this was fun," Owen said as he opened the door for me.

"Yeah," I agreed. "Thanks again for the milkshake. Best milkshake ever." I gave him a wide smile, hating myself for being so weird.

"Okay, see ya around."

"Yep. Bye! Later Iz," I said with a final rub to the dog's head. I was almost halfway down the front walk and five seconds into an angry internal monologue in which I chastised myself for being such a coward when I heard Owen's voice behind me.

"Annie!" he called out. "Wait up." Then he was jogging toward me.

"I forgot to get your number," he said, like it was the most natural thing in the world. "I don't want to have to come knocking every time I want to talk to you."

"Oh, right," I said, like I'd forgotten too. "Hold on a sec." I had to dig my phone out of my pocket and scroll to the section under "Contacts" that listed my number. "I still don't know it by heart," I explained. "They just gave it to me yesterday."

"Here, we'll do it this way." He took my phone from my hand and began dialing another number—his own—and a second later his phone started ringing.

"Perfect," I said, but he wasn't relinquishing my phone. I

peered at him pointedly, but he was busy fiddling with my interface. Was "interface" the name of the phone display? Who knew. "So whatcha doing over there?" I asked.

"One minute," he muttered. "Okay," he said a second later, extending my phone toward me. "Now you have both my number and the most spectacular game ever to grace the smartphone. So now we can play each other."

"Cool," I said, trying to be casual, even though our interaction had effectively ended even better than I'd hoped, with *the promise of continued communication!* "See you soon." I jogged back to the house, willing myself not to look back. He couldn't know how excruciating leaving him had felt, or how ecstatic I was now. I ran right up to my room, sure I was sweating and flushed enough to warrant an interrogation from Libby if I didn't clean up first. My body was fireworks. It was rapids. It was the Grand Prix. It was racing ahead of me and I couldn't control it, but I didn't want to.

**I SPENT THE REMAINDER** of the evening playing Owen in Words with Friends, the Scrabble-like game he'd downloaded to my phone just after programming his number into my contacts. I never thought I could feel such profound ardor for a cell phone. If there was a better feeling than the one I felt then, I wasn't sure I could live to handle it.

# CHAPTER
# SEVEN

**RIGHT AFTER ZOE'S** oatmeal and strawberries, I broached the subject of sidewalk chalk. "Do you have any?" I asked Zoe.

"Mommy," she said in a slurpy voice around the lip of her sippy cup, a tiny dribble of milk rolling down her chin.

"Mommy has it?" She shook her head, yet pointed to Libby's office. It was a mixed message, but I walked over anyway and rapped gently on the door.

"Yes?" Libby's voice was curt. I instantly regretted approaching her.

"I thought I could take Zoe outside and play with some sidewalk chalk," I told her. "Do you happen to have any?"

"We just moved here, Annie," she sighed. "Do you really think we had time to stock up on sidewalk chalk, of all things?"

"Okay. Well . . . maybe we'll play in the sprinkler, then." I smiled over at little Jackson, who was enjoying tummy time in his Pack 'n Play. Apparently babies were supposed to lie on their bellies for a while every day in order to strengthen their necks. Jackson couldn't stand not looking at us—it was cute to see him struggle to lift his neck in my direction.

"I'm happy to help out with Jackson more, if you want," I said hopefully.

Libby looked up at me, her eyes suddenly suspicious. "Jackson's fine here with me. And why do you want to spend time outside all of a sudden?" she wanted to know. "Is it the boy next door? I know you went over there yesterday," she said disapprovingly.

"I did . . . just to thank him. But no, that's not it. I just want to enjoy the warm weather while it lasts. Didn't you say this is unusual for San Francisco?"

"Yes," Libby said. "It's usually much cooler than this." I could tell she wasn't completely satisfied, but I wasn't sure why it mattered; why should I feel guilty for making a friend? Or even a boyfriend . . . if it ever got that far? Nevertheless, I felt a little uncomfortable, as though I'd let her down. "Well, you're welcome to set up the hose and sprinkler," she said reluctantly. "They're both in the yard."

"Okay, great." I turned to go.

"Annie . . ." Her voice sounded wary, concerned. I stopped at the door and looked back at her, waiting for her to go on. "It's just . . . we don't know anything about that boy. I don't want him to hurt you. You know, if you get involved with him." She held my gaze in hers. "I know you're vulnerable, and I don't know if I'm prepared to help you mend a broken heart."

I took a deep breath, forcing a smile. "I'm fine," I said. "Really. It's not an issue. But if it were, I'd be fine."

"Okay," she said, turning back to her paperwork. "Please keep Zoe far away from the street."

A few minutes later, Zoes and I were outside running through the sprinkler. We were having so much fun that I almost forgot why I'd wanted to come outside in the first place (which of course was to entice Owen out, too). But I couldn't get Libby's words out of my head. Was she being protective? Or did she not think I was good enough for Owen? I tried to convince myself that she'd just been looking out for me. That she was being protective because she'd grown to care about me.

Fifteen minutes later, when Zoe and I had turned off the sprinkler and were sitting on towels eating apple slices as we dried off, I heard the distant sound of a door slamming. I couldn't see the front of Owen's house from where we sat, at the bottom of the hill that formed the front lawn, but I held my breath anyway, hoping it was him.

Izzy rounded the bend first, loping past the hydrangea bush. She was off-leash. Zoe froze up mid-bite, and I wrapped my arm around her protectively. Izzy came right up to me, planting one paw in my lap and licking my face aggressively.

"No!" Zoe shrieked from beside me. "Bad dog! Go away, dog!"

"Shhh," I told her, stroking Izzy's head. "She's a nice doggie. See?"

"Doggies awe bad!" she insisted.

"No, sweetheart. Who told you that?"

"Mommy," she said, looking at Izzy suspiciously. Izzy sniffed at Zoe's apple slice and Zoe held it out, allowing the dog to take it gingerly from her palm.

"See, Monkey? Not all doggies are bad. This one's very nice," I told her as Owen came around the corner.

"Sorry!" he called. "She slipped out without a leash. She's not bothering you two, is she?"

"Not at all," I said. And I meant it: Zoe had begun stroking Izzy's fur of her own accord. "I think somebody's made a new friend," I told Owen with a smile.

"Awesome," he said. "So who's this little lady? I don't think we've ever met."

"Really?" I asked, surprised. "Well, she's been your neighbor longer than I have. Zoe, meet Owen. He lives next door. Owen, this is my friend Zoe."

"Hello," he said, kneeling on the grass. He took Zoe's hand in his. "It's nice to meet you."

"Hi," she mumbled, still transfixed by Izzy, who was now slobbering all over her face.

"Zoe, Izzy's so big she's almost like a pony. I bet you could sit on her back and she'd carry you around the yard."

Zoe looked at Owen without saying anything, then turned back to Izzy.

"I think that was a no," I told him.

"I think she won't deign to talk to me," he said.

"Can't blame a girl for having standards."

Owen swatted my shoulder, making me blush. Something about him lit me up. He made me feel like I was about to laugh all the time whenever I was around him. I felt both prettier and more self-conscious all at once, in particular since I was wearing the red one-piece-and-tunic combo, still wet from the sprinkler.

"Where'd you go on Words with Friends last night?" he wanted to know.

"I fell asleep," I told him. "I had to get up early today to watch Zoe. Why, did you want to further humiliate me?" When we'd stopped last night, he'd just scored seventy-two points on *placate*. My WWF vocabulary was mostly three-lettered.

"Nooo," he said. "I just missed you after you disappeared." I felt the beginnings of a serious blush spreading across my face. He cleared his throat and looked down at his shoes. "Seriously, though," he said then, "what's the deal? Are you babysitting for them full-time? Doesn't Mrs. Cohen work from home? My mom said she's an interior designer, but her car's always in the driveway."

"She has a home office," I replied, a little wary of telling Owen too much. I had the feeling the Cohens liked their privacy, given the fact that they had promised to value mine. "And I'm in school. I just started at SFSU. The hours are different every day depending on my classes, but Libby promised me it wouldn't be more than twenty-five hours a week when she hired me. She just wants to make sure she can get some work done without having to worry about the kids. And what they're paying me is amazing—I wouldn't be able to afford college without it." I stopped short, worried I'd said too much. But Owen didn't seem bothered. He was listening carefully, but there wasn't any judgment in his expression.

"And I don't know, Libby's just gone above and beyond to be as supportive as possible," I continued. "And she seems totally comfortable having me around Zoe."

"What about the baby?"

"Jackson's mostly with her, so far. I barely ever look after him. He just sleeps and feeds all the time, so she keeps him in her office. But anyway, another thing she did was help me pick out my courses and get me registered. I had no idea what I wanted to study when I came here a few weeks ago. I just knew I wanted to do something kind of creative. But I never thought about interior design, and I'm pretty sure it's *perfect*. I mean, look at Libby's life! Look at her *job*." I paused, aware that I'd been going on for a while. "Sorry," I told him, eager to change the subject. "Guess I got carried away. It's been a while since I've talked to someone who isn't just out of diapers."

"No worries," he said, looking thoughtful.

"Why did you ask?" I wondered aloud. "They're really great, you know."

"I don't doubt it," he said. "I only asked because I wanted to get an idea of your schedule." He fidgeted a little, looking nervous. "I was thinking maybe we could go out sometime. I could show you around San Francisco a little. You know, since you're new here and everything." I wasn't sure if he was suggesting that we go on a date, but I almost didn't care. Whatever he was asking was enough to make my face flush and my heart pound out of my chest.

"Sure," I said. "Yeah, that would be great."

"Okay. Great." He smiled, relieved. "That's awesome. Just, you know, let me know when you're free."

"I have Sundays off," I told him.

"Oh . . ." He trailed off. "That's almost a week away. Will you have any time during the week?"

"I'm not really sure. It's kind of a play-it-by-ear situation."

"No set hours?"

I shrugged. "Not really. I mean, once I get started with classes it'll probably even out, I would assume. But for now it's just whenever they need me."

"Just be careful," Owen said.

"What do you mean?"

"Nothing, really. I just mean that I could see that situation getting a little weird."

"Weird how?" He sounded so negative, and it was starting to irk me. As much as I liked Owen, I didn't want him ruining my high. Everything was going so well. The last thing I needed was for someone to plant a seed of doubt.

"I don't know, what if you want to change majors and Libby gets pushy or insulted? Or, like, what if they start asking you for more hours and you feel awkward saying no? It all seems great now, but when you're working *and* living with someone, things could get weird. It's like that thing people say about not eating where you sleep, or something."

"I'm pretty sure it's 'Don't shit where you eat.'"

"Same concept."

"Not at all," I said stiffly. "And anyway, I'm used to working hard. I think I can handle this."

**87**

"Look," he said again. "I'm not trying to piss you off. I just know that I've had some situations where friends and I have worked together and it hasn't panned out, and things became complicated and it was harder to sort out than if it had been strictly friendship or strictly professional. So I guess what I'm saying is, set boundaries. Don't be so in love with that family that you let them take advantage of you."

"'That family' wouldn't do that," I told him coldly, my voice shaking. I clutched my hands together tightly in my lap, so Owen couldn't see how upset I was. "And you don't know what you're talking about. You don't even know them, and as far as I can see, you don't know a whole lot about keeping a job, either. And you don't even go to *college*." I regretted my outburst as soon as it was over. My cheeks were flaming for what seemed like the millionth time that day, and I was so upset I'd begun to shake. He didn't respond, and his face looked stoic, but I could tell from the pained expression in his eyes that I'd hit a nerve.

"I should probably walk the dog," he said, standing up.

"Owen," I started.

"I've got to go," he interrupted. "It's cool. It's not like you said anything that wasn't true." He brushed off his shorts and hooked Izzy's leash onto her collar.

"Okay."

"Come on, Iz," he said. "Nice meeting you, Zoe. Catch you guys later." Then he was off. It occurred to me belatedly that I might have ruined my first and only chance at going on a date with Owen. I struggled to hold back the tears I felt forming in the corners of my eyes, while Zoe babbled about her new-found love for "doggies."

It wasn't until I headed up to my room later to get cleaned up, though, and suffered the minor frustration of not being able to slam the door behind me—a frustration I'd borne all my life—that I wondered why I'd reacted so intensely. Was it because I finally found a place where I belonged and people who cared, and I was eager to protect that? Or was it just because Libby and Walker knew my secret, and that bound us more tightly than I'd realized? Either way, I felt bad. The trembling, the anger—that kind of thing hadn't happened since I was a kid. It couldn't start happening now. Maybe I'd blown my chance with Owen, but I wouldn't let my emotions get in the way of my position at the Cohens'.

# CHAPTER EIGHT

**"STORIES?"**

Zoe shook her head adamantly. It was the day after I'd completely ruined everything with Owen forever, and babysitting was not going well. It was only two P.M.; Libby and Walker were out, the baby was sleeping, and we'd already run through most of our typical go-to activities. We'd made a craft—pumpkin-shaped votives to line the front yard at Halloween; we'd baked cutout cookies in the shape of stars, which Libby would likely throw out for their dangerous nutritional content; we'd read five *Fancy Nancy* stories and three *Amelia Bedelia*; we'd watched an episode of *Dora the Explorer*; played a game of Red Light, Green Light; built a tower with Legos; and Zoe had gone down for a brief nap only to awaken twenty minutes later, restless and crying. We didn't have use of the car, so I couldn't take Zoe to the park or zoo. I was running out of ideas.

"What about a walk?"

Zoe looked excited for a second, offering me the beginnings of a dimpled grin. "What about my twike?" she asked hopefully, making me laugh.

"Sure. Is it in the broom closet?"

"No," she said, shaking her head and laughing.

"In Mommy's bedroom?" I asked, making a game of it.

"Nooo!"

"In the microwave?"

"NO!" Now she was full-on giggling, and I sighed with relief. I'd learned over the last month or two that keeping Zoe's spirits up was a big deal. If she had a crying fit or sank into one of her inexplicable spells of toddler grief, nothing but the coming of a new day would snap her out of it. It was kind of worrisome, definitely stretching the bounds of normal childlike emotion, but it was something I hadn't felt comfortable talking about with her parents.

"Well then, where?" I threw my hands up in confusion. "If it's not in the refrigerator, I don't know what I'll do," I informed her.

"The gawage!" she shouted, collapsing with laughter on the floor of the family room, a room ironically named, since Zoes and I were the only two who ever saw its interior.

"Okay, okay, on to the garage we go." I took her hand in mine, feeling it press trustingly into my palm, our two heartbeats merging. I felt a brief pang. It had been happening more lately, these nagging reminders of my Lissa. I shook my head to clear it. In order to move forward, I *had* to give her up. If it took forgetting her entirely, then that's what I'd do.

It was immediately obvious that the seemingly simple task of unearthing Zoe's tricycle from the depths of the garage was going to be way harder than I'd anticipated. The garage was a war zone of stuff—all kinds of stuff filling a space that would normally accommodate four cars—with an SUV-sized space carved out. It was weird—I'd never seen the inside of the garage until that moment. Libby always parked outside; and if Walker drove us, he made sure to let us out before pulling into the garage, maybe for this very reason.

"I don't know about this," I said. The sobering news did not sit well with my girl, who promptly screwed her face up into the purple beginnings of hysteria.

"Okay," I told her. "We'll take a look. Fine. But you've got to stop this tantrum thing. For real. You're way too old for this."

"I'm thwee."

"Exactly," I told her mock-sternly. "You're basically an adult."

"No," Zoe said.

"Don't argue," I told her mildly, beginning to pick through the rubble. "You have much to recommend you, but I'm both older and wiser than you are." Zoe popped her thumb in her mouth in response and followed me across the garage.

"Stand there," I said, pointing to the center of the SUV space, "and don't move. I don't want you to wind up buried under a pile of old CDs, or whatever they keep in here." The light in the room was garish, creepy. It cast its sinister glow over the boxes and bags and bins. I already didn't like garages—they were worse than attics. They housed spiders and all kinds of unwanteds. I crossed the floor again and pressed the red rectangular button next to the door to the muck room. The garage door lifted with the groan of mechanical gears, and natural light flooded in. I watched it travel up Zoe's flip-flops, knees, dimpled elbows, and head. She smiled trustingly and sat down in the center of the floor.

"I don't see it," I told her skeptically. "Are you sure it's in here?" What I wasn't sure of was why I was asking a three-year-old anything and expecting a reliable answer.

"Back thewe," she said, pointing toward a corner that was completely obscured by a tower of plastic bins. I leaned closer and barely detected a tasseled handlebar.

"Ugh, Zoe, I don't know. I'm going to have to pull all those boxes out. Maybe we should just wait for Daddy to get home. We can go on a walk now, bike ride tomorrow—how's that?" Zoe screwed up her face again and began gasping for air. I groaned inwardly and felt something like frustrated anger well up in my chest. But really, I asked myself, how was I going to spend the rest of the afternoon? May as well spend it lugging boxes around. Even manual labor was preferable to a tantrum.

I lugged a few boxes aside, and divine intervention led me to a bucket of sidewalk chalk (they had some after all!) that I handed to Zoe—she might have a while to keep herself entertained until the tricycle was unearthed. After about twenty minutes of this, I could see the bike beginning to emerge, little by little. I pulled at the handlebars, but it still wouldn't budge.

"*How* are you going to do this?" I whispered to myself, forgetting my present company. Zoe glanced up at me, but seemed unconcerned. My habit of talking to myself on occasion apparently wasn't going to get me in any trouble with her. I turned my attention back to the massive load of boxes rising in front of me like the Andes.

I'd have to rearrange several heavy stacks that sat at the bike's base, trapping the wheels. I was getting sick of the whole endeavor. I lunged for a pile and kicked it hard, trying to move it to the left. It stayed firmly wedged. I leaned my body weight against it, my hands resting on my knees, feeling sweat trickle down my ribcage.

"*Shit.*" I glanced at Zoe. Thankfully, she hadn't heard me that time: she was absorbed in drawing what looked like water, a long stripe of squiggles colored in blue. She hummed her signature tune under her breath, seemingly unaware. I barely noticed it myself by now, she hummed so much. It was part of who she was, just another element of her developing personality. Maybe she had a future as a musician, who knew?

"How badly do you want to ride your tricycle?" I asked her in an even tone, trying to hold my temper. Before I had the sentence out, her eyes had begun to well.

"I want to wide my twike," she told me. "Pwease." If she hadn't added that "pwease," I might have resisted in the name of discipline. But her face was so plaintive, so sweet, those curls framing her face in just the way my dead sister's had. . . .

"Okay. Fine." I gave the stack a final shove with my hip, fully expecting to meet resistance. But in the world of physics, something in my first couple of shoves had upset the balance. And when I leaned just so with my hip, shifting the boxes a fraction of an inch, the stack gave way and tumbled down, the taped sides of the lower boxes bursting under the weight of the upper, their contents spewing onto the dusty cement floor. I stifled my urge to let out a frustrated scream-slash-screech-slash-grunt. But there it was, the tricycle: the golden nugget. Was this what miners felt like? I grabbed its tasseled handles and gave it a tug. It was still wedged behind some stuff, and in that moment I both cursed the Cohens' disorganized ways and felt a rush of pride for my own tenacity. One more good pull and I was holding it aloft.

"Zoe! Look! I got it." I held it in the air for another second in a dramatic display of victory. Zoe's humming merely grew louder, but at least she turned toward me.

*Rockabye Baby, on the treetop. When the wind blows, the cradle will rock. When the bough breaks, the cradle will fall. . . .*

"Zoe," I said calmly, "you are getting on this tricycle even if it's the last thing in the world you want to do right now. Unhand your chalk." She stopped humming and looked up at me, confused.

"The chalk, Zoe, put it down," I said as calmly as possible. Sensing I was near my breaking point, she relinquished the chalk mid-rainbow and came over to me. I helped her aboard her tricycle and gave her a shove. To my satisfaction, she seemed content to pedal around the garage for the time being. It would be a while before we actually left the property. I turned back to the mess.

Clothes, papers, and knickknacks surrounded me.

But they were beautiful, these clothes. Intricate patterns reminiscent of India and Sri Lanka, gold-embroidered silks and cottons, unlike anything I'd seen on Libby. I held a silk scarf aloft. It was a vibrant blend of greens and blues, bright even against the afternoon sunlight that filtered into the garage.

"Mommy!" Zoe cried out, noticing my find. She climbed off the tricycle and toddled over to where I was now sitting, piles of clothing surrounding me. She clutched the scarf in her fists, playing the puppy in our tug-of-war.

"Does Mommy wear these?" I wondered aloud, sifting through the vibrant fabrics.

"No, not now."

"Do you think she would mind if I borrowed this scarf?" I asked. It was one of the loveliest things I'd ever seen, like the ocean and its many hues encapsulated in one piece of silken material. I imagined how it might look against my olive skin and dark hair, and how Owen might look when he saw me in it.

"No. Mommy won't mind," Zoe confirmed.

"Probably not," I agreed, given how much she'd given me from her own closet. I folded it and put it aside, making a mental note to ask Libby for permission later. Maybe these were donations bins. Maybe they'd want to donate to me—I was definitely a worthy cause, my wardrobe consisting mainly of T-shirts and jeans beyond what Libby had given me already.

"Here, hon," I told Zoe, leading her back to the trike. "Pedal around for a little while longer, okay? But stay in the driveway area, where I can see you. I have to clean this mess up." There were at least two boxes of papers to reorganize. I felt a slight flutter of panic, worried Libby would think I'd been snooping.

She'd been so temperamental lately: warm and supportive, mostly, but I was beginning to see hints of a moody streak that I worried was largely due to my presence.

I scooped up a stack of papers, shoving them back into their manila envelope. It looked mostly like receipts and documents, but I didn't want to look too closely. If there was one thing I supported, it was the concept of privacy. Two other folders next to me, though, had spilled all over the place. Their contents were definitely mixed. I'd have to sort through them. One of the files was labeled "lawyer," another read "receipts," and the last read "vacations."

"No big deal," I muttered under my breath. "It'll be easy. Quick and easy." Yep, that was the way. I'd worry about whether to tell Libby about this later, or whether to let sleeping dogs lie, as my mother would have said.

I sat down cross-legged on the cold cement, tucking my ankles up under my calves. I went for a handful of what looked like receipts. They were labeled in foreign currencies, so I put them in the "travel" folder. There was an e-mail printout of itineraries to Spain and Greece. Even though I was doing my absolute best only to identify the information needed to file the papers away, rifling through everything was like getting a secret glimpse into the life I wanted for myself—and a life I'd never seen up close until now.

There was a deed to the house: that went into "lawyer." A Harry Winston receipt from Turks and Caicos (a place I couldn't even pronounce). An airline ticket stub for Walker Cohen to Madrid, seat 4C, business class. Despite myself, I found it fascinating—the places they'd been, the life they led. Maybe one day I'd get to accompany them on a trip in order to watch the kids. I felt a streak of jealousy wend its way through my heart and settle in my gut when I realized that was probably the best I could hope for. I would probably never have a life like this for myself; I'd always be the tagalong au pair. It was irrational, that jealous feeling. But I wanted so much from this—so much more than just a job.

Only a few minutes had elapsed, but I was aware that Zoe wouldn't be satisfied making figure eights in the driveway forever. Thankfully, there were only a dozen or so documents left to identify.

A quick glance at a pay stub from Walker's architectural firm told me that his gross yearly income was a lot. But not the kind of "a lot" that I'd thought it took to live in a place like this. I felt a sharp pang of guilt—I hadn't looked on purpose, but this was way outside the bounds of appropriate and professional. I bit my lip and forged ahead—what was I supposed to do, leave it for Libby to clean up?

The next item was bound by a paperclip. A bolded statement across the top of the first page read, "Last will and testament of Adele Cohen."

"Adele Cohen?" I whispered it aloud, and Zoe looked at me curiously. I peered closer at the paper, which obviously belonged in the "lawyer" envelope. I wondered who Adele was—Walker's sister, his mother? Whoever she was, the numbers that flashed in front of my eyes indicated that she'd had a tremendous amount of money. More money than I could imagine. I'd never liked dipping into people's private lives, mostly because I'd never wanted anyone to dip into *mine*. I didn't like knowing anything about the Cohens' money or their relatives' money or anyone's money at all. It made me squeamish.

I shoved the paperwork into its appropriate folder. I filtered through the rest of it in two minutes flat; suddenly, I wanted to get out of there. I felt dirty, like I'd done something illicit, and I had the urgent need to put as much space as possible between me and the documents. I stared down at the folders in my hands, about to place them back in the box; but at that moment, a car pulled into the driveway. Zoe pushed the brakes on her tricycle, but it was almost too late; the car was pulling toward us fast. At the end of the driveway, just before the garage, it slammed on its brakes.

Libby exited the car and strode toward me, an angry expression on her face.

I buried the folder at the bottom of the box before she reached the inside of the garage, while she was still squinting against the sun. But it didn't matter; she'd seen me. I only hoped she didn't think I'd been snooping around on purpose.

# CHAPTER NINE

**WALKER WANTED TO FIRE ME;** Libby said no.

"This is beyond unprofessional," he railed. "Anyone else would be fired instantly for this kind of transgression."

"Walker, really," Libby scolded, "this isn't your office. No need for the lofty vocabulary."

"She rifled through our *files*, Libby. She's completely lacking in discretion. The girl isn't like us! Even you've said that. Now I'm saying she can't be trusted."

"Don't be ridiculous," Libby said calmly, but with a hint of anger in her voice. "Do you know how many opportunities she's had to steal from us if she wanted to? And you're mad because she accidentally knocked over a few files? What reason would she have for snooping through our boxes? Everything she could possibly be tempted by is right in front of her! Do you understand that I literally leave wads of cash out on the countertops, and she doesn't touch it? Not only that, but she's amazing with Zoe. Zoe adored her from the start. And god knows I've needed help with Zoe." Libby's voice faltered a bit at that, as though she was struggling to maintain her composure.

As much as my heart swelled at Libby's obvious trust for me, Walker's comments stung. I was listening from the hallway outside my room, not that it could be called eavesdropping. Zoe was long in bed, but Walker wasn't doing anything to adjust the volume of his voice. I probably could have heard it from inside my room with the door closed. If I'd had a door, that is. Libby still hadn't been able to locate a repairman whom she trusted with the antique wood.

*The girl isn't like us.* How stupid I'd been to think I could fit into their world.

"She found some things she shouldn't have," Libby continued in a cool tone. "Some things that shouldn't have been there at all. I thought you'd gotten rid of Adele's stuff, Walker!" Her voice was shrill, thick with potential sobs. "How *dare* you! Do you still love her?" There was a pause that probably only lasted seconds, but to me it may as well have covered the space of an hour. Because in those seconds, something fell into place. Something that, for reasons unknown, drained my entire body. Walker had been married before. The file I'd found—it was his former wife's. *That's* why Libby had reacted so sensitively. I'd unwittingly unearthed something that reminded her of the woman her husband had loved before her. And as for Walker . . . no wonder he wanted to fire me. Who knew how raw his wound still was, how much pain he still felt over his dead wife? Everything was starting to make a lot more sense.

"Of course not!" Walker shouted. "And how could I get rid of the will? We need a record of it."

"Stop yelling!" she said, crying then. "You've woken the baby!" Sure enough, Jackson had begun to cry through his monitor. Walker lowered his voice then, and I heard sounds of his murmuring and her quiet assents. "Sweetheart," he crooned. "Please. I love you. You're my life now." Libby quieted finally, and after a few minutes, Walker declared, "I want her out. I want Annie to pack her bags and go back to wherever she came from. She's caused enough trouble."

"Walker. Listen to me." Libby's voice was as commanding and steady as ever now, as though she was talking to a child. "Let's not lose our heads. Annie is the best thing that's happened to us since we've moved here. I will not let you fire her. She is fantastic with Zoe, she's incredibly mature, and I like her. I know she's trustworthy. I *know* that what happened was an accident. I believe her." She was speaking confidently, louder now. "And what of it? She's living with us. She's bound to hear or see things that are personal every now and again. It's not as if we've got any skeletons in our closet. What does it matter if she knows how much money we have or that you were married before? I know you value your privacy, but the worst that can happen is the neighbors know how much money we have, which they've all been dying to know for months anyway." There was a pause, and finally Walker responded, his voice strained.

"You're right," he said evenly. "We have nothing to hide. But it's the principle of the thing. The girl isn't family, Libby. She's a sweet kid, but accidentally or not, she's crossed the line."

"I'll speak to her. I'll make sure it doesn't happen again. Remember what we talked about. We need her here. God, Walker, the baby's still crying! I have to get him. We can talk about this later."

As I heard her start up the stairs, I slipped back into my room and curled up in bed with my book. The relief I felt at hearing Libby say they needed me was immeasurable. Because I needed them, too. I loved Zoe. And I'd begun to think of Libby as a sister. But more than that, I was afraid of what would happen if I left. Without their recommendation, I wouldn't be able to get a job anywhere. If they revealed the truth of my past—and my sister's death—to another family, I'd be ruined. Who else would take a chance on me the way they had, knowing my past? And for the wages they were paying me? No one. I'd have to quit school, move back home, work a minimum wage job at the diner or grocery store, just like everybody else. The Cohens knew too much about me for me to leave. *And,* I realized as I snuggled underneath the fluffy down comforter that enveloped my bed, the light from the hallway pouring into the gaping hollow of my doorway, *now I knew something about them.*

# CHAPTER
# TEN

**THE DOOR STILL WASN'T FIXED.** I didn't even know what was wrong with it in the first place that required an entire week of repair, but I was finding it harder and harder to fall asleep at night. Owen might have had something to do with it; I hadn't seen him since two days ago. I could see now that I'd over-reacted. Maybe it wasn't his place to judge the Cohens or comment on my job here, but it's not like he was being rude. Just presumptuous. And then I responded by being . . . well, *rude*. I had raised myself on *Tiffany's Table Manners for Teenagers* and *How to Be a Lady*. Books I'd coveted, thinking they gave me insight into a world I'd never know. It was not like me at all to be unnecessarily mean.

But I'd been super stressed lately. My initial classes were difficult, and I wasn't making friends easily on campus. I only had one class with Morgan, who'd looked at me blankly after the night of Dis-O, as if she barely remembered hanging out together (and she probably didn't). I wanted to please Libby, but she'd been short-tempered, and it seemed like I was always screwing up: putting the wrong baby formula in the bottle; giving the baby a swim diaper instead of a regular one; washing Zoe's laundry on hot instead of cold, letting the colors run together and all over the whites. It's not that I couldn't babysit—I was awesome with kids and knew exactly what I was doing—it was that I was so distracted.

"So how did it go? When you went out to talk to that boy, I mean," Libby asked in a friendly tone. Two days had already passed since the incident with Owen. It was strange that she was bringing it up again, especially after she had expressed disapproval the first time. She was making coffee in the Nespresso machine and I was preparing Zoe's peaches-and-cream oatmeal while simultaneously feeding the baby bananas from a jar. I patted the corner of the baby's mouth where a chunk of banana puree had dribbled out.

"It was fine, I guess." Although it wasn't fine, not at all. The last thing I wanted to think about was Owen and the Date That Never Was.

"Just fine?" Libby raised an eyebrow.

"I think Zoe had fun with his dog," I said carefully, uncertain whether she'd approve. I felt my throat constricting a little as I remembered how much fun we'd had joking around. Before the incident on the lawn, when he'd become a judgmental asshole. *Or was I projecting?* I tried to ignore the little voice in my head.

"Hey," Libby said, placing her cup gently on the marble surface of the countertop and removing Jackson's spoon from my hand. "You can tell me anything, remember?" She skillfully maneuvered the bananas into Jackson's sparrow mouth, wide open and waiting now that Libby was at the spoon's helm.

"It's no big deal," I said. "He's just not that great. I mean, I guess I kind of hoped we'd be friends." I shook my head and tried to smile. "It was stupid. I just thought it would be cool to have someone so close by to hang out with."

"So why can't you? Did something happen?" she pressed.

I sighed. I didn't really want to tell Libby what had pissed me off. The last thing I wanted to do was cause tension between them and their neighbors, or to make her feel bad.

"I don't know, I guess I just decided he was kind of immature," I admitted, twisting the truth a little. "I mean, who lives with their parents at age twenty? He doesn't have a job, and he's not even in school."

"Walker says he's running his own tech startup," Libby said. "Apparently that's why he skipped out on college. He got some investments and wanted to throw himself into the company. Apparently it has, just in the last six months or so, started to take off. He just does the EMT thing once a week because he likes it," she continued. "I guess he's always had an interest in medicine and thought about going to med school for a while. Walk really got a good impression from him."

"Oh," I said, feeling guilty as the significance of what she was saying began to hit me. "So he's running his own business?"

"Yeah, I guess so. I think he wanted to put his savings into the company rather than funneling it all into rent."

"Oh."

"So maybe he's not as immature as you thought." She smiled knowingly, scraping the last of the baby food from its jar.

"Maybe." I officially felt terrible. I had judged Owen based on . . . pretty much nothing. And now even if I apologized, it wouldn't matter, because the damage was already done. He'd think I was apologizing just because I thought his job was "up to my standards" or something. But none of this would have happened at all if he hadn't mentioned Libby. I normally didn't even care about stuff like getting a slow start—if anything, I understood it better than most. But he'd never see it that way.

"There's something else, isn't there?" Libby asked, appraising my face.

"Not really," I said. "Pretty much just that."

"Did he say something you didn't like?" Libby's voice had become graver, more intense. "I thought we had an understanding, Nanny. I thought you understood you were to tell me everything." I felt confused, lightheaded. She was trying to be supportive, so why did it sound weirdly like a threat? And why was she calling me by my title?

"I—"

"Did you sleep with him?" she asked suddenly.

"What? No, of course not. God!" I couldn't mask my shock. I hoped desperately that she wouldn't be offended.

"Are you a virgin, Nanny?" I looked toward Zoe to see if

she'd heard, not that she was likely to know what the term meant.

"Mrs. Cohen, I really don't like when you call me 'Nanny.'" The words escaped me before I had a second to think about it.

"What?" Libby set her mug down abruptly. It hit the counter so hard that I was afraid it would break. Zoe looked up from her cartoons and stared at us curiously.

"I—I just—"

"No." Libby cut me off in a stern voice, lifting a hand to silence me. "What's with this 'Mrs. Cohen' thing all of a sudden? And what do you mean, 'when I call you "Annie"'? What else would I call you?"

"Annie would be great," I told her. "But you just called me 'Nanny.'" Suddenly, though, I wasn't so sure. The look on Libby's face was a cross between shock and confusion.

"No," she said slowly. Then in a sharper tone, "Zoe! Go watch your *Dora*. Mommy's iPad is right over there. Nanny and I are having a conversation." There it was again. *Nanny* where I should have heard *Annie*. "That's ridiculous," she continued, turning to me. "I would never do something like that! I'm insulted that you'd even suggest it. I would never treat you like you're . . . I don't know, a *servant* or something." She seemed genuinely appalled.

"I don't know," I stammered. "I thought maybe I'd done something to make you angry—"

"That's ridiculous. You probably just heard wrong. 'Nanny' and 'Annie' aren't exactly on opposite ends of the spectrum, you know. But I would never call you by anything but your name."

I nodded. I felt my eyes well up. I was overwhelmed by confusion; I had heard it several times, I was sure of it. But why *would* she do it? None of it made sense. Libby moved to the stool next to mine and draped one arm around my shoulder. "Listen," she said. "You've had a rough couple of weeks. The stress of school, the thing that happened the other day . . . it's no wonder you're giving everything a negative spin. I minored in psychology, you know. And it seems to me like you're interpreting things wrongly. Hearing what you want to hear."

"Maybe you're right." I felt too weak and confused to argue. Maybe she *was* right. If there was one thing I believed, it was that the mind could play tricks on you if you let it.

"Now stop trying to change the subject," she said with a wry laugh. "Are you a virgin or aren't you?" I didn't know how to respond. The whole thing felt so weird.

"I'm not sure I'm comfortable talking about that," I stammered. Libby's jaw tightened.

"No secrets," she told me. "I'm asking for a reason, you know." Thinking back to the garage and how she'd stuck up for me to Walker, I decided she was right. No secrets. Even if I couldn't possibly imagine what her "reasons" were for wanting to know such a thing.

"I'm not technically a virgin, but I think of myself as one," I admitted finally. Now Libby's laugh was more like a bark, loud and raucous.

"Don't we all," she said. "Or at least that's what we try to tell ourselves when we're your age."

"It's just that it was only one time," I started—but Libby was already thumbing through a magazine, apparently uninterested now that I'd given her my answer.

"There was more," I admitted finally, grasping for things that might please her.

"More?"

"Owen. He said some other things. He said his mom had tried to reach out to you and you hadn't been that friendly."

Libby took this in, her jaw stiffening and then relaxing rhythmically, as though she were clenching it tightly over and over.

"Well," she said finally. "I guess I've been a little distracted, what with trying to build my business out here and having Jackson and all."

"That's just what I told him," I said. "I don't even know why he mentioned it, it's ridiculous. His mom's probably just a busybody or something."

"I'm sure she's perfectly nice. I suppose I'll have to make more of an effort to reach out to the neighbors."

"Libby, I—"

"No, no," she said, silencing me. "There's probably some truth to what she said. I haven't made enough time for making friends, and it would probably do me some good. I'll swing by their place today. Or, I know! I'll invite them over for dinner. Would you like that?"

"I don't know. I was pretty rude after he told me that."

"There's always time for an apology. And I appreciate you defending me. Remember, we're on each other's sides."

"Thanks." I smiled up at her. Libby really was amazing, and incredibly kind. A little quirky from time to time, that was all. Besides, who was I to judge what was normal and what wasn't? I'd never had a reliable barometer for social graces. Maybe asking about my virginity was totally normal and noninvasive in Libby's world. It really was a whole different culture, this sphere of wealth and good breeding. I was just a visitor, and she had welcomed me. I had no right to be critical. I didn't deserve her.

"Why don't you take the day off to rest?" she continued, unaware of what I'd been thinking. "It seems like maybe you're exhausted. Maybe I'm pushing you too hard."

"I'm fine," I protested.

"I insist."

"But what about Zoe?"

Libby glanced at Zoe in surprise, as though she'd forgotten about her. "Hmm." She tapped one finger against the counter-top, deliberating. "I'll drop her at her father's office. It'll be fine."

"Oh, I couldn't let—"

"It'll be *fine*," she cut in, more sharply this time. "He's her father, after all. Surely he can spend a day looking after her."

"I'm going to Daddy's?" Zoe asked, her eyes wide and hopeful.

"Yes. Now finish your food and go get your shoes."

"I'll drive her, I don't mind," I told Libby. "You've already taken up a half hour just talking to me. I don't want you to waste half your day." I'd driven the car already a couple of times to campus, and I relished the feeling of being behind the wheel.

"That would be great. I'll just plug his address into the GPS."

I put together a bag of books and toys for Zoe and packed her a lunch. I was so excited about driving Libby's brand-new BMW around the city that I didn't notice until after the fact that Libby hadn't kissed Zoe goodbye. But Zoe hadn't noticed either, thankfully—she was so excited by the prospect of spending the day with her dad, it seemed, that she'd temporarily forgotten about her mom. It was pretty obvious that Zoe favored her father, but that was normal for kids that age—the dad, rarely home, was the novelty. And Libby had her hands full with the baby. It was all completely healthy.

After I dropped Zoe off at her father's architectural firm, I drove aimlessly through the city for a long time, following signs for the Marina District. The weather was gorgeous for fall. The marina was picturesque. People my age were tossing Frisbees and footballs in T-shirts and cutoffs by the shoreline, laughing and sneaking booze from their backpacks. San Francisco was a sleepy little town, as far as I could tell. It was so different from what I'd left in Detroit. I sighed. It was going to take a while for me to make friends . . . but I told myself I may as well start close to home. I knew I had to apologize to Owen; I just hadn't quite figured out how. I thought it over for hours as I drove. I passed cable cars snaking through the streets and roadside musicians playing everything from the accordion to the saxophone to the kazoo. I drove aimlessly through Union Square, past Saks Fifth Avenue. I wanted to get lost in the city.

I drove through Chinatown, where short, crowded buildings jammed up against each other, each storefront displaying its wares prominently through windows and on little stands outside. I made a giant zigzag down Lombard Street, laughing because I'd seen it in pictures but had never dreamed of seeing it in person. I drove past the Alemany flea market, where dozens of vendors had set up stands under tents to ward off the heat wave.

I went to the Haight, a colorful little community that I immediately loved. Its houses were vivid pinks and blues and reds and greens, with elaborate trims on the houses. They reminded me of enormous Fabergé eggs. The alleyways and storefronts there were covered in graffiti, the kind that looks like art rather than vandalism. The Haight was my favorite part of San Francisco up to that point. I could have driven around for many more hours than I did—even stopped off and wandered by foot—but finally the threat of Libby's suspicion was enough to keep me going, taking all the right turns back toward Belvedere Island, which had begun to feel a little bit like a stifling prison because of all the hours I spent working there.

**SEVERAL DAYS LATER,** I was still mulling away. I hadn't seen Owen, thank god; I didn't want to see him before I'd devised a plan. Something that would show him how sincere I really was. I only had one more day to mull; he and his parents were coming over for dinner on Friday night. Problem was, I couldn't focus. The damned door, or lack thereof, was like a gaping hole that taunted me. It made me feel exposed. It took me back to places I didn't want to be. Every time I closed my eyes, there they were: the images I couldn't get rid of.

*The sound of the floor creaking . . .*

*Someone stumbles outside my doorway; my St. Christopher medal falls from my wardrobe to the floor.*

*My mother passed out in her room. Her loud snoring filling the house.*

*Dean's hot, sweaty breath against my neck.*

*Panic.*

I'd tried everything. I'd gotten rid of my bulky wardrobe, put a lock on my door. But it didn't matter; none of it mattered. The day I put in the first lock, it was gone again by the time I got home from school. *"What are you hiding, Annie?"* That's what my mother had said. *"You doing drugs now? What are you keeping from me?"*

*"No lock,"* he'd said. *"It's the only way you raise a teenager."*

This room, in my head, in the dark of night when I couldn't see anything and it could have been anywhere, was turning into that room. I hoped it wouldn't be much longer. I couldn't sleep. I couldn't do anything but lie awake and pray for that door and its sturdy metal bolt to come back. I was so, so afraid. I hadn't wanted to admit how leaving might affect me, how maybe I couldn't leave my demons behind me after all. And during the day, I could pretend—but at night there was no hiding.

I must have lain there for at least an hour, drifting in and out of a troubled sleep, before I heard the first cry. It was the kind of sob you hope a child will never experience—deep and hopeless. The kind I didn't even know a child was capable of until then. But it was undoubtedly Zoe. I lay still, waiting for her mother to run to her—Walker was away for a few days on business, so it would have to be Libby that went to her daughter. I flipped on my bedside lamp and looked at the antique wall clock that I'd slowly gotten used to. It was the vintage sort of thing, large and brassy, that ticked the time away second by second. It read four thirteen A.M.

Zoe's shrieks became louder, and I realized she wasn't caught in a dream anymore; she sounded fully awake and lucid. My heart began to pound as I wondered where Libby was. Wondered if it was overstepping my boundaries to go to the little girl in place of her mother. Finally, my fear that something was happening to her won out. They weren't cries of alarm or terror, but I couldn't stand to hear her sobbing for another second. It was possible, I reasoned, that Libby couldn't hear Zoe from the floor below. *But then why put a little girl all the way over here? Had she been crying like this all alone at night before I showed up?* I couldn't stop the thought, even with its glimmer of betrayal.

I stood up and pulled on my robe, switching the light off behind me as I padded down the hall toward Zoe's suite. Her cries got louder and higher-pitched the closer I got, afflicting me with sharp bursts of fear so strong that I had to will my feet to move closer to the room rather than flee. By the time I reached her door, she'd already risen from bed. Her tiny form looked like a specter's in the moonlit glow of her window, her wild curls askew and floating over her tiny, shaking shoulders; her nightgown floor-length and ghostly pale.

"Zoe, sweetheart?" I whispered. She flung her arms around me in response and buried her hot, sodden face in my shoulder.

"What's wrong, baby?"

She couldn't tell me for several long minutes. She was so distraught that she'd worked herself into a frenzy, hyperventilating and choking on her heavy, grief-laden sobs.

"What is it, sweetie? Did you have a bad dream?" Zoe nodded yes.

"About Mommy," she finally said.

"Oh no, baby, what happened to Mommy?"

"Mommy went away," Zoe told me, her sobs quieting to hiccups.

"No, Zoe. No, no. Just in your dream, do you understand?" I took Zoe's face in my palms and looked into her eyes. "Mommy's just downstairs. Do you want to go see her?" Zoe shook her head and wiped at her nose with her hand. She seemed to be calming down; her eyes looked brighter and more awake. I led her to the bathroom that adjoined her room and held a tissue to her nose. "Blow," I instructed, and she blew with all her might. Then I wet a washcloth and toweled her face off, blotting away her tears. Zoe let out a big yawn when I was finished. She still looked a little upset, but sleep had begun to take its hold.

"Are you sure you don't want to go down the hall and find Mommy?" I asked.

"No," she said definitively. "Annie, not Mommy." I drew a big breath, touched but also a little bothered that she preferred me. *It's just because I'm here,* I told myself. *Because I'm here and I'm a novelty.* Little kids were always like that, latching on to new babysitters with the infatuation and curiosity of discovering a new friend. Zoe had my hand in hers; she tugged me toward her bed and reached her arms out wide. "Hold you," she told me in a plaintive voice. So I crawled in next to her and smoothed her damp, matted curls until she moved her thumb sleepily into her mouth and fell back asleep.

# CHAPTER ELEVEN

**MY LIT CLASS WAS SMALL,** only twelve students in all. We met twice a week on Tuesdays and Thursdays for two hours and forty-five minutes. It was a more intense study of literature than I'd expected. We followed the Socratic method, and everyone was required to engage in conversation about the texts. But I'd been falling behind on my reading already—I was finding it difficult to balance the job and school. I was determined to do it all, but I needed to create a better strategy.

The other problem came in the form of my classmates. Everyone in the class seemed a little goofy and out there, outspoken hippie types. But they were all brilliant, serious students. I felt way out of my league among them, and I stood out both for my silence and for my mainstream look, my good-girl clothes, and the fact that I hadn't been to any of their symposium parties yet. I didn't quite trust myself at a party after what had happened my first week. But these symposia were supposed to be something else entirely—it was rumored that the liberal studies majors (I was one of only two double-major kids in the program) used their parties as an excuse to drink wine, burn term papers, and philosophize. They did old-school drugs like LSD. They stayed up all night reading to each other and inventing brilliant new ideas.

They were the weirdoes of SFSU. The weirdoes and the geniuses. They walked in a pack and no one touched them. I didn't quite fit into their pack—I was way too conformist, way too normal. I didn't like to stand out. But I also didn't quite fit in at the rest of the school, where almost everyone partied and hung out when they weren't in class.

"Annie?" asked Professor Malone. "Did you have any thoughts about the reading?" I did have thoughts. I thought the five-hundred-page Russian novel we'd been assigned was way too long to read in two weeks and simultaneously reach any level of comprehension or insight.

"I'm fascinated by the character of Alexei," I tried. "I couldn't stop wondering whether he was a product of his faith or whether his conflict with his father informed it." I'd gotten this from CliffsNotes and prayed Professor Malone wouldn't notice. Out of my periphery, I saw at least one smirk from someone who probably also had read up on CliffsNotes.

"Yes," agreed Professor Malone kindly. "The age-old nature versus nurture debate. Anyone care to comment on Annie's insight?" No one said a word. A few of the smarter kids adopted expressions of undisguised derision. I wondered for the tenth time whether I should drop the class. That was the only comment I offered. I suffered the following two hours in silence, watching the minute hand tick by.

"Okay, that's it," Professor Malone announced finally. "A little something lighter for next week's reading. Or at least shorter, thought notably complex, I think you'll find. We'll be starting our fem lit unit. It's a big change from Russian lit, but Charlotte Perkins Gilman is one of my favorite female writers of the nineteenth century. I think you'll find her work rewarding."

I sighed inwardly and gathered my things. I'd checked out *The Yellow Wallpaper and Other Stories* when the curriculum was first assigned, and I was beginning to think Professor Malone's taste in feminist literature drastically differed from mine. I'd expected to read the Virginia Woolf and Anaïs Nin fare that had packed the sample syllabus I'd studied before signing up for this course. But at the last minute, they'd brought on Professor Malone, a new teacher who had her own vision of what constituted the very best feminist reading.

"I know, right?" a blonde, gum-chewing girl said as she caught up to me in the hallway. "I was totally not expecting this when I signed up for this course."

"There's still a week to drop it," I told her unsympathetically. I'd pretty much put my need for friendship aside when I'd accepted that my college experience wasn't going to be a typical college experience, due to my job. Also, I didn't want to get my hopes up after what had happened with Morgan.

"I'm Trista," she informed me, walking quickly to keep in step with me.

"Annie."

"Where are you from?"

"Texas," I lied.

"Oh yeah? I'm from San Antonio," Trista said excitedly, nearly dropping her Starbucks iced coffee in her enthusiasm.

"I'm from outside of Dallas," I hazarded, already regretting my lie.

"That's so great. Did you drive up? I did. Maybe we can carpool over breaks."

"I don't know," I told her as we reached the front of Hastings Hall. "I don't see myself going home a lot."

"Oh," Trista said, obviously disappointed. "Well, what are you doing now? Wanna go out for coffee or something?"

"It looks like your engine's still full," I said unkindly, gesturing at her cup. Trista blushed.

"Sorry," she said. "Am I being annoying? I don't mean to be annoying. I'm just nervous. I don't know anyone here. And my roommate's awful. She doesn't even shower. Maybe, like, once a week, tops. And she sprays this really gross cologne to cover it up, and I'm really having a hard time with it. I never had to share a room before, and—"

"Hey, Trista," I interrupted, "I'm really sorry, but I have to get home. Back to the place I'm staying, I mean. I'm off-campus, and we're kind of having a get together tonight, so . . ."

"A party?" Trista asked eagerly.

"No, no, nothing like that. Just some people over for dinner." I began to feel guilty as she gazed up at me hungrily. She seemed like the kind of girl who had been pretty dorky but well-meaning in high school. The kind of girl who was totally oblivious to social cues, but who was so naive you couldn't bear to quash her. I gritted my teeth. "Would you . . . want to come?" I asked. "I'll have to check with the family I'm staying with, but—"

"I'd love to!" she gushed. "That's so great! Thanks for inviting me. I had no plans, and I don't want to sit in on a Thursday, and, I mean, this is just great."

"Don't get your hopes up. We'll be the only teenagers there. And Owen. But it's not going to be very exciting."

"I don't care at all. I'm just excited to hang out. Who's Owen?" This girl was too much. I revised my previous assessment: maybe she'd been homeschooled. I'd been a loner in high school, but I had one thing Trista didn't have—my *pride*. It figured that the only other girl in the liberal studies concentration who stuck out like a sore thumb wanted to be my friend.

But I'd heard her talk in class, I reminded myself as I typed out a text to Libby, asking if she minded if Trista tagged along for dinner. She was smart. *Really* smart. Her eager personality fell away when she was talking about our reading, and she became someone different, someone confident and articulate and poised.

I didn't hear back from Libby right away, so I made the decision that it would be fine. Surely she wouldn't care if I brought back a potential friend from college.

"I'm heading back now, if you need a ride," I told Trista. She followed me into the parking lot and whistled as she clambered into the passenger seat of Libby's BMW.

"Nice," she said admiringly.

"It's not mine," I said. "My housemate just lets me borrow it sometimes. I'm picking out my own car next month." Next month was when I'd finally have enough money. I couldn't keep borrowing Libby's car, no matter how much she insisted she didn't mind. It just didn't give me the freedom I needed— I felt guilty taking it out for anything other than classes, and eventually I wanted to start taking advantage of the city more. Maybe on fall break, when things slowed down.

"Holy crap," said Trista when we crossed the bridge to Belvedere Island. "You live *here?*" Trista had talked on and on for most of the ride—about her family, her dog, her love for jazz dance. I hadn't had the chance to explain my situation.

"I live here, but it's free. Kind of," I explained. "I mean, I work for the family that lives here. I babysit when I'm not in school."

"You're, like, a nanny?"

"Yeah, like a nanny." I gritted my teeth, trying not to sound irritated.

"Cool." I could tell she was being falsely diplomatic. I sighed despite myself.

It was only as I was pulling into the driveway that Libby pinged back: "No," the text read. That was it. I didn't know what to do. Zoe was already running out of the front door. Trista opened her car door and stepped out before I had a chance to say anything.

"Oh, hi there," she said to Zoe delightedly. "Aren't you cute in that flowery dress?"

Libby appeared in the doorway, her arms crossed over her chest. Her mouth was set in a grim line.

"Hey, Zo," I said, getting out of the car. "One sec," I told Trista, walking quickly in Libby's direction.

"Libby," I started, "I only just got your text."

"Why would you bring her back here without first waiting to hear from me?" Libby's voice was loud. Loud enough to carry. I glanced over my shoulder at Trista, who had straightened up, looking confused.

"I just thought you wouldn't mind," I said quietly. "Can she stay? Please?" But Libby ignored me entirely. Instead, she stepped around me and approached Trista.

"Hello," Libby said, her voice cloying. "I'm Libby. I'm so sorry, but Annie didn't tell me to expect any visitors. And she's on the job now. I'm afraid there's been a miscommunication." I watched, my cheeks burning. I was mortified. As annoying as Trista was, she was the only person who had bothered to pursue a real conversation with me since the night of the party. She was sweet, if overeager.

"Oh," Trista stammered. "I'm so sorry. I'll be on my way. If Annie could just give me a lift back to campus . . ."

"That's impossible," Libby interrupted. "I'll call you a car. Annie is on the job. She needs to look after my daughter now. And she'll have to help me with dinner." Trista nodded as if she understood, but I could read the confusion in her eyes as Libby turned toward the house and marched past me without a word.

"Listen," I began.

"Don't worry about it." Trista's voice was wooden. "You'd better go inside."

"Don't you want to wait inside for the cab?"

"I'm fine out here," Trista said from where she'd perched on the brick steps that led to the front stoop.

"Then why don't I wait with you?"

"Annie," Trista's voice was uncharacteristically sharp. "You heard her. She wants you to work right now."

"Yeah." I stood there awkwardly for a few seconds before Trista spoke up again.

"You know it's going to cost me at least thirty bucks to get back to campus," she said.

"I'm sorry. I'll give you the money."

"Don't bother."

And so I turned and walked inside with Zoe at my heels, shutting Trista—and my embarrassment—out of the house.

"*Why* would you do that?" Libby hissed her words as I entered the kitchen. She was busy pulling foil-covered platters from two large paper bags with a "Vic's Catering" logo on them. She unwrapped each carefully and placed as many in the oven as the oven could hold. But there was a certain rigidity to her shoulders, a stiffness in the way she carried herself.

"I just thought . . . you're always encouraging me to make friends," I stammered.

"Let me be clear about something," Libby said. "This is not your house. You may not invite people here without first checking, particularly not to a dinner I'm preparing. Maybe I've blurred the lines a little too much, Nanny. You're our *staff*. I don't know what you were thinking."

I took a deep breath, fighting back tears. Apparently the relationship I'd seen developing between me and Libby—what I'd thought was a sort of mentor-friend type of thing—had only existed for me. My heart pulsed in my ears.

"Another thing," Libby said, her voice getting louder. "I do *not* want strangers poking around this house. Not now, not ever." Walker poked his head in the room as she was finishing her sentence. He approached Libby, adjusting his tie as he entered. His eyes darted from me to her, taking us both in.

"Sweetheart?" he said to her. "Annie. What's wrong?"

"Annie invited a stranger over—to dinner—without having asked."

"I asked," I protested.

"You brought her here without my permission!" Libby's voice was cold and furious. Her normally porcelain skin was even paler than usual, almost as if, in her anger, it had been drained of pigment.

"Where's the girl now?" Walk wanted to know.

"Outside," I said. "Waiting for a cab."

"A cab? That's ridiculous. I'll drive her. I'll be back in half an hour."

"Walker! You most certainly will not," said Libby, aghast. "I'm sure the girl will be perfectly fine in a cab."

"But the money, Libby. Why make her pay for a cab when we can easily drive her?"

"I need you here," she told him. "I need your help preparing for our guests."

"All right," he sighed, throwing his hands in the air. "Fine. What do you need me to do?"

"First off, I'd love for you to talk with Annie," she said, as though I wasn't standing right there. "I'm tired of having to lay down all the rules around here, like she's another child." I winced. Her words cut me deep.

"We can't have strangers in the house, Annie," Walker said, turning to me. "At least not without asking us first. Even if you *were* our child, that's a courtesy we'd expect. We want to include you in our daily lives—in dinners like this and days at the beach—but you really need to ask about other things. You can't just assume that you can treat this like it's your home."

I nodded, trying hard not to cry. "I'm really sorry," I told him. "I won't do it again."

"It's fine," he said, while Libby glared from the corner by the stove. "It's all fine. It's over, so let's just move on and enjoy the night." He looked extremely stressed out, as if conflict wasn't at all his strong suit. "I'm going to go get cleaned up, splash some water on my face, do a shooter . . ." He paused. "Not funny? Yeah. Okay. I'll just be upstairs. Libby, holler if you need me."

"Please get cleaned up for dinner, Annie, and put Zoe in something nice, too," Libby said stiffly. I nodded and retreated to my room. I wasn't sure what had happened; I only knew that I'd done something to profoundly upset Libby. And now I was shaking all over, as if my body had experienced an intense shock. I gripped my hands together, trying to make them stop trembling. But I couldn't. I was sweating, too. And now Owen was coming over, and I had to act normal. I didn't know how I could pull it off. I hadn't heard a word from him in days, not even a move on Words with Friends. He had disappeared. And now with Libby's anger, I'd never felt more alone. I needed to cry, to scream, something . . . but I didn't even have a door to slam or hide behind. The thought of acting normal, saving face—it was inconceivable. But I would have to find some way to hold myself together.

One thing had become clear: I knew that I wouldn't be able to have a normal life here, or at least not the kind of life other college kids considered normal. I went into the bathroom that adjoined my room and closed *that* door. It was the only place I could go to have privacy: my bathroom, my sanctuary. I laughed miserably at that. Everything had turned into a night-mare, and it seemed like Libby hated me, and I didn't know how to fix it.

But then something occurred to me: it said something that Libby hated the thought of strangers in the house, but she'd embraced *me*. Me, whom she'd known for less than a month. She trusted me. She cared about me. She had to. All of this anger, it was because she knew I was better than I was behaving. I was letting her down.

I couldn't let her down.

I blew my nose and wet my face with a cold cloth. Then I walked up to Zoe's room calmly and began rifling through her closet. I was flooded with conflicting emotions. Anger, confusion—but predominantly guilt. I didn't want to be a troublemaker. All my life, I'd screwed things up. Not this time.

**"THE PINK ONE,"** announced Zoe.

"Don't be a goof. There are at least seven pink ones," I informed her. "Come on, narrow it down for me." After a few minutes of arguing with Zoe about something as banal as what dress she'd wear to the dinner party, I felt much calmer. Zoe brought me back to earth.

"That one!" she shouted, pointing at an outfit I was all too familiar with—I'd seen the frilly pink number in her Halloween pictures from last year. It had blue and purple sashes woven through and silver sparkles scattered across.

"Zoe, that's a costume," I said. "You need to pick a nice dress for Mommy and Daddy's visitors."

"THAT ONE," Zoe said stubbornly. I weighed my options. The Oswalds were due to arrive any minute, and I still hadn't changed. I could stay here and duke it out with Zoe, or I could put her in a costume everyone would probably think was cute anyway, and I could go down and get myself ready. I chose the latter.

But I also didn't really get what the big deal was. I knew the Cohens were from a different world—a world in which there were social rules and dress codes I'd never dealt with in real life—but it all seemed a little excessive for a friendly dinner with the neighbors. Libby had been obsessing over the menu all week, and she'd wound up ordering a bunch of food from their favorite Italian restaurant. That morning before I'd gone to school, she'd made me help her polish the good silverware and rinse their wedding china. She'd bought new candles for the candlesticks, which she scrubbed to a shine. She'd thought about hiring someone to help serve, but changed her mind when I assured her I'd be there to help out with whatever she needed. It seemed so *elaborate*. It seemed really weird.

Then again, what did I know about it? I grew up in Detroit. Maybe this was totally normal for Belvedere Island. And anyway, I admired her desire for perfection. When Libby did something, she did it 110 percent right. And maybe that was the way to achieve what she had. I rooted through my chest of drawers in a quest for an outfit that would please her. Finally I settled on a simple black pencil skirt, a red silk blouse, and ballet flats. I pulled my hair up in a ponytail, added lip gloss, and turned to Zoe for approval. She'd been sitting on the edge of my bed playing with my lipsticks while I chose an outfit.

"What do you think? Pretty?"

"Pwetty," she confirmed, her mouth covered in RahRah Raspberry. I hastily wiped off her lipstick, and we hurried downstairs just as the doorbell rang.

"Daddy!" shouted Zoe, running down the stairs to hug Walker, who wore a suit jacket with his khakis.

"Bean!" he greeted her back, scooping her up in his arms. Libby glanced at Zoe and me, and her face hardened into a disapproving line.

"You couldn't be bothered to get her properly dressed?" she wanted to know. I didn't have time to answer, because she was already opening the door. A feeling of dread—and a little resentment—overwhelmed me.

"Don't worry," Walker whispered with a tense smile, patting me on the shoulder. Zoe smiled down from his other arm. "She just gets a little stressed out when she entertains." The Oswalds were all wearing jeans. I watched as Mrs. Oswald took in Libby's pristine white pants, her black off-the-shoulder top, and her strand of pearls.

"Oh my," said Mrs. Oswald carefully after we'd exchanged greetings. "I feel terrible that we're so underdressed! We were expecting a patio grill-out."

"I changed my mind," Libby said with a bright smile. "I wanted to make up for my self-imposed solitary confinement of the past couple months." The adults all chuckled politely. "Anyway, you couldn't help but look fabulous," Libby added. It wasn't much of an exaggeration: for fifty or so, Mrs. Oswald looked healthy and fit, and her naturally pretty face was tanned and smooth. She and her husband seemed to share their son's interest in the outdoors. The family looked like a poster for the active Californian lifestyle.

"What can I get you to drink?" Walker asked. "Scotch? Wine?"

"I'll have some red, if you have it," said Mrs. Oswald. "And scotch for Terry, neat."

"I believe you kids already know each other, is that right?" Mr. Oswald was asking with a friendly smile.

"Annie," Libby interrupted, before I had a chance to respond, "why don't you show Owen the entertainment room. Maybe you kids can shoot some pool while we wait for dinner to heat?" I nodded, stinging from it. Libby had sounded so patronizing; but then, apparently we weren't really friends. Her tone was, I supposed, appropriate for an employer.

"Annie!" Libby said sharply as we headed off. "Aren't you forgetting someone?"

"I'm so sorry," I replied. "Zoe, come on, hon. Let's go downstairs."

"Zoe just takes to Annie so well," Libby said as we moved from the room. For my part, I tried to act composed with Owen walking behind me. Wasn't I technically off-duty right now? Why was she insisting I watch Zoe? I'd thought I was attending this dinner not as a babysitter, but as a guest.

"She always make you work all evening?" Owen asked, giving voice to my fears.

"No, not usually. Hey, what about air hockey?" I asked quickly, eager to change the subject. I couldn't defend something I didn't understand myself. And I didn't really want to get into touchy territory with him again. For some reason, being with Owen triggered this feeling I sometimes got, when someone challenged me about something I believed without being able to articulate why. It had happened only a few times in the past, and when it did, I wound up feeling cornered, like there was no way out. Sometimes it made me uncharacteristically bumbling and inarticulate. I hated that feeling of stammering, searching for words. I desperately wanted to avoid feeling flustered like that again.

"Or foosball?" he suggested.

"Sure." I was historically terrible at foosball, but I had

vowed to be agreeable. To show Owen a different side of me. "Zoe, you and me on a team, okay? I'll work one handle, you work the other." I moved a chair over to the table so Zoe could stand on it. She turned out to have a pretty intense competitive streak for a three-year-old, judging by how excited she got when Owen let her score. But he wasn't one to let anyone *win*, not even a toddler. After losing four games in a row, games in which the high scorer for our team was Zoe, I knew I couldn't avoid it anymore.

"What's up, Phillips?" he teased. "Can't handle it?"

"There's actually something I wanted to talk to you about," I said, unable to meet his eyes.

"Oh, sure." He suddenly looked uncomfortable, and I was willing to bet anything he'd been hoping we could just skate right past the elephant in the room.

"Zo, how about some cartoons?"

"*Dora*?" she asked hopefully.

"Sure thing." I set her up on the sofa, wrapping her in an afghan, and popped in her favorite *Dora* DVD. Within seconds, she was transfixed. "She never gets tired of it," I told Owen. "It's kind of amazing." There was only one sofa in the basement, an anomaly in an otherwise immaculately furnished house. Thankfully, it was a large one. Our thighs would not be brushing anytime soon. Zoe was curled up on one end, and I settled in the middle next to her. She wormed her feet under my legs absentmindedly. Owen was seated in the opposite corner with an expression of unmasked dread.

"Relax," I told him. "It's no big deal. I just wanted to apologize for the other day."

"Oh," he said, visibly relieved. "No need to apologize. Seriously. It wasn't my place to say anything about the Cohens. And it looks like I was wrong, anyway—they seem great."

"They are," I agreed. "But I really want to say this. I assumed you were just some kind of lazy waste of space, like some of the guys I knew back where I'm from. They were like leeches. They'd just suck their parents' money away until they'd drained them. And then they'd keep living in their parents' houses, getting fat and collecting unemployment."

"Wow," he said. "So in your head, I'm a fat, lazy leech."

"You weren't there yet," I laughed. "But you were well on your way."

"Then I guess you *do* owe me an apology, for you are sorely mistaken." When I found the courage to glance at his face, I realized he was more amused than anything else, thank god.

"I'm really sorry," I told him. "I'm sorry for assuming I knew who you were without actually bothering to get to know you. And I'm sorry for judging you. God." I shook my head. "I, of all people, am in no place to judge. And I'm not usually like that."

"You don't need to explain."

"No, really. I've just been a little overwhelmed. But I feel terrible. You didn't deserve any of it."

"Apology accepted," Owen said softly, holding my gaze. "And if you want to make it up to me, that's fine too."

"Ew," I said.

"'Ew' wasn't the answer I was hoping for. However, I was thinking you could repay your debt with brownies or other delicious edibles. I don't know what *you* thought I meant. . . ."

I felt my face turning beet red for the millionth time since I'd moved there, and Owen burst out laughing. "I know," I said. "I know. It would almost be better to have a permanent sunburn."

"It's cute," he replied. "I wouldn't change it." I bit my lip and turned away from him, suddenly shy. I'd never been good at flirting . . . if that's what he was doing.

"Zo, how's *Dora*?" I asked, eager to fill the silence. But Zoe ignored me. She wasn't listening to our conversation at all; she was watching Dora and Boots swing from a rope into a lagoon.

"Oh, to be three and blissfully unaware," Owen remarked. I smiled at him. There was something about him that was just so open and honest. It put me at ease in a way no one had—not that I had a lot of experiences to hold it up against.

"I don't know how blissful. She had a doozy of a nightmare last night. It was sort of scary."

"Monsters? Ghosts? What do toddlers dream about anyway? They can barely form full sentences."

"Mommy went away," Zoe said offhandedly, her attention still focused on the screen.

"What?" Owen started to say something else, but I shook my head sharply, and he clamped his mouth shut.

"Nothing, nothing," I said, as the *Dora* credits started rolling. Zoe hummed along with the theme song, but soon her humming turned to "Rockabye Baby," as it always seemed to.

"Cwadle and all," she sang under her breath.

"That's enough," I said mock sternly, reaching over to tickle her armpits. She squealed, laughing so hard she rolled off the sofa.

"No, NO!" she shrieked happily as I pretended to chase after her. Finally I collapsed on the floor melodramatically, allowing her to tickle me back.

"I forfeit," I laughed. "Forfeit, I say!" But she kept at it, laughing happily until Owen stepped in, grabbing her by the armpits and spinning her in the air.

"Unhand the lady," he commanded her, tossing her finally onto the couch where she lay, giggling still but more quietly now, as though she were losing steam. While Zoe was sprawled out on the couch, I was sprawled out on the floor. Owen lay down next to me on the carpet, his body far enough from mine that we weren't touching, but close enough for me to feel his heat.

"Zoes, how about a game of Simon Says?" I suggested once I caught my breath, again desperately trying to ignore the feeling of Owen's body just inches from mine.

"Annie," Owen cut in, "there's something—" But then the familiar squeak of the basement door sounded from above us, and Walker shouted down, "Come 'n' get your grub!" Zoe let out a happy shriek and dashed up the stairs. I stood up and ran after her, making sure she didn't fall.

"Seems like she's your number-one fan, Mr. C.," said Owen as Walker scooped up Zoe and placed her on his shoulders.

"She's my buddy," he replied. "Best pal, this little gal. Right here." Owen flashed me a smile and, when Walker's back was turned, reached behind him for my hand, helping me up the last few stairs. Was he chivalrous? Was he some kind of lady-killer? Or—it hardly seemed possible—did he like me? What had he been about to tell me? He'd sounded so . . . serious. So sad. I forced the questions out of my head when I realized one important fact: it didn't matter. Right in that moment, he was holding my hand. He gripped it a few seconds longer than necessary and gave it a little squeeze before letting it drop. My heart felt like it was about to explode. It was beating so forcefully I was sure everyone in the house could hear it.

Dinner raced by after that. Every time I took a bite of mashed potatoes or reached for my water glass, Owen was there to distract me: His hand, reaching for the serving knife. His eyes, meeting mine over the table. His voice, his grin, his smell. It was like my senses were on overload. While we were at that table, Owen was everywhere. He enveloped me in a warm, protective shield. He wasn't mad at me; not even close. There was still a chance.

I was so distracted by the dynamic between Owen and me that I didn't even notice Libby's cold silence through the meal. I finally recognized that something was amiss when she stood up from the table halfway through dessert, claiming she had a splitting headache and needed to lie down. But it still didn't seem all that unusual. Maybe it should have, I don't know, but that's what happens when you start to fall in love. Love blinds you to everything. All the signs you should see, all the details you'd never normally miss—they give way to the only thing you really want to see: his face. And the warnings, the things you would have perked up to in the past? You don't hear them, because they're not the sound of his voice. Love is a very beautiful, very dangerous thing.

# CHAPTER TWELVE

**SUNDAY WAS MY DAY OFF,** but I had way too much homework to actually *take* a day off. By the time I woke up at ten A.M., got dressed, and wandered downstairs, Walker, Libby, Zoe, and Jackson were already gone. Libby had left a note for me on the kitchen island. "Back around 4," it read, without the usual details or smiley face.

It was good that they were gone, though. I had a lot of homework to finish, and Owen and I had made tentative plans to hang out that night. We'd seen each other only a few times since he and his parents had come over for dinner, but those few times were enough to make it hard to concentrate on anything else. And I had a critical essay due the following week in my lit class. To my surprise, the feminist unit had quickly become my favorite. As a whole, the class was far and away more interesting than the Elements of Design class I was now only taking because I felt terrible letting Libby down.

*The Yellow Wallpaper and Other Stories* was really good so far, but I'd only just started reading "The Yellow Wallpaper" itself, and that was supposed to be the basis for my essay. We'd been talking about a period of female oppression in which women were sent to asylums for pretty much any reason at all—for being "slutty," even if they were victims of rape; for having anxiety; for being troublesome—and this story was supposed to illustrate the feminine psyche being driven mad. We'd talked a lot in class about mental illness as a product of the era and environment rather than chemical imbalance, and how it was used as an excuse to control women who bothered to speak up or act in a manner that was considered rebellious.

*The Yellow Wallpaper,* my professor said, was interesting because it was written by one woman who was nearly driven mad by the real-life advice of the doctor who was treating her. Then when she wrote the story—about a woman whose husband prevents her from working and encourages isolation and bed rest as a cure for depression/nerves—it changed the way that doctor treated his patients from then on. So in her own way, this writer made huge strides for women.

I was really into the background—I was interested in literary theory as a whole—and I was psyched to sit out on the upper balcony of the Cohens' house, with its gorgeous view of the Pacific, and drink iced tea and read the story. What I wasn't prepared for was how creepy the story would be.

Half an hour in, I was sufficiently freaked out. The heroine in the story had begun to see a creeping woman behind the pattern of the wallpaper. By the end of the story, I was so jittery it may as well have been midnight and not midday. I actually missed Zoe's normalizing—if slightly whiny—presence. The woman in the story had become convinced that *she* was the woman trapped in the wallpaper. She crept around the room, dragging her shoulder against the wallpaper, and she tore the paper off the wall in shreds. When her husband finally found her, just a day from leaving the awful prison of the room, she'd already gone completely crazy. She'd turned into a literal creeper. It almost made me grateful for the lack of privacy in my own room.

Just as I was reaching the end, my cell phone rang. Hoping for Owen, my heart leaped; ever since the dinner party, we'd been back on texting terms. But a call would have been a new thing. I looked eagerly at the name lighting up the display: Libby Cohen.

"Hey, Libby," I said, trying to mask my disappointment.

"I need you to do something for me," she said without bothering with a greeting. "Turn on the oven to three-fifty and throw in a pot roast, okay? The meat and vegetables are in the fridge and you can just grab a can of stewed tomatoes from the pantry. It shouldn't take longer than fifteen minutes." I knew it would take longer, but that wasn't my concern.

"Will you be home to take it out?" I asked.

"Why, will you not?"

"I'd planned to meet Owen at—"

Libby sighed loudly from the other end. "Fine. Just hook up

the slow cooker. It won't be as good, though. God, I haven't used that since . . . ever. It's at the bottom of the pantry, toward the back. Just hook it up and I'll take care of it when I'm home." She made it sound like I was doing her a disservice by allowing her to "take care of it" herself. And besides, wasn't the point of slow cookers that they do all the work themselves?

I sliced up tomatoes, onions, peppers, garlic, potatoes, and zucchini for the stew. I hoped that would be okay. I added some stewed tomatoes from a can and a little salt and pepper. I sliced the meat into cubes and added a dash of rosemary. I'd used a slow cooker many times before, all those times when my mother couldn't. I'd woken up early before school and thrown everything in so that Dean would have something to eat when he got home from the parts store in the afternoon. I didn't even have to think about what I was doing anymore.

By the time I finished, I needed a change of pace. I could work on my paper later, I decided. Why not go find Owen right then? It was kind of ridiculous that we didn't see more of each other, given that he lived right next door. Unless he didn't like me? The thought was ridiculous; I hated how insecure I was about Owen. It's not like there had been any other girls coming and going over the past few weeks—I knew very well there weren't, because I'd become a vigilant spy in my downtime. But there was something about him that was so confident, so secure—it had the very opposite effect on me. It derailed me. It made me feel like I wasn't good enough.

I swallowed my paranoia—the awful fantasy I had of showing up unannounced and finding him with another girl—and threw on my swimsuit. I'd pack a picnic, and maybe we could drive down to the shore.

I packed us two turkey sandwiches on focaccia, some cheese, a bunch of olives, fresh cherries, banana bread, and San Pellegrino. One of the benefits of living here was that Libby was a food nut, but she didn't eat any. She was obsessed with buying good food and always foisted it on me, hating to see it go to waste. As a result, I'd eaten more types of cheese in the last month than I previously knew existed. It kind of put those billowy shirts from the garage in perspective . . . if they were in fact hers.

I was halfway down the driveway when my phone rang again. I switched the picnic basket awkwardly over to my right hand, fumbling in my jeans pocket. I picked the phone up just as it went to voicemail. Libby again. I pressed "call back" before she could leave a message.

"Nanny, I'd appreciate it if you would pick up the phone a little more promptly when I call," she told me. I bristled. I'd gotten to it as fast as I could, and . . . had she really called me Nanny again?

"I'm sorry," I told her through gritted teeth.

"Before you leave, I really need you to make sure Zoe's lunch is packed for tomorrow morning's play-date," she said. "Who knows what time we'll be back tonight, and I don't want to have to worry about it before bed."

"Okay," I said, sighing inwardly. "Is there anything else?"

"No," she said, after a pause. "Not right now. But I'll call you if I think of anything."

ANNA COLLOMORE

I decided to leave the picnic basket in the driveway while
I prepared Zoe's lunch. When I finished a few minutes later, it
was only a half an hour 'til I'd planned on meeting Owen in
the first place. I wondered briefly if I should just wait it out in
the house, but decided I didn't want to lug that picnic basket
any more than I had to.

"Just the girl I was hoping to see." Owen swung the door
open seconds before I pressed the doorbell. "And bearing food?
How did you know this was my fantasy?"

I laughed. "How did you know I was at the door?" I asked.
"Stalker."

"It's just that we're so connected," he replied. "Plus, I happened to see a strange basket lying abandoned in the middle
of your driveway.

"Oh. Right," I said.

"Ohhhh, someone thought I was keeping an eye on her!
Getting cocky, are we?" He flashed me a playful grin that illuminated his green eyes.

"So I just swung by to ask if you had any soda," I said seriously. "I was bringing this picnic to a guy down the street and I
realized, gosh darn, I'm clean out of refreshments. . . ."

"Okay," he said. "Okay, I get it. I'll stop. Assuming you're
joking about Mystery Boyfriend, where shall we go?"

"You got wheels?" I asked. "Hanging out at your place has
been great, but I'm dying for a tour of this city. It seems all I do
these days is work."

"At your service, madame. Just give me a sec." I nodded,
moving into the foyer as he ran up the stairs, taking them two

at a time. I liked Owen a lot. I liked that for all his banter, he was open and honest. I liked that he wasn't afraid to show me he liked me. Maybe it was because he was twenty. Maybe older guys were just like that. But then I thought of Dean, and somehow I doubted he was the exception. Owen emerged from the kitchen a minute later carrying a Ziploc bag full of cookies. I tried unsuccessfully to hide my giddy pleasure. He'd thrown on a button-down shirt over his T-shirt and shorts, and he'd rolled up the sleeves over his tanned forearms. He was so different from the guys I'd dated back home. They'd had a raw, sexy energy, but Owen was real, and he was sweet, and he was *good*. It all combined for a more powerful want than I'd ever felt.

"You dressed up for me," I blurted out. And instead of saying something witty back, it was his turn to blush.

"Just didn't want to embarrass you," he said mildly. "So, these are my mom's famous chocolate chip cookies." He extended the bag toward me, obviously eager to change the subject.

"What makes them famous?" I wanted to know.

"They just are. Once you taste them, you'll get it." Owen gestured toward the front door and we walked out together, climbing into his Jeep. I loved that Owen was probably the last guy on the planet to drive a Jeep Wrangler. It made him even cuter.

"But did you ever notice that the word *famous* automatically makes a thing more appealing?" I asked him. "Like, if I were going to open my own restaurant, I'd call all of my creations 'Annie's Famous Green Beans' and 'Famous Apple Crisp' or whatever."

"What are you running, a Southern diner? I've got news for you, little lady. These cookies actually *are* famous. They won the Hershey's bake-off in 1987." I burst out laughing; I couldn't help it. "Hey now." He looked faux-wounded. "It's a big deal! They fly you out to New York for those things."

"I believe it," I said soberly. "What was the grand prize?"

"Cash award," he said. "Plus a cookbook with recipes from all the other contestants."

"So basically . . . a cookbook with all of the losing entries," I clarified.

"Yep. I'd say that's pretty much it."

"Hopefully the cash award was generous."

"It's not polite to discuss money," he said. He was only kidding, but his words reminded me of the incident in the Cohens' garage.

"Ugh," I said aloud. My resolve weakened, and I reached in the bag for a cookie. "Oh my god! These are amazing!" I wasn't lying. The chocolate chips were somehow still melty inside the soft, chewy dough. Yet the cookie itself was cool, like they'd been baked hours or maybe even a whole day before. How did the melty chips exist within cool dough? It was a science miracle.

"Why the 'ugh'?" Owen wanted to know.

"Oh, nothing," I said, waving it off. "Just something you said reminded me of this thing that happened a while back. I accidentally stumbled across some files I wasn't supposed to see, and I almost got fired over it."

"Unbelievable," Owen said, visibly bristling.

"What? I shouldn't have been snooping through their stuff."

"Well, were you? Actually snooping, I mean?"

"No. I was trying to move some boxes in the garage, and one of the boxes broke and everything fell all over the place. But I should have been more careful about letting my eyes wander where they shouldn't have been."

"Well, what did you see?"

"Just some financial information," I hedged. "Nothing terribly personal."

"I can't believe they'd fire you over what was obviously a total accident," Owen muttered. We were driving along Highway 1, watching the coastline breeze by. Owen was an expert driver, dodging traffic with confidence, one arm resting on the open window.

"What? It's not like they actually fired me." I hadn't even told him the bad part, but his mood had turned darker within seconds.

"You're right. Just a knee-jerk reaction, sorry. I think they're good people, I just . . . I don't know what it is. Something doesn't sit well. But I'm probably just reading into it." He turned up the music, nodding his head along with Fun. But in my periphery I could see his eyebrows knitting together, the way he rubbed his bottom lip with his index finger, controlling the wheel with his opposite hand. And then my phone rang. I fished it out of my pocket and motioned for Owen to turn down the music.

"Hey, Libby," I said, with a pointed look in Owen's direction.

He pursed his lips disapprovingly. "No, I'm with Owen. No, we're pretty far away right now. Yeah. Okay. All right. It's not a problem. I put the green one in the wash yesterday. All right. Okay, thanks, sorry for leaving it out. Yep. Thanks. Bye."

"What?" I asked defensively when I hung up. "She needed to know if one of Walker's shirts was clean. And I guess I left my lit reading on the deck, and she brought it inside for me."

"They make you do housework too?"

"Not really. Just light stuff here and there when the maid cancels, or if it builds up before her day off. They cut her schedule back a little since I can do a lot of it myself pretty easily." I avoided his eyes, knowing what he'd have to say about that.

"Did she give you a hard time for leaving it outside?" he wanted to know. "It sounded like you were apologizing."

"Not really, she just doesn't love it when there's clutter. I totally get it," I said defensively.

"Are you their babysitter or their maid? And isn't this supposed to be your day off?"

"You're acting sort of weird," I informed him. "Just relax." He let out a frustrated noise akin to that of a baby lion in distress. A bereaved sort of growl that made me laugh. I liked how Owen was just Owen around me, no pretension, no real efforts at being someone other than whom he'd always been. I'd only known him a few weeks, but I already felt closer to him than I'd ever been to anyone, really. I'd hung out with a couple of guys in high school, and of course I'd had those few months with Daniel, but those other guys were just faces.

Bodies. Ways to pass the time. It was hard to explain, but those people were just hands holding my hands, lips pressed against mine, people to watch movies with and go to parties with and make out with. Owen was different: more and better in ways I didn't fully understand. And then it hit me: I didn't feel like an outsider around him. I didn't feel damaged, bad, deformed. *But he doesn't know about Lissa,* said the ever-persistent voice in my head. *He doesn't know who you are, not really. And what will he think of you then?* I decided to ignore the voice for as long as I could. Besides, Owen was different from Daniel. I could let Owen in.

"And you know, even my dad was a little offended," Owen went on. "She was kind of critical. And I mean, she's, like, twenty-four. My mom's in her fifties. She knows a little more about life than Libby."

"Wait, what?" I'd zoned out while he was talking. "Who's twenty-four?"

"Libby. You didn't know that? God, just look at her." He let out a low whistle.

"Um, obviously *you* have."

Owen rolled his eyes. "I don't know if you've noticed, but I'm not into hyper-maintained women. I mean, Jesus. She probably sleeps in her makeup. She's definitely not my type." I thought it over. I'd thought Libby was around thirty. The way she dressed, the way she carried herself . . . she just seemed thirtyish. She was beautiful and young-looking, sure. But twenty-four? It seemed impossible.

"She can't be twenty-four," I argued. "That means she

graduated from college, like, three years ago. Walker's not that creepy. And Walker is *definitely* not twenty-four."

"He's thirty-three," said Owen.

"Okaaaay. But how do you know all this?"

"My dad was their real estate agent. He filed all their paperwork when they bought the place."

"He clearly has high standards for client confidentiality," I noted stiffly. I didn't want to get in another fight with Owen. But I was feeling a range of emotions. For some reason, Libby's age bothered me. I don't know why, but it didn't gel with this image I had of wife number one, whom I'd begun to deify despite myself. The fact that Libby was that much younger just felt so slimy. So underhanded. A betrayal of Walker's wife's memory. And Walker and Libby had seemed . . . perfect. But here was Owen, drilling little holes in their idyllic façade. I didn't like that, either. I was already feeling stretched thin with everything the Cohens expected me to do. It was a lot more difficult than I'd anticipated. The last thing I needed was pressure from Owen, too. I wanted him to serve as my escape.

There was something else that bothered me about it. The more I was forced to confront, I realized, the harder it would be to keep all this up without feeling like their slime was rubbing off on me. But it was only a job. I had to think of that. What they did had nothing to do with me.

"Oh please." Owen, annoyed, rolled his eyes. "My dad only mentioned it because my mom was prying. She couldn't believe they had a three-year-old kid. I don't even know how much the place cost. Or any of the other details. Except that they paid for the whole thing in cash. But you can find that information on public websites."

"A wee bit curious, are we?" I said, trying to make light of it.

"My job is the Internet," Owen said with a shrug. "It's not that hard to figure these things out."

"So what do you know about me?" I asked sharply. "What sort of research did you do?"

"Just a basic background check, where you grew up, your IQ, that sort of thing." I felt the blood drain from my face. I dug my fingernails deep into the palm of my other hand, fighting panic. "Jesus, Annie," Owen said, looking alarmed. "I was only kidding. I'd never in a million years check up on you like that." It took a second for his words to sink in, a long second in which I struggled to breathe normally again.

"That was really crappy," I told him through the beginnings of tears. "That was really, really crappy."

"Hey," he said with concern, placing a hand on my knee. "Hey, shhh. What's wrong? I was just kidding."

"It's fine," I said, trying to pull myself together. He probably thought I was nuts. "I'm sorry. I don't know why I'm getting so upset."

"No, no, you're right. That was mean. Here." He rifled around in the glove compartment and handed me a pack of tissues. He steered the car into the parking lot of an In-N-Out and cut the engine. Taking my hand in his, he began to sketch semicircles on my wrist with his thumb. "I really didn't mean to upset you. It was only a joke."

"No," I said. "It's really not a big deal. As long as you *swear* you would never actually violate my privacy like that."

"I would never," he swore, his eyes earnest. "I'm serious. I never check up on people. Even with the Cohens, I was more curious about the house than anything else."

"Okay." I was feeling a lot calmer. In retrospect, the last fifteen minutes seemed more intense than they'd needed to be. "I just . . . I don't know. My emotions have been all over the place lately. I'm really sorry. Don't think I'm a freak. I'm just not sleeping well, and—"

He placed his hand gently on the side of my face, stroking my cheek, my neck, the hair at the base of my scalp. He leaned forward and kissed the side of my cheek once, then again. "You're not a freak," he whispered next to my ear, sending goose bumps down my spine. "You're perfect." His left hand cradled my jaw; I let him turn my face toward him. When our lips met, it was pure, perfect, surreal. My body felt so electric that I almost couldn't feel a thing. His lips moved against mine, softly but with a gentle rhythm that pulled me closer, made me want more and more. As the thing I'd fantasized about ever since I met him five weeks ago materialized, it became briefly impossible to separate fantasy from reality. It all blended into a beautiful, chaotic mess. I allowed it to sweep me up, content to relinquish all my self-control.

**FORTY-FIVE MINUTES LATER,** we reached our destination: Dolores Park, a beautiful expanse of grass in Mission Dolores. We found the perfect spot to plop down in the grass:

secluded enough that it felt like its own private oasis among a sea of picnic blankets and sheltered by both a palm tree and an oak. The city rose up beyond our grassy island, making the contrast of elements all the more stark. I had to laugh; the city was so unexpected, a hodgepodge of hundreds of completely different elements that somehow blended together to form a beautiful, chaotic picture. It was a Chex Mix of a city.

"Fooooood," Owen said then in a low, guttural voice, interrupting my reverie. Apparently all of our making out had made him hungry. "This bad boy needs some." He grabbed a handful of would-be belly (he didn't have an ounce of fat on him) and squished it together in a mass. "Its name's Garth," he said. "A derivative of the Latin *Girthius maximus.*"

I rolled my eyes. How could he switch from super sexy to childish in ten minutes flat? I couldn't figure out if I thought he was funny right then, or gross and immature. Whatever it was, it was ruining my post-make-out buzz. "You're getting weird looks from the person at six o'clock," I informed him.

"That's not a person," Owen stage-whispered to me. "It's only a kid. Hey, what's up, kid?" Owen waved to a little boy, maybe about four years old, who was clutching his mother's fist and staring at us while his mom chatted away on her cell phone. My buzz was fading . . . fading . . . gone.

"Yep. Terrified. You've changed his life for the worse. You've damaged him."

"As long as I've changed yours for the better . . ." Owen let his sentence hang between us like a half-teasing, half-serious promise. And there they were: the tingles. Back again.

"So, you never told me," I said quickly, breaking the silence, "what it was your mom didn't like about Libby. I mean, you told me, but I was totally zoned out. Tell me again?"

"Can we please table the Cohen talk for the rest of the afternoon? I've learned my lesson. And besides, I'd way rather talk about other stuff."

"Okay," I said reluctantly. "Like what?" I busied myself putting our sandwiches out on the tray, arranging the cheese and fruit next to the paper-thin crackers, pouring us each some sparkling water.

"Like, who were you before you came to California? Where are you from? What brought you out here? What do you like to do when you're not selling your soul to Libby Cohen?" He could not have asked a more difficult question. So I decided to do what I always did: deflect it.

"You go first," I said. "What kind of a guy is a volunteer EMT? And tell me about your business. I've barely heard a word about that."

Owen puffed his cheeks and let the air out in a sigh. "Tough questions," he said. "Okay, I'll go. But don't think you're getting off the hook."

"Don't worry," I hedged.

"Okay, so, I guess I'm what you'd call a huge science nerd." I burst out laughing. Rugged, tanned, all-American, wholesome, well-rounded Owen? Right.

"No offense," I told him. "But I can't picture you hunched over a beaker."

"No beakers," he agreed. "Computers all the way. I don't

know why you're surprised. I'll model my wire-rimmed glasses for you later." I caught myself mid-laugh. It appeared he wasn't joking. Suddenly, I was fascinated. I wanted to know everything.

"So it's always been just you and your parents?" I asked.

"Yep. Me, my parents, math competitions, science fairs, and the National Spelling Bee." At that, I nearly choked on the piece of cheese I'd been shoving in my mouth.

"No," I whispered. "You were one of those kids on television? The weird ones?"

"I was," he said gravely. "It was the seventh grade. I got out in the fourth round on 'verisimilitude.' *So stupid*," he groaned, tossing his head back in a gesture of woe. "I rue that day. Had I only asked for the origin, I would have won the whole thing. I knew all the words after that."

"Do you think your life would have been different if you'd won?"

"Maybe," he told me. "Yes, it probably would have been. What National Spelling Bee winner doesn't get into Harvard?" I raised an eyebrow. I didn't know the answer to that. "But if I'd won, I wouldn't have met Rebecca Carver in the crying room."

"What's the crying room?" I had never known it was possible to be filled with simultaneous dread and glee.

"It's where you go to cry when you miss a word. Rebecca Carver lost on 'oscillate.' The easiest word in the English language." He shook his head scornfully. "But I didn't hold it against her, because she had pretty hair."

"Naturally."

"I dated Rebecca long-distance for all of eighth grade. It

was very serious. She lived two states away, and she knew how to use a transistor radio. We had dozens of late-night conversations in Morse code."

"You're joking."

"Maybe," he grinned. "Wouldn't you like to know?" His hand inched closer to mine on the blanket.

"I don't know any Morse code," I confessed.

"I can teach you."

"I don't want to know Morse code." His pinky crossed over mine.

"I like you despite your shortcomings." He leaned closer, his eyelids drooping a little as he looked at my lips, then my eyes, then my lips. I could feel his breath on my cheek. I ducked my head, letting his cheek touch mine. Then I turned back toward him, and his lips were there, waiting. This time when his mouth met mine, I knew what to expect, but it was no less exciting. I wasn't as nervous as before, and so I could pay attention to the pressure of his tongue as it moved with mine. I sensed the whole of him: his smell, his taste, the roughness on his chin, the way his bravado hid a tentative quality that I hadn't known he possessed. When he pulled away, I leaned my forehead against his. My heart thudded wildly, and all I wanted was a world where that moment could freeze forever. He trailed his fingers up and down my arm, and goose bumps rose in reaction all over my body.

"Now you," he said softly. "Tell me everything."

And the moment was over.

"I can't follow that," I replied.

"Try." The way he said it, I knew it wouldn't matter what I told him. I could have sailed across the world on my own or spent high school staring at a blank wall, and it wouldn't have mattered. He liked me because he liked me, and nothing I did or didn't do before we met would make a difference.

"I grew up in Detroit," I said. "In a two-bedroom house the size of your kitchen. My father left when I was three. He ran off with a waitress from the Steak 'n Shake down the street, where he liked to go binge-eat after he binge-drank. My mother raised me and my sister Lissa on her own for a little while . . ."

And so the story unraveled. I talked and he listened . . . and listened . . . and listened. He didn't pry, or look sorry for me, or even look surprised. Somewhere in the middle, though, he laced his fingers through mine and pulled me back against the blanket we'd spread out. While I was talking, he cradled my head against his chest. That's how we stayed until I was done. And when I was done, nothing awful happened. Everything was much the same. Except when we pulled our hands apart, an invisible net remained, binding us together even though our bodies were no longer touching. That was the only difference. It wasn't at all what I expected. It was much, much better.

**I DIDN'T REALIZE** we had dozed off until I woke up to find a dozen ants crawling over the cheese.

"Oh god," I said, sitting up. "Owen! Wake up." He rose and rubbed his eyes.

"Wow," he said, looking at the cheese. "Damn. I was really looking forward to eating that."

"Well at least the rest of the food is safe," I said, relieved.

"Yeah, because I'm starving." He started unwrapping the containers eagerly. "Let's eat quick before it gets dark." He was right—the sun was setting fast, and as if by magic, dozens of white lights had appeared on the bases of the palm trees bordering the park. It was lovely.

"You prepared quite a spread here," Owen said.

"Most of it was pretty much ready-made. I just put the sandwiches together."

"What's this?"

"Libby brought home banana bread last night. Told me to eat it. Begged me, really. I think she's a little weight-obsessed. She's one of those people who buys things and then makes other people eat them."

"There are things I could say now, but in the spirit of not talking about the Cohens, I decline to remark."

"I appreciate it," I replied, fixing him with a stern look.

"So, hey, right after this they're showing a movie at the other end of the park." Owen unwrapped one of the other cheeses and set it on the small wooden board I'd packed. "Want to go? It's outside and free."

"Oh yeah? That sounds great."

"It's one of my favorite things to do in the summer and fall. They put up a huge projector screen. It's a lot of fun."

"What are they playing tonight?"

"I'm not sure. I think I heard something about *The Muppet Movie,* but I could be mistaken."

"I guess it doesn't matter," I said without thinking.

"Why is that?" Owen had a smug grin on his face. I was getting the feeling he was starting to enjoy my awkward, completely un-smooth self.

"I just meant that I'm not picky about movies," I said lamely. I quickly spread some cheese on a cracker and stuffed it in my mouth in an effort to forcibly eliminate further awkward language from the conversation. The cheese had a strange, woodsy aftertaste that I wasn't crazy about. I broke off a hunk of the banana bread and popped it in my mouth to chase it. That, on the other hand, was delicious: moist, buttery, and sprinkled with chocolate chips.

"Anticipating as much, I brought a bottle of wine with me," Owen told me. He took a huge bite of his sandwich and let out a big sigh of satisfaction. I was about to tell him exactly what I thought of his confidence when I felt my throat tighten. I swallowed hard, forcing the last chunk of bread down my throat. But the feeling got worse even after I'd swallowed the food; it felt as though a fist had reached within me and was squeezing my esophagus. I couldn't breathe.

"Annie? Are you okay?" Owen sat up from his relaxed position atop the blanket, his eyes wide with concern.

I nodded. Then shook my head. I wasn't okay. Panic was descending too quickly for me to think. My whole body felt heavy and itchy, even as my head grew lighter. Owen's voice began to fade. I struggled harder for air, but the narrow tube in my throat had closed to what felt like a pinhead. Like mounds of cotton had been stuffed down me until there wasn't any room for oxygen to seep through. I'd never been more terrified.

Lissa flashed through my head, as she always did. But this time, her breathing became my own. Her body, struggling to stay afloat, was my body. Her lungs and mine were the same. Together, we couldn't breathe. We were drowning.

And then I realized: I was about to die.

# CHAPTER THIRTEEN

**"I ONLY WISH YOU'D INDICATED** that you were allergic to nutmeg," Libby said the next day, her face looking more drawn than I'd ever seen it. "I would have double-checked the ingredients. My *god*."

"I did," I insisted. "At least, I thought I did." I could have sworn I'd mentioned it, but my head was so foggy that I couldn't be certain of anything anymore. My throat still felt swollen and scratchy, but the welts in my mouth had completely disappeared. Yet I couldn't argue about it. I didn't feel like suffering Libby's anger. I was too exhausted. I'd been allergic to nutmeg for as long as I could remember, so it was weird that I hadn't been clearer about it with the Cohens. I always made a big deal out of it and even wore the information on a thin, silver ID bracelet, which is probably how Owen knew exactly what was happening. Nutmeg, for me, was the culinary equivalent of being bitten by a black widow. It could very easily have become lethal. It was actually kind of miraculous that he'd gotten me to the emergency clinic on time. From there, once they'd administered epinephrine, I'd been transported to the hospital, where I'd spent the night.

Now I was back at the Cohens'. I felt extremely exhausted. But more than that, something like depression was wrapping its talons around me. I'd had to skip classes today because of the episode. I'd skipped classes before because Libby had needed me at the last minute. I was falling behind at school and failing at my job, and it was only the first semester. I could feel everything—the life I'd waited so long to live—slipping from my grasp.

"Don't." Libby's voice was cold. "Don't make excuses. And don't think you can blame it on me. We have done *everything* to make you feel welcome. Everything! We have overlooked every incident that should have given us pause. We've accepted your eccentricities, we've—"

"What . . . eccentricities?" My voice was faint-sounding. It came from another universe a million miles away.

"The sleepwalking, the way you whisper to yourself, all of it! Don't you think this worries me? You're sleeping under our roof, handling our children . . . it's unthinkable! Yet we've made every single concession. I have actually fought with my husband over whether to keep you on. And now this." I couldn't focus; her words were like thick sludge I couldn't wade through. Sleepwalking? I'd never sleepwalked, not that I knew of. And although I did have a habit of talking to myself on occasion, I never did it around other people. Or at least not usually. And I didn't remember any times where they'd caught me doing it when I thought I was alone. Her words weren't making sense.

"But remember that first time we talked?" I insisted. "During my phone interview. You asked me if there was anything you should know about me, and I mentioned my allergy. I mention it everywhere I go, anytime I eat anything I don't prepare myself. Maybe you forgot?"

"I would never forget something like that." Libby looked enraged. "It must have been some other interview you're thinking of." But there had only been one interview.

I fidgeted in the navy blue velvet armchair in which I sat, my fingers trembling more than they should have under the intensity of Libby's gaze. She tapped the arm of her chair impatiently with carefully manicured nails. *Tap. Tap. Tap.* Before Lissa died, back when she was a concerned parent, my mother had always made me tell everyone about my allergy. She was certain there'd be nutmeg slipped in somewhere, and she was constantly afraid that I'd unknowingly ingest it. She used to keep an EpiPen zipped in my backpack as a kid, but I'd stopped carrying one once I'd gotten older and started trusting myself to stay away from complex foods that might contain the spice.

"I'm just not sure what to do with you," Libby said, after a long silence. "How could you blame me for this, Nanny? We're hitting so many bumps lately. So, so many rough spots. I just don't know how to handle you anymore."

"You can fire me," I said. "Just tell me if that's what you

want to do." I couldn't stand the torture of sitting there, not knowing.

"Oh, but I can't," Libby said softly. "I can't let you go when you owe me so much. You have quite the debt to pay, Nanny. Think of all I've done for you! All we've done, but also all the ways I've stuck up for you. Walker wanted to fire you after the incident with our files. But you already knew that, didn't you?" Her voice took on a soothing, almost melodic quality. "Yes, you knew that, because you're trickier than you look. You slip around here looking wide-eyed and innocent, but you and I know the truth. All you've caused is hardship. No, Nanny. You're not going anywhere. You're staying with us as long as we need you. And I envision that being a long while. You owe me that."

I shuddered, beginning to cry softly. It all felt so surreal, like a nightmare. I was still exhausted from the drugs they'd given me at the hospital and confused by my memories of what I'd told Libby versus what she was saying I'd omitted. Maybe she was angry with me, maybe I'd made some mistakes, but she'd never have purposely given me a substance that could have been lethal. So either I was forgetting or she was forgetting. But right then, it felt as if my brain had turned on itself; I doubted everything I thought I knew. There was a reverse side to everything, other possibilities that hadn't been explored. What I thought was the truth no longer felt certain at all. I felt my body clench up. My tears trickled down my cheeks, leaving salty, itchy streaks everywhere they touched.

"Nanny," Libby soothed. "It's okay. Maybe I came down too

hard on you. It's okay." She rubbed my back with one hand, using the other to wipe away my tears. Despite myself, I leaned into her.

"It's Annie," I said quietly, so quietly I wasn't sure she could hear. "Please call me by my name."

"I always do," Libby told me carefully. "I always use your name." I relaxed against her, crying harder, and she wrapped her arm tightly around me, resting her chin on my head. "Don't worry," she soothed. "We're not going to fire you. We'll keep you here, Nanny. We can help you. I just need you to work with me. Just trust me, and it will all get better, I promise. You need to stop fighting me. You just need to let me take care of you." I nodded as she stroked my hair, pushing back damp, sweaty tendrils from my face. I didn't protest when she led me upstairs and put me to bed as though she were the nanny and I was the child.

I didn't even ask her what had happened to the paisley-printed wallpaper that I'd grown to love; why it had been stripped off, revealing angry blue paint below; and why there were large, plastic-encased tubes of yellow wallpaper resting on my floor. Instead, I let myself drift to sleep.

# CHAPTER FOURTEEN

**THE WALLPAPER WASN'T A DREAM,** even though every aspect of my life had begun to feel off-kilter. The wallpaper was there when I woke up at seven A.M. for class. It was in my head so much on the way there, even as I carefully navigated through the dense fog that settled around the city in a cool, misty blanket in the mornings. The wallpaper didn't go away all day, not as I fidgeted with my coffee cup while my Eighteenth-Century Political Philosophy professor droned on, and definitely not as Morgan passed me a note in Design that read, "U alright? U look like shit. Mani/pedi's after class?" I was tempted to crumple up the note and ignore it. "No time," I wrote back instead. "Gotta get back 2 the kids." She read it and made an annoyed face. And on my phone's screensaver, the yellow wallpaper flashed and swirled.

My desk was covered with yellow-patterned wallpaper. The

classroom began to resemble a yellow prison. *Why my room? Had she decided to play some sick mind game with me after she saw what I'd been reading? But why?* I felt like I was high, but I hadn't taken anything. I felt like I hadn't eaten or slept for weeks. I felt like something had shifted inside me and I was too weak to figure out what it was.

I hadn't had any texts from Owen all morning. But he had played *pirate* in Words with Friends. I tried to convince myself that his seventeen-hour silence was normal. I spent a lot of time composing texts and then deleting them instead of listening to the lecture. I drank peppermint tea from a Thermos to stay alert. My hands shook. They were shaking pretty constantly now, because I was always so tired and on edge. I wondered when Owen would text me, and why he hadn't yet. I wondered if he didn't think about me as much as I thought about him. I thought he probably didn't, because if he did then he would have gotten in touch. What if he just thought of me as a little kid he could mess around with and then discard? These thoughts, they crushed me. They wormed their way into my mind and nested there. I decided I wanted Owen to be in love with me. It didn't really matter whether I was in love with him.

Morgan caught up with me after class. Some other girl— one of her friends, I guessed—loitered awkwardly behind her. She gave me a half smile and hugged her books to her chest. "Dude," Morgan said, "where have you been? I haven't seen you in, like, forever."

"I've just been working a lot. Hey." I nodded my chin at the friend.

"Oh sorry, this is Lily," Morgan said. "We're on the pom squad together. I made the pom squad! You should come to a football game, it's awesome."

"I don't know," I hedged.

"Well, look, whatever," Morgan said brusquely. "I know you're busy and all, but I just wanted to tell you about this party we're hosting at the Pom House on Friday. It's going to be great, we're going to have four kegs, there's going to be tons of cute guys, and I haven't seen you out all semester. Will you come?"

"Sure," I said, knowing full well I wouldn't. I was just so tired lately. "I'll definitely try."

"Awesome!" Morgan's face brightened, like she'd forgiven me for something I didn't know I'd done. "Gotta fly. Practice. Hey, you should come over early on Friday. We're doing a pre-game at the house."

"Cool, yeah. I'll definitely try." Morgan rolled her eyes at my response.

"Annie, at least pick up your phone once in a while," she said. And then she was off. Lily gave me a little wave. "Nice meeting you," she said before tagging along after Morgan, her high-heeled boots clicking lightly on the surface of the sidewalk.

I hadn't even talked to Morgan in at least a month. It was weird that she was all of a sudden being friendly. And was she pissed at me for not getting in touch with her? Why would I call her when she hadn't even bothered to call me?

"Morgan!" I shouted after them, and she paused, turning

halfway back toward me. I jogged after them to catch up. "Hey, I just—um." I wanted to ask her why she'd dropped me after Dis-O. In the end, I couldn't ask. "Have you done the reading yet for the fem lit unit? In Lit Sem? The *Yellow Wallpaper* thing?" Morgan looked at me strangely, furrowing her brows.

"I'm not in that class," she told me. "Sorry." Then they turned and walked away, leaving me stunned.

**"YOU'VE BEEN SKIPPING A LOT** of classes," Libby pointed out as if it were my fault. As if she hadn't begged me to skip class here and there to take Zoe to birthday parties or because she had an appointment she "absolutely couldn't miss," something that usually wound up being the all-important treatment for her invisible cellulite or laser bikini hair removal. "It would probably be way easier to make friends if you went to school more often." She didn't bother looking up from her paperwork. She'd pushed her glasses down to the bridge of her nose and was peering intently at a bunch of forms.

"I just think it might be good for me to get out more," I said uneasily. I'd decided that maybe Morgan's party wouldn't be so bad after all. I was thinking I should make a last-ditch effort at a normal college social life. As Libby talked, I stared at a crack that was beginning to form in the ceiling above her. It looked like water damage. I couldn't believe I'd never noticed it before. I couldn't believe Libby hadn't noticed it yet. "I think I'd be a little less stressed if I started hanging out with more people," I mentioned. The crack spread from one edge of the molding all the way to the other, almost the whole length of the wall. It had little offshoots, like fingers. The paint bubbled out from under the offshoots in fat white blisters.

"I'm sorry, Nanny, is there something I'm missing?" Libby looked up from her paperwork with a frown. "In the past several weeks, you've skipped out on babysitting nine times. Now obviously I'm not blaming you for your calc exam." She waved one hand dismissively. "That couldn't be helped. But this whole nutmeg-allergy thing could have been avoided. I mean, really! And is it in my imagination that it occurred when you were *out on a date with your boyfriend?* Hence, time off? Maybe if you were a little more responsible, these snafus wouldn't happen! Maybe if you managed your time better . . ." She stopped and took a breath, apparently in an effort to calm herself. I rubbed absently at a smudge on her desk with the corner of my T-shirt. I looked up, and she gave me a hard glare.

"Do you know what this is?" she asked quietly, indicating the stack of papers in front of her. I shook my head. I'd only asked for Friday night off, so I could go to Morgan's party. Zoe would be in bed anyway, and Walker and Libby had a nonexistent social life. Why was it such a big deal?

"It's our bills," she said. "More specifically, your hospital bills. Do you even *know* how many extra hours you owe us to make up for this?"

I raked my fingers through my hair. She had a point—I'd been nothing but a burden to them since I'd arrived. After they'd gone out of their way to make me feel comfortable. "I'll make it up to you," I said. "I'll figure it out. I'm sorry. I'll work harder."

"Nanny, just sit," she said with a sigh, indicating the damask chair in front of her desk. "There are a couple of things."

"Okay." I sat. My headache had already begun to over-whelm me. I'd felt its onset shortly after we'd started discussing the party, and now it was beginning to feel all-consuming.

"First, I'm wondering if you should cut back your hours at school to part-time. Before you protest"—she silenced me with a palm—"just listen to my logic. One, lots of kids can barely manage school *without* part-time jobs. And the ones who do work usually wait until their senior years, when they have more flexible schedules. Would it be so bad to take an extra year to graduate? It seems like the most logical move to me." She paused as if to gauge my reaction. *Part-time jobs*, she'd said. It was laughable; I'd been working full-time hours since the day I'd started, with the exception of the days I'd taken off because of the allergy incident. But I only had one day off per week, normally. And I wasn't guaranteed to have even that whole day. It was hardly part-time. *Which makes her argument all the more valid*, the voice inside my head argued.

"I'd have to talk to my professors . . ." I started.

"Fine," she interrupted. "Whatever works. I'm sure Walker can talk to them, too, if need be. One of his contracts is the new engineering facility. They're very grateful for his contribu-tions; I'm sure they'd be receptive to our suggestions for your curriculum." There was something off-putting but also comfort-ing in the way the Cohens were making decisions for me. If I'd had more energy, I might have fought. But there was relief in floating through it, allowing things to happen. The alternative was just too exhausting.

"What else?" I asked. Libby sighed again, rubbing her temples. She got up and filled her electric teakettle with water, pulling a bunch of tea bags from a drawer in her desk.

"It's Owen," she said abruptly, just as the water started to boil.

"What about him?" I tried to keep my tone even, not too guarded.

"I'm just not sure he's good for you."

"What are you talking about?" I forced out. "He's my only friend here."

"Darling," Libby laughed. "Don't be so dramatic! And besides, aren't we friends?" I nodded faintly in response, although I was still confused about that. "I just think he's taking up what little extra time you should be devoting to your schoolwork. Like you said, you should be leading a normal college life. But also, I feel responsible for you. I can't imagine what your parents would think if they knew you were having a sexual relationship with someone so much *older.*"

"He's only twenty. And we're not having sex." I was too thrown by the thrust of her argument to make sense of any of it or even bother to mention that it wasn't her business either way.

"Then where did these come from?" Libby wanted to know, rummaging in her desk to produce a packet of condoms. "Zoe apparently found these in your *room.* Thank goodness she's too young to know what they are. But I'm not sure I'm entirely comfortable with you bringing strange boys into this house. Around my daughter! How well do we really know him?" My mind felt thick, clogged. I took the condoms from Libby and turned them over in my palm. I'd never even held a pack of condoms before. I was still basically a virgin, if you didn't count that one mistake with Daniel.

"These aren't mine. And we haven't had sex."

"Well, they're certainly not ours, if that's what you're implying," Libby said, looking shocked and furious. "Walker and I haven't had sex for months. Because of the baby," she clarified. "Not because there's anything wrong. But even if we were, we certainly wouldn't be using condoms. We're trying to build a family."

"Maybe they're leftovers," I suggested. "From before."

"Don't be ridiculous," Libby snapped. "Take ownership for your mistakes."

"Libby," I protested, "I don't even have a door on my bedroom. How would I be having sex?"

"At his place! In the pool house! In the car! In the myriad of rooms available to you. How should I know? That's not the point."

"The point is that they're not mine," I tried again.

"Then what's this?" she asked, producing a receipt from her drawer.

"I have no idea! It's a receipt from the drug store. How should I know? It could be yours."

"The credit card number doesn't match any of our cards," she informed me. I looked down. The receipt was numbered

6686. I shuffled in my purse for my wallet, pulling out my credit card. The last four digits read 6686. I looked back up at Libby blankly.

"Well?" she wanted to know.

"It matches," I whispered. The receipt trembled beneath my fingertips. *I didn't remember buying these.* But if I didn't buy them, who had? Libby, in a conspiracy to frame me for . . . sex? That was completely bizarre. None of it made sense.

"Tell me, Nanny. What do you and Owen talk about when you're together?"

"I don't know," I managed, squirming in my seat. "Just normal things. His family, my family . . ."

"Us?" Libby interjected. "Your life here?"

"Sometimes," I stammered. "But nothing specific. Just normal things."

"Do you two talk about me and Walker? Do you laugh about us? Does Owen tell you how mean I am, how you shouldn't have to put up with it? Does he tell you that you should work less? Is that why you've been so lackadaisical lately?"

"What? No," I insisted. "No! Never."

"Maybe he wants to get you to quit, to run away with him," she suggested. "Maybe he tells you he'll stay with you forever, if you tell him everything."

"I don't know what you mean," I whispered. She was speaking so calmly, but her words were shocking and completely unwarranted. The tears were streaming silently down now. There was nothing I could do to stop them.

"I really don't like living with liars," Libby said, holding up the condoms. "So I'm going to assume you forgot about buying these. It's an awfully shaky memory you have, Nanny. I'm starting to wonder whether you weren't forthright about being up to the task of nannying. I think maybe it's time we looked into getting you some help." The wall behind Libby blinked and faded. It was marigold and sunshine and the color of my mother's wedding ring. And in it were faces. Layered over and over, their mouths gaping as if screaming from under a pool of liquid gold.

"I don't have a door on my room," I said finally. "Why are you putting up yellow wallpaper?"

"Nanny!" she snapped. "Focus! What do either of those things have to do with anything?"

"Annie," I said. "My name is Annie."

"Which is exactly what I said," she seethed. "It is exactly what I have *always* said. I'm starting to think there's something seriously wrong with you, Nanny. I'm this close to firing you." She indicated how close between her thumb and forefinger. There was a space wide enough for perhaps a piece of paper to slip through. "I feel like my hands are tied."

"Don't," I heard myself pleading. "Please don't." If she fired me, I would have to leave. There would be no Owen. There would be nothing. The idea of Libby hating me was unbearable.

"I won't—for now—only because I know you have nowhere to go. Would those deadbeat parents of yours even take you back? Especially in your condition? No, Annie. I'll let you stay only because I feel sorry for you. And because I wonder if maybe I can help you."

"Yes," I said. My voice emerged from the dark tunnel of

my brain, worming its way through muddy, cottoned clumps. "Help me."

"Drink this," she told me, handing me a mug of tea. "And take this." She held out a little white pill on a napkin. "It will calm you down."

"What is it?"

"Just a Valium. Nothing to worry about." I took the pill from her and swallowed it down with a gulp of tea. The warm, peppermint-flavored liquid scalded my throat, making me gasp for breath.

"What did you mean about Owen not being twenty?" I wanted to know once I'd taken a moment to calm down. "Why did you say that?"

"What do you mean?" Libby's face wore a confused expression. "When did I say that?"

"Just a minute ago . . ." I stammered. "I thought . . . I mean . . ."

"You must have misheard me," she said crisply. "Twenty seems about right. His mother mentioned something about how he'd be a junior in college if he'd gone."

"But then what about my parents?" I asked. "You said they'd be upset if they knew I was sleeping with someone older?"

"My goodness," Libby laughed. "I know your parents don't care what you do, so why would I say that?" Then she paused as if something had just occurred to her. "Oh god," she said. "Oh, Annie."

"What? What is it?"

"I wonder if you misinterpreted something I said because of your stepfather."

"What are you talking about?" My pulse quickened and I felt the world swirling around me. The tea had had a soothing effect, or maybe it was the Valium. I could feel my panic but it had been muted, as though someone had thrown a blanket over it. It was there somewhere but far enough below the surface that it didn't bother me anymore. Nothing bothered me anymore. The Valium was lovely, it really was.

"Darling," she said softly. "Of course I know all about your stepfather. He was a vile man. Don't be afraid to admit what he did to you. The abuse. Of course that's why you'd be afraid of older men."

"Dean didn't—he never did anything. I blocked the door." My soft voice curled around us. *It's okay*, it told me. *Don't be angry with her. She only wants to help.*

"I understand," Libby nodded, pity in her eyes. "I know. We have more in common than you think, you and I. We're both used to being manipulated, pushed down. Taken advantage of by older men." The fury underneath her words was unmistakable.

"No," I protested feebly. "Dean never got a chance. I never gave him a chance." But the world was fading out, and my eyelids were growing heavy. It was only nine o'clock, and Zoe needed to be put to bed. I couldn't be falling asleep again. I couldn't cast aside my duties.

"Where's Zoe?" I asked, my thick tongue making it difficult to force out the words. "I need to tuck Zoe in."

ANNA COLLOMORE

"I'll take care of it," Libby said. "She's upstairs with her dad. Hey," she continued, as though experiencing an epiphany, "maybe you and I can have some bonding time this weekend. We can finish redecorating your room! Won't that be fun?"

I couldn't have explained why Libby's words struck fear into my heart as she draped an afghan over my shoulders and led me away. I couldn't explain exactly what I was dreading when she tucked me into bed, stroking my hair as lovingly as I'd ever been touched.

# CHAPTER FIFTEEN

**THE FOLLOWING WEDNESDAY,** Owen rang the doorbell at nine P.M. I heard it from my room, but it was Libby who answered; I'd already changed into my sweats and a T-shirt and was ready to head to bed early. I'd been feeling so exhausted ever since Libby's and my confrontation over Owen. Everything was starting to seem bigger and more confusing and out of my control than I could handle, despite all my efforts to make everything right again. All I wanted was to return to that time of happiness I'd felt during my first few weeks on the island. But I was reminded of something my mother had told me long ago, back when I was a little girl and my best friend had started hanging out with someone else—someone with more money and all the right things—leaving me in the dust. She'd said, "Sometimes when things are broken, baby, you just can't fix them, no matter how hard you try." That's how I'd been starting to feel about my relationship with Libby for the last couple of weeks. Things were beginning to feel cracked in ways that pointed to an imminent and irreparable shatter. I was struggling to bind those cracks, but it was becoming increasingly difficult.

I wouldn't have heard Owen at the door except that I'd been returning to my room from the bathroom. The murmur of Libby's chilly voice—the one she reserved for unwanted guests—was unmistakable. I paused at the landing, and when I heard Owen's familiar lilt, I dashed down just in time to hear Libby tell him, "I'll let her know you stopped by."

"I'm here," I said breathlessly. "Hi." I didn't even care that my hair was disheveled and I was wearing polka-dotted pajama bottoms and a *Rolling Stones* T-shirt with no bra. Owen glanced at Libby, obviously confused, but she just straightened her shoulders and made her way out of the room. "If you go anywhere, Annie," she told me, "please be back by midnight. This is not your day off." I didn't bother responding. I just flew into Owen's arms and felt the comfort of him wrapped around me. I loved how I had to stand on tiptoe to reach his face as he pulled me in for a kiss.

"Hey there," he said softly. "That's the way to greet a guy."

"Sorry," I told him. "I'm just so happy to see you. It's been a rough couple of days."

"Well," he said, trailing off, taking in my bedtime wear. "I hope not too rough to go out for a little while? I wanted a take two on the picnic. There's this place I really want to take you to. It's one of my favorite places in the city, and I think you'll love it."

"Just give me five minutes," I told him, leaning in for another kiss. "Don't go anywhere." I ran upstairs as fast as I could—we only had three hours to hang out, although my curfew was arbitrary, given that the kids were in bed. Still, I was in no mood to argue with Libby again. I threw on some jeans and flats, pulled up my hair, brushed my teeth, and slipped on a bra and tank top. Owen was . . . ugh, I hated how he made my heart beat. I hated how intoxicated I felt around him. But I couldn't get enough of it. I wanted him and hated him for not being with me every single second.

"You look adorable," he told me once we were in the car. And then suddenly he was leaning toward me again and kissing me, and it was different this time, more intense and passionate. I didn't recognize the sounds I was uttering. They emerged from some place deep inside of me that felt as if it had been locked away until then. His hands moved through my hair and down my lower back, and I felt insatiable, heady, and unaware of what I was doing even as my hands moved independently of my brain, touching his shoulders and face. Finally we pulled apart, both breathing hard.

And then I saw her.

Libby was standing on the second-floor terrace, looking down at us. I wasn't sure what she could see, but I jumped anyway.

"Holy shit," Owen said. "I guess we should have saved that for later."

"Let's just go," I told him, my adrenaline from our make-out turning into adrenaline-fueled anger at Libby. What had she been doing out there? Was she deliberately spying on us? I glanced over at Owen, and he seemed creeped out, too. He was drumming a beat on the steering wheel with his fingers, and his brow was furrowed in a way I was beginning to find familiar.

"Why is she like that?" he wanted to know as we drove off the island. "Is it me?"

"No, no," I assured him. "It's me, I guess. I mean, I don't know. Things were really great for a while, and then I found those files, and it's like our dynamic shifted."

"What files? The ones you mentioned before? When you almost got fired?"

"Yeah," I said, sighing. "I don't know why, but things have been different since then."

"Well . . . what was in them?"

"I feel bad saying, Owen. It's not really my business."

"No problem," he said, his mouth drawn into a firm line.

"Oh, whatever. It's not even a big deal, that's the weird thing. I just think Libby's a little jealous. Walker was married before. He had an ex-wife who died, and I think Libby has some sort of complex about him not being over her yet."

"How do you know she died?"

"The files I found . . . there was a will."

"Ah."

"Can we change the subject, please? I really, really don't want to think about this, and you're my escape. Let's not ruin it." He smiled slightly and took my hand in his, but I could tell that he wasn't completely satisfied. Owen's brain was working hard the whole way to our surprise date, which turned out to be at the Audium. I could tell from his silence, and from the worry lines that creased his face, that he hadn't stopped thinking about it.

By the time we got to the Audium, though, all was forgotten. The Audium wasn't what I'd expected—but then, I hadn't known what to expect. It was a circular space with plain, cream-colored walls and a ceiling covered in speakers. All in all, there had to be at least a hundred speakers surrounding us, maybe two hundred. There were red chairs set in a circle, and once we entered the space we weren't allowed to talk. Within a minute, the whole room went black. Owen had smuggled a bottle of sparkling wine and some Dixie cups into the theater in his backpack, and over the sound of the musical sculptures, it was impossible to hear the cork pop. I wasn't sure how he managed to pour it without spilling a drop—maybe he put a finger under the stream to follow its path to the cups—but the thought of it seemed normal, given the atmosphere. Nothing was weird in the Audium. We spent the next two hours submerged in impenetrable darkness, letting music from almost two hundred speakers radiate above, around, and beside us until we felt consumed by a whirlpool of sound that contained only us. The sound filled me. The only thing keeping me tethered to reality was Owen's hand in mine.

"That was incredible," I breathed when it was over, our footsteps sounding inept compared to the cacophony we'd just experienced.

"It's one of my favorite places in the city," he told me as we reached the car.

"What are your other favorites?"

"The movie theaters in the Castro," he said. "We'll go there sometime. They're old-timey theaters, with velvet curtains and opera seats and stuff. And the Musee Mecanique. I definitely have to take you there." He looked at me out of the corner of his eye, grinning devilishly.

"What is it?" I asked, his smile making me suspicious.

"It's this huge collection of antique arcade games and, like, mechanical puppets and stuff."

"Mechanical puppets."

"Right. Like the fortune-teller from *Big*. It's pretty great."

"Because what's better than creepy automatons," I said.

"Exactly."

"I'm personally very glad we came here, at least this time," I told him.

"Yeah," he said in a more serious tone. "Ever since my first visit, I try to go when I need something to remind me why life is more than just us. It's the only place I can go where I feel transcendental."

"Thank you for taking me," I said softly. He turned toward me, leaning his back against the side of the car, pulling my waist close to his. I wrapped my arms around his shoulders and I felt his lips on mine.

"You're the only person I've ever taken," he told me. "You're the only one I've ever wanted to share this with." He leaned his forehead against mine and kept my hands tucked tightly in his. It was then that I wondered if I loved him.

We were home twenty minutes later, just in time for curfew.

"Thanks," I told him as I climbed out of the car. "I'd better run in right away before we start making out again and unwittingly put on a show for Libby."

"Hey, Annie," he said, that worried look crossing his eyes again. "About that . . . something about it feels a little off."

"What are you talking about?"

"Just how upset she got after the files. How upset she gets about everything. How she's been treating you since then."

"Owen," I warned, knowing where he was headed with it. "Don't do anything stupid."

"Just a little poking around on the interwebs," he said, smiling. "I promise I'll stay out of trouble." I sighed. I knew there was no stopping him once he got something into his head.

"Fine," I said. "But just remember: your trouble is my trouble in this. So please, god, don't you dare ruin my job for me."

"Not gonna happen," he assured me. "C'mere, babes." I leaned in for one more kiss, and he waved goodbye as I slammed the door. The last thing I saw before I ran into the house was his adorable, crooked smile.

**LIBBY NEEDED ME ALL THE TIME** over the course of that week. She even had me taking care of Jackson and changing his diaper, "privileges" she usually reserved for herself, since she almost never let him out of her arms, let alone her sight. But that week was different. It was as though I was on call, ready to spring up to assist in the event of any crisis. But instead of bullet wounds or aneurysms, the crises I needed to attend were scraped knees or pots that threatened to boil over. I knew I should insist on some hours to rest—to do my homework, at least—but I didn't have the will to resist her. So I leaped when she called, I answered when she buzzed, I was perpetually tied to my intercom like a harnessed animal. It was almost as if she was purposefully trying to keep me from Owen.

I was tired.

But it would be over soon, the busy week. And then I would get some rest.

The house, though, was growing smaller as I scurried relentlessly through it. Sometimes I was able to step outside myself and see what I looked like from afar: a rat running through a maze, one room to the next, never really getting anywhere. All the rooms and their grandeur had begun to fade for me. The yellow wallpaper, which we'd put up on my day off, mocked me from my bedroom. I couldn't feel safe anymore because of that wallpaper. Every morning when I woke up, I had to fight the urge to tear it down. But it wasn't just that.

The heated tiles in my bathroom, which I'd found so soothing when the weather first began to turn, scalded my feet. I checked the thermostat over and over; I even turned it to "off." But I still emerged from my bathroom red-soled and wincing from the pain. My room had begun to take on a shabby tinge under the gaze of the yellow wallpaper. Instead of bright and cheerful, it looked forced and macabre, like a big, false smile. Like my mother's smile when unexpected visitors came to the door.

Owen was the only thing keeping me normal.

I woke up around six on Thursday morning to the pinging of my phone. It was still dark out, the sun just barely beginning to press its gray morning light through my bedroom blinds; but Owen was up too, apparently, because the chime was signaling a new move in Words with Friends, which he'd playfully dubbed "Ultimate Warrior." I needed more sleep. But I wanted Owen. Want versus need. I'd always thought I had remarkable self-control, I'd thought I was a logical person—until I met Owen. And then he became all I wanted and needed, both.

Owen had played *candid* for seventeen points. I had a *z* in my stash, as well as a blank tile. I could save them or use them. In the spirit of being candid, I went for it. I played *dizzy* for seventy-eight points, both because it gave me an awesome lead and because "dizzy" was how he made me feel. I smiled at my private joke. I waited a few minutes, rolling on my side to doze until he responded. Finally my phone chimed and I lifted my aching, heavy lids. I laughed: he'd played *you* for seven points. I wondered if he knew he'd created a double entendre.

My next move was *hug*. Now that I had a lead, I was content to have fun with wordplay. I burrowed under my comforter until I'd made a dark cave for myself, my phone offering the only illumination.

He played *hot*. I let out a low whistle. Was he aware that he was upping the stakes? I decided to get risqué and play *thigh*. My heart thudded rapidly. Had I been too bold? But no. I hadn't been. Because his next word, using the *n* from *candid*, was *naked*. My heart stopped. Tingles spread from my center outward, down my arms until the whole of me felt light and wobbly.

Instead of responding, I slipped out from under the covers and made my way across the bedroom, grabbing my robe from where it hung on the back of the bathroom door. Maybe if he saw me outside, he would come down. And then we would . . ..
*What? What did I plan to do, get naked on the pool deck?*

I just wanted to see him. To touch him, to have him touch me. The rest of it wasn't enough anymore, and I was tired of waiting days and days for a stolen couple of hours when he lived right next door. I was tired of playing outside with Zoe in the hopes that he and Izzy would walk by. I wanted him right that second. I wanted to run my hands through his hair, touch the side of his jaw where he felt a little scruffy, pull him closer, feel his arms and stomach and chest muscles press against me, feel his lips on my neck and the chills that would follow. I couldn't wait any longer. It was an urgency I'd never felt before, a sense of immediacy that made me disregard any concern for consequences.

So I ran downstairs in Libby's castoffs: a cotton robe and a matching boxer/tank set. I wasn't worried about who would see me, as long as he saw me. I ran down the back staircase and out through the back door and through the pool gate and down the driveway. I snuck alongside the fence that divided the two properties. I trailed my hand over its wooden slats as I walked, feeling the dew wet on my toes. Dragonflies buzzed around me, but I didn't bother swatting them away. They were everywhere in San Francisco, and I'd gotten used to their presence. It was cool out, colder than I thought California could be in the fall, and it showed how much I hadn't known about what I was doing by moving out here, even the basics. But I liked it, the way the droplets of water wet my toes and tickled the bottoms of my feet. I liked the roughness of the wood fence under my fingertips, and the way the wind blew my robe open and caressed my skin under and around my pajamas. I looked up at his window, and there he was, looking down at me. I drew closer to the fence, hugging my body to it as if I could slip right through and up into his room.

I watched as he pressed his hand to the glass. Then both hands were there, and his face receded as his fingertips met to form an image. He bent his fingers together and I squinted, trying to read his message through the ever-present fog that decorated the island. Finally it was clear. A heart. He'd formed a heart with his hands, just for me. I laughed, and then his face was back, and I could see that he was laughing, too. I motioned for him to come down, but he held up a finger: *one minute*. I was starting to get cold from the wet, so I decided to head back toward the pool terrace. The pool was heated, and I could control the temperature of the stone tiles around it too. At least if someone woke up, it wouldn't look like we were trying to hide anything. It crossed my mind that Libby would be mad at me for inviting someone over . . . but this was different. This was Owen. She knew him now.

I turned slowly from the fence and moved toward the

pool, focusing on the reflection of the sunrise on the bay as I went. When I reached the gate, I reluctantly tore my eyes from the gorgeous vision I still hadn't gotten used to. I hoped I never would. I never wanted to take something so beautiful for granted. I unlatched the gate, my heart wild with anticipation. I started counting down from sixty to mark Owen's arrival.

That's when I noticed the figure in the pool.

It was dark and small. At first I thought maybe it was a raft left out from the day before; it was hard to tell, because it bobbed under the overhang of the floor above, and the sun hadn't come up enough to illuminate that end of the pool yet. I moved closer, feeling my heart accelerate as it did whenever I was near swimming pools.

My palms began to sweat. The form looked more solid than it had from the other side of the deck.

I took another step, and realization washed over me in a cold wave.

And with it came memories.

*A gate unlatched. I was fourteen. I'd forgotten to lock it.*

*A tiny form in a pink bathing suit bobbing near the surface.*

*Lissa begging me to take her swimming just an hour before, but I'd grumbled and turned away, wanting to read a while longer.*

*"Lissa!" I called, laughing too hard, pretending she was playing dead. But she hadn't stood up and laughed, hadn't told me, "Fooled you!" in her little baby voice. She was supposed to turn seven that summer.*

I sank to my knees at the edge of the pool, staring at Zoe's floating form. The same thing was happening again: my curse, my nightmare, the thing I'd tried to run away from. The thing that had driven my mother mad. I wanted to curl up and sleep right there, but I willed myself to get up, strip off my jacket, jump into the pool.

"Zoe," I heard myself shriek over and over as I paddled toward her, the icy water lapping at my tank top and shoulders, slowing me down, mocking my attempts to save her. "Zoe!" I screamed it over and over, making my way closer. I prayed there was still time. My tears mixed with the water, blending together until I wasn't sure whether I was crying at all.

I felt a supreme aching in the back of my skull. An emptiness in my chest. I wasn't going to make it. I wasn't going to reach her.

Then the back door swung open and I met Walker's eyes, saw Libby standing behind him. I watched the expression on Libby's face morph from confusion to alarm to horror. I barely had time to wonder why she was wearing a bathing suit under her robe—had she slept in it?—before I felt my panic overwhelm me.

Time stood still.

I gave in to the blackness.

I felt the world slip away.

# CHAPTER SIXTEEN

**AS IT TURNED OUT,** Zoe wasn't dead. Not even close. Her body had hung there, just under the surface of the water in that curious way bodies with a little extra baby fat do, but her mind was alert as ever. And to her, my screams had sounded muted, as though I was playing along. It was only when I jumped in the water that Zoe pulled herself up and saw my face and the way I grasped at her. And then her screams matched mine, her shriller voice twisting with my mature one in a discordant harmony.

But I didn't remember any of that. After I saw Zoe's floating form—after I felt panic consume me—I blacked out. I awoke to the sounds of tense murmurings.

"... had quite a shock."

"... to the hospital?"

"... go then."

I waited a beat before allowing my eyes to flutter open, to face the reality of whatever had happened to me.

"She's awake." The pronouncement came from the tanned face of a boy about my age, his ruddy skin framed by a mass of wavy, sandy-brown hair. I saw him first because he was bent over me, his eyes lit with concern. It took me what seemed like an eternity to register him as Owen. I allowed myself to look around then and saw Walker standing to my left, wearing sopping wet pajamas and looking more strained than I'd thought his normally tranquil visage capable of.

"Where's Zoe?" I asked, sitting bolt upright, overcome by one of the many waves of nausea I'd become accustomed to. I'd just had a flashback to little Zoe's body, floating prone and lifeless in the pool.

"She's fine," Walker replied tensely. "She's inside the house."

"But—"

"She was just playing, Annie," Owen said gently. "She was fine the whole time. But man, you've got some killer maternal instincts. Looks like you hired the right girl for the job, Mr. C."

"Thanks, Owen," Walker managed stiffly. "We were lucky to have you around."

"I was happy to be," he said.

"Owen, you can leave now," Libby told him in a terse voice.

"Yeah," Walker agreed, putting a palm on Owen's shoulder. "We've got it from here." Owen looked at me, reluctant. He didn't move his hand from where it rested on mine. But one look at Libby convinced me it would be better for him to leave.

"I'll talk to you later, okay?" I said.

"You're sure you're fine?" At that, Libby rolled her eyes.

"I'm fine," I assured him, forcing out a small smile for his benefit.

"Okay. See you later on then. I'll check in." He gave me a quick kiss on the cheek before walking off. When he reached the fence that separated our houses, he leaped over it like a pole-vaulter.

"Sorry, Mr. Cohen," he called behind him. "Way faster this way."

"Hopefully that won't become a habit," said Walker under his breath. "Apparently he heard you screaming and was over here pulling you out of the pool before I even made it out of the house. Good thing, too, because you were out cold, Annie. What happened to you?" Walker squinted at me suspiciously. "You look so wan. Are you using drugs? I know college can be crazy, but you know how we feel about that. . . ."

"No, no." I shook my head firmly. "I just . . . I thought . . ."

"Zoe was *playing,* that's all. She and her mom were up early this morning for a swim."

"I'm sorry." I struggled to my feet, and it was only then that I realized how awful I must look to them. My clothing was drenched and clinging to my body, my shirt nearly see-through. I wrapped my towel tighter. I was blowing it. At this rate, I would never last the year.

"Sit, Annie," Libby commanded.

"I'm talking to her," Walker said. Some unseen communication passed between them: a desire on Walk's behalf to take control. "I'm handling it."

"It's fine, Walker," Libby said calmly, firmly. She gave him a long glare, and I watched his shoulders slump in acquiescence before he even bothered to speak.

"I'm just not sure—"

"It's fine. Don't you have to leave for the gym, anyway? It's already seven-thirty. If you don't go now, you won't make it before work." Libby sat down without waiting for a response. The conversation was over, as far as Libby was concerned. I both sympathized with Walker and admired the way Libby carried herself, the way she took control. It was so rare to see that kind of balance. If my mother had been that way, my life might have turned out differently. Besides, I was glad to talk to Libby. She'd understand why I'd been so freaked out. She'd stood up for me in the past. She knew what haunted my nightmares. Walker stooped to kiss her cheek and waved goodbye to me as he made his way through the back terrace toward the driveway.

Libby patted the empty space next to where she sat on one of the several taupe lounge chairs that decorated the terrace. "It's better for us to talk with Walk gone," she told me. "Woman to woman. I'm guessing this is hard for you." I nodded, sensing it was the right response, but I was too tired and overwhelmed to feel much of anything. I just wanted it to be over. "I didn't realize you were still so sensitive to scenarios that involve pools, Annie, but I should have known," Libby's voice was gentle, caring. She wasn't angry. She was concerned.

"I'm not, I just—" But she raised one hand to quiet me. "It's totally normal, hon, and something we should have anticipated.

And we understand if . . ." She trailed off as though searching for the right words. "I'm only saying that you shouldn't feel pressured to stay with us anymore if it really is too much for you." I felt overcome by a wave of nausea; she was telling me to leave. I must have looked stricken, because Libby was quick to finish. "We *want* you to stay, Annie! I see this as a good thing, in a way. You were quick to react . . . even if you did wind up passing out. But if this had been the real deal, your screaming would have alerted us, and I guess a watchful eye is better than the alternative. And as I said previously, you *are* in our debt."

"I'd really like to stay," I said tentatively. "You have to understand that this kind of thing never happens, I—"

"You don't have to explain it to me." Libby said. "And I don't mean to suggest that you should go home. I was just thinking . . . with a trauma like this, maybe you'd be better off getting professional help. I've mentioned it before, and I need to know your thoughts." There was a long pause. Was she suggesting that I see a doctor?

"I'm fine," I repeated.

"Okay then," Libby said with a resolute smile. "As far as we're concerned, this never happened. And I'll make sure I'm available if Zoe ever wants to go swimming, so you never have to worry about taking her. You two can just steer clear of the pool area." Maybe it was for the best to avoid the pool. As much as I wanted to feel capable, to feel like I'd gotten past that day with Lissa, apparently I hadn't. And the sight of Zoe . . . I shuddered. It was the kind of thing I didn't want to experience again. "I think I'm going to go upstairs and nap for a few hours, if it's okay."

"Sure. Don't forget, I have a call at noon, and my yoga trainer's coming after that. I really need you bright-eyed and bushy-tailed by noon sharp."

"No problem."

I slept for a few hours, and the rest of the day passed by in a blur. I had a few texts from Owen of the "R u ok?" variety, but there was no return to the intimacy we'd had before my freak-out by the pool. I hoped I hadn't scared him away. I hoped he'd understand why I'd panicked the way I had. But when I called him later that night after my babysitting duties were over, I couldn't get in touch with him. I didn't want to be para-noid, but his silence made me anxious. That night, I slept rest-lessly, and the yellow wallpaper entered my dreams, blending my waking and sleeping states into some kind of suspended, nightmarish haze.

# CHAPTER
# SEVENTEEN

**LIBBY AND WALKER GAVE ME** Friday night off to go
to the pom squad party—which meant they let me leave the
house once Zoe was in bed. The rationale was that (after the
pool incident) I should get out and have some fun.

"She's a kid, Libs," Walker had told Libby the previous afternoon. "Let her get out, it'll do her some good. Things have been
so tense around here lately." Then he tickled her neck, making
her laugh. "Plus, we could use a little alone time," he said in a
voice that was low, but not so low that I couldn't still hear it
from where I was cutting Zoe's ravioli into bite-sized pieces.

Libby pretended to think it over, but I knew she'd say yes.
Even though she ordered Walker around, she was like Jell-O
when he got all romantic. She liked the attention, I had begun
to realize. But not just attention from her husband—any kind
of attention. It was obvious by the way she lit up whenever I

asked her exactly how she wanted her coffee fixed or what sort of pattern she wanted for the kitchen tiles or what kind of food I should use to feed the baby.

I'd made Owen promise to come to the party with me. I still didn't know Morgan all that well, and I didn't want to stand there alone like the last time.

"Seriously," he groaned. "I can't believe I agreed to this. I thought I was getting out of lame social events when I decided not to go to college. That was kind of one of the perks."

"You never miss having a social life?"

"I've got friends, babe. You just haven't met them. And you know I'm not really into partying."

I knew he didn't mean anything by it, but his words stung. We were sitting in the sunroom playing Memory with Zoe.

"Ha!" I said, "Friends? A likely story." I was trying to make light of it so I wouldn't dwell on why exactly I hadn't met anyone in his life and why we hung out at his place only when his parents were gone. I turned over a bunch of cherries and reached for the third card down in the far left-hand row. More cherries.

"You got a match!" Zoe exclaimed, bouncing up and down a little. She got more adorable every day. She was a funny kid—always happy to see other people happy, if a little serious. She'd had her moments, sure, but I'd seen how other kids screamed at their parents in public, lied to get what they wanted, demanded constant attention.

"Zoes, I've only got two more than you," I said.

"Yeah, you're about to kick our butts," offered Owen.

"We got butts," said Zoe.

"Thanks. Really mature, Owen. Zoe, it's not nice to say 'butt.'" Zoe just looked up at us from under her long eyelashes and smiled.

"*Butt* wait, there's more!" Owen reached over to pinch my butt, sending Zoe into a fit of giggles. I swatted his hand away, but I couldn't help smiling. Being around Owen restored my equilibrium—I was feeling more myself than I had in days. I was even getting excited about the party. This little dose of normalcy gave me hope.

"Time for bed, Zoes," I told her. "Let's get this cleaned up." She hummed under her breath as she gathered her tiles. The nursery rhyme had become so familiar to me by then that I thought it as much a part of Zoe as her glossy brown ringlets.

I tucked her into bed reluctantly—I worried about being away, even for just a few hours. She'd woken up in hysterics two more times since that first awful night. Once Walker had come to her, and the other time I'd waited five minutes before going myself. Five minutes of hearing her piercing cries split her in two, of wondering what could possess a little girl so painfully. It had been almost as awful for me as it was for her.

"Sweet dreams, little one." I kissed her on the cheek and ran back down the corridor, giving Libby a quick wave as I passed the great room. She smiled at me from the sofa, where she sat playing with Jackson. Things between us had normalized since the pool incident, and I had reason to believe the difficult period might be over.

"She's asleep," I called out, even though Libby hadn't asked.

Then we set off in Owen's Jeep, twisting our way down the hills of the island, over the Golden Gate Bridge to San Francisco and toward campus. Owen reached over and clasped my hand in his, rubbing my fingertips with his thumb. I looked out my window at the twinkling city reflecting over the water and felt something like peace. I had had a rough start, but things were going to get better, I was certain of it.

"Remind me again who these people are?"

"Person. It's Morgan, this girl I have some classes with."

"Morgan. What's her last name?"

"I don't know, why?"

"No reason. Just curious." He squeezed my hand reassuringly. "Sorry about complaining. It'll be fun."

But as soon as we walked in, I knew it wouldn't be fun. It was packed. I didn't step more than two feet into the dilapidated house before my drunk classmates were spilling beer on my shoes and jeans from both sides of my body. The music was deafening. Owen yelled something in my ear, his hot breath lacing my neck. I felt sticky, hot, overwhelmed. I couldn't hear him.

"What?" I yelled.

"Where do you want to go?" he shouted again. I shrugged in response, and he took my hand and led me back through the house and out through the kitchen to the backyard.

"Where's your friend?" he asked once we got out back. One of the four purported kegs loomed a few feet to our right, and people swarmed around it like flies around a dead animal. I shuddered; it was cold outside, and ever since we'd arrived I'd had a strange, anxious feeling.

"Not sure," I told him. "We'll be lucky to find her at all in this crowd."

"I'm guessing it'll actually be pretty easy," remarked Owen wryly. He pointed none too discreetly toward a girl nestled up against the shoulder of a huge, brawny guy who leaned against the front porch railings. She was wearing a short blue skirt and a tummy-bearing top. His hand rested against the bare skin of her waist. "Think they're all in uniform," Owen asked, "or is this one just extra spirited?"

"Stop!" I elbowed him in the ribs and tried to stifle my laughter. "Surely they're not all in uniform. Surely not."

"I wouldn't be so confident," Owen said under his breath just as I felt a tap on my shoulder. I swiveled around to find Morgan grinning at me.

"Heeyyy!" she cried out, throwing her arms around my neck. "*So* glad you could make it!" I could tell from her flushed cheeks that she was already pretty buzzed. And sure enough, she was in full pom squad apparel, complete with little white sneakers and a purple ribbon in her hair. I was about to answer when I saw that her attention had shifted. She squinted over my shoulder and cocked her head to one side, frowning at Owen.

"Owen?" she asked in disbelief. I extracted my shoulder from her grasp and turned Owen's way, lacing my hand through his. His expression looked wary, uncomfortable.

"Hey," he responded.

"You guys know each other?" I looked from one face to

another; the sight of Owen had apparently sobered up Morgan pretty fast, and Owen had lost his easy smile.

"We went to high school together," he said. "Morgan was a couple of years behind me."

"Small world," I said faintly, eager to ease the tension. "But I thought you were from Kentucky?" None of this was making sense to me.

"Boarding school," Morgan confirmed. "You've got a real catch on your hands, Annie." It wasn't immediately apparent from her tone whether she was being sarcastic or sincere. "And how did you two meet?"

"We're neighbors," Owen said quickly, removing his hand from my grasp to rake it through his hair. The absence of his hand left me feeling naked and insecure. Had he dropped it because of Morgan? Why was he so uncomfortable?

"You didn't tell me you were dating someone, Annie!" Morgan's tone was suddenly bubbly again, as if the awkward moment had never happened.

"Sorry," I said. "We hadn't really—"

Before I could finish, she grabbed my hand and tugged me toward the door. "Bathroom break?" she asked, tugging me away from Owen before I could answer.

"No problem," he told me. "Go catch up. I'll grab us some drinks."

Morgan didn't say anything until she'd dragged me through the throngs and up the stairs and shut me in a second-story bathroom. "How long have you been dating Owen Oswald?" she asked, arms folded across her chest.

"Um, maybe a month," I said. "Why?"

"You've got to break it off, Annie. He is seriously awful. I'm only telling you this because I'm your friend. He'll totally screw you over. He'll screw you *and then* he'll screw you over."

"What are you talking about?" I asked, my face flaming. Morgan's own face was contorted into a singularly nasty expression, something residing in between hatred and disgust.

"Look," she said. "He dated my older sister for a while. He totally broke her heart. He acted like they were so in love, like everything was perfect, and then—" She trailed off, leaving her sentence open-ended.

"Then what?"

"Then he moved to California, and he broke her heart."

"Okay," I shrugged. "So they broke up. That doesn't make him a bad guy."

"It was the way he did it, Annie. I'm telling you, he's *cold*. The guy doesn't have a heart." I stared at her, completely speechless. None of this sounded quite right.

"It's nuts, I know." Morgan's tone had softened, and now she looked sympathetic. "I just don't want to see you get involved with some shady bastard."

I nodded. "I'm glad you told me," I said, though I wasn't sure if I meant it. My head was throbbing the way it always did when a situation became overwhelming. None of what Morgan was saying matched up with the guy I knew Owen to be. But then, I hadn't really known him for that long. And my instincts about people . . . they hadn't always been right. I couldn't trust my instincts. The truth was, I had loved Dean before my mother married him, before he'd moved in with us. *I never knew the difference between right and wrong, because I couldn't even trust my own gut. I'd loved Dean, and he'd turned out to be a monster. Owen could just as easily be the same.*

"You know, I'm not feeling great," I said to Morgan, "and honestly, I have to be up early tomorrow. I really only came out to see you. But you should go back out there. I'll have Owen drive me home. I'm just going to take a minute, maybe splash some water on my face first."

"Okay. Want me to stay with you?"

I shook my head. "Can you just tell Owen I'll be down in a minute, if you see him?" All I wanted was to be alone for a minute to clear my head.

"Sure." Morgan hugged me and gave me a light kiss on the cheek. "I'm really glad you came, you know? I knew we'd be friends. I just had that feeling when I first saw you." I managed a weak smile.

"We'll do it again," I said. "Have fun." And then she was gone, and I was standing in front of a mirror, looking into eyes that didn't seem mine anymore but a stranger's. I looked tired; even I could see that. I had faint purple circles under my lower lids that no amount of makeup could banish. I'd gotten thinner, and my cheekbones were more prominent than ever. My hair looked slightly greasy, and it occurred to me that I hadn't washed it since the previous morning. Even when I was living in our tiny Detroit house—even at my absolute worst—I'd been meticulous about hygiene. I didn't have great clothes, but I'd made sure I was clean and fresh-looking.

Now as I stared into my own blank eyes, I noticed for the first time how unkempt I looked. I'd brushed my hair and worn mascara and lip gloss and put on a fresh, figure-flattering T-shirt, but my skin was uneven where I'd started compulsively picking at it, and my hair hung around my face in limp, greasy strands. I took a quick sniff under my arms, and the smell was rank. I'd forgotten to wear deodorant. When in the past weeks and months had I forgotten how to take care of myself? When had it stopped being a priority? And what could a guy like Owen possibly see in me, even if I *was* just a temporary thing to him? Owen could have chosen anyone, but he'd chosen me.

I stared so long and hard at my reflection that it began to morph in front of my eyes into something uglier and uglier until I couldn't stand the sight of myself. I turned from the mirror and sank down onto the floor instead, hugging my knees to my chest as I leaned against the cabinetry. And then, finally, it hit me. Owen was dating me because he needed something. There was no other possible reason. That had to be it. But what was it he could want? I didn't have money, or powerful friends, or anything, really. Did he want access to the house? Was he hoping Walker would invest in his tech startup, and this was the easiest way to get to know the family? Or worse, did he have some sort of sick fascination with *Libby*? I thought back to all the times he'd made fun of her—had there been some sort of weird sexual passion underneath his disdain? It *was* really weird how intensely he claimed to dislike her, how her presence was always looming over our conversations. Was that disdain actually just a cover for unrequited lust? After all, he'd mentioned her age and her body more than once. He wasn't unaware of her physical presence. *Was I actually just some kind of pawn through which Owen hoped to get closer to the one he really wanted?*

I leaped up and bolted downstairs. I was going nuts. I needed to get out of there. I needed to get away from all of these normal college kids thinking about normal things like exams and drinking and hooking up. They were carefree in a way I couldn't really imagine being, not ever. I was going to call a cab; I wasn't about to ask Owen to drive me home, not after everything. For god's sake, maybe he was *dangerous*. I shivered and pulled my thin cardigan more tightly around my T-shirt. It was early November and beginning to get chilly. The sky was cloudy and there was a thick layer of fog adorning the road in front of me. Soon the heavy rains would start, as Libby had warned me they did every fall and winter. I wished I'd brought something warmer, but I'd assumed I'd be heading straight from the party to the car, that I'd be outside for all of two seconds.

I dialed 411 and had the operator connect me to the number for a car service. I was just dialing the car service when Owen jogged up.

"Hey! Annie!" he called out. "What's going on? I've been waiting for you for the past twenty minutes. I thought you ditched me for some other guy." He tried to crack a smile, but I could see through it to the confused hurt that lay underneath.

"You knew I was talking to Morgan," I said. "You had to have known she'd tell me about you and her sister."

Owen sighed. "I thought maybe she'd keep her mouth shut out of respect for your feelings," he said.

"What, so you could continue to manipulate me?"

"Annie," he said a little angrily, "how am I manipulating you? I dated her sister four years ago for, like, two seconds. Why would it have been worth mentioning? I didn't even know you and *this* Morgan were friends."

"I'm fine calling a cab," I told him, unwilling just yet to get into the rest of it. I wondered exactly how long "like two seconds" really was.

"It'll be close to eighty dollars from here! Just let me take you. Please." I eyed him suspiciously. It would be a lot easier to get a lift home with Owen. Was I angry enough to spend an entire day's paycheck on a cab?

"Okay," I said. "I'll let you take me. But I don't want to talk about this anymore, and I want to go straight home."

"Done."

When we pulled into the driveway, though, Owen fidgeted in his seat and turned the music down a little instead of cutting the engine. A light rain had started to fall, a prediction of what was to come.

"What?" I asked. "Is it something about Morgan?"

"No," Owen said slowly. "But there is something that I think I should talk to you about."

"Okay." I wondered if he was interested in someone else.

If he didn't want to date me anymore. If he were about to confirm my fears about Libby.

"I really didn't want to bring this up like this . . . after a night of fighting."

"Can you please just say it?" I asked. "It's really excruciating, the way you're dragging it out like this."

"Sorry," he said. He unbuckled his seatbelt and moved closer, grabbing my hand. "It's nothing bad. I mean, I think it's good news. Great news, actually. The thing is," he took a deep breath, as if he was nervous about whatever it was he was about to say. "I was recently contacted by a big investor who likes what I'm doing with the company."

"Okay," I responded, still dubious. "That's great."

"Yeah, it is," he agreed. "This is everything I've wanted for . . . I don't even know how long. This is really my chance to do something big. But . . . it would mean moving."

"Off Belvedere Island?" I asked.

"Out of San Francisco," he replied. "To Durham."

"North Carolina," I said flatly. "Congratulations."

"I thought you'd be happy for me."

"I am happy for you," I told him angrily. But the fact was, I felt like he'd just ripped my heart from my chest.

"It's not like we can't be together just because I'm not going to be leaping over fences to come to your rescue anymore," he told me, rubbing his thumb along my cheek. I didn't answer him. I was struggling not to cry. Just when I thought I really had something great, it was going to disappear.

"Babe," he said. "Don't be upset. Be happy for me, please? This doesn't need to be a bad thing for us. And it's not even for sure yet."

"How can it not be a bad thing?" I asked, before I could help myself. "I already barely have time to see you. I hardly have time to get out of the house!" I couldn't imagine taking a plane to Owen's for the weekend. Libby would never let me have that kind of time off. *At least he could come visit his parents*, I thought hopefully. *It's not like he'd have to stay at the Cohens' in order to visit me.* But I knew, deep inside, that this was what would happen: we'd keep in touch, and we'd see each other from time to time, and then it would fizzle out. We hadn't even had time to get to know each other, not really. We could never sustain a long-distance relationship.

"When do you leave?" I asked him. At least—I hoped—we could enjoy it while it lasted. Owen tightened his jaw, and when he answered, he was careful to avoid my eyes.

"I'm going out to meet the guy in three weeks," he said. "It would move pretty fast after that."

"Three weeks! Why are you only telling me now?"

"What did you want me to do, bring it up on our first date?"

"Maybe. Or maybe you should have realized that it was stupid to *have* a first date when you were about to change your entire life!" My voice was all choked up and I couldn't help it: the tears started spilling over onto my cheeks and the front of my white T-shirt.

"Wow," he said coldly. "I really thought you'd be happy for me. I thought maybe you even cared enough to want to support me, to give this a real shot." He was saying it, but in his words I heard something else. I heard that he was doing to me the same thing he did to Morgan's sister. Tossing me aside when he got tired of me and something better came along. At least Morgan had warned me.

"Cut it out," I told him. "Of course I'm happy for you. Stop trying to make me feel like the bad guy. I didn't plan for this. You, on the other hand, knew all along. But you pursued a relationship with me anyway."

"I honestly didn't think it would be that big of a deal," he told me.

"Well, it is. It is a big deal," I said, opening my car door. "It's a huge deal."

"I see that now," said Owen flatly. He looked up at me and I stood there next to the car for a second, avoiding eye contact.

"Good night," I finally said, slamming the door behind me and striding toward the Cohens' front door.

The second I slipped into the house, I knew something was wrong. It was one of those gut feelings you get. It was the same feeling I'd gotten the day I found Lissa floating facedown in the swimming pool.

I took off my shoes by the front door and walked quickly up the stairs toward my room, trying hard not to make any noise. As I got higher, I heard what sounded like Zoe crying faintly. I walked toward her room, and the crying intensified. I opened the door gently and went in.

"Sweetheart?" I asked, "It's me." Zoe's sobs had the tired, weary, hiccupping quality of a child who's been crying for a very long time. She was sitting up in bed, and through the glow of her nightlight I could see that her face was tear-streaked and blotchy. As soon as I sat down next to her, she threw her arms around my neck and sobbed into me, pressing her wet cheeks against mine.

"Zoe," I said. "Zoes, sweetie, calm down. What's the matter, honey?"

"I'm all alone," she said finally in little gasping breaths. "Where's Mommy?"

"She's here, sweetheart. She's just asleep." Stroking her hair gently, I wrapped her back up in her covers. I swung my legs up on the bed and lay down next to her. She nestled close, looking perfectly angelic with her little fists curled right up against her throat and one thumb in her mouth. And there we lay together, each of us lost in her own little world of night-mares until morning.

# CHAPTER EIGHTEEN

**"I HEARD YOU COME IN LAST NIGHT,"** Libby said over pancakes the next morning. Walker had made them, an unusual treat. Zoe was having hers with whipped cream and strawberries and powdered sugar, and it had formed a sticky mess that she'd managed to get in her hair and all over the front of her pajamas. I would normally have loved pancakes, but I had no appetite. Ever since the night before, it felt like a rock had settled permanently in my stomach. I glanced out the kitchen window toward the water and sighed inwardly. The weather matched my state of mind: mostly cloudy with a hint of gloom.

"You were back early; did something happen?"

"Not really," I mumbled. "It just wasn't that fun."

"Did Owen join you?"

"Yes," I told her, taking an enormous bite of pancake to forestall the conversation.

"Well, did it achieve its intended purpose? Do you feel unencumbered and rejuvenated?"

"It wasn't a spa trip, Libby," said Walker. "She probably feels hungover."

"I didn't really drink," I said. I glanced at Zoe to make sure she wasn't paying attention. She was doodling happily on her plastic tray, using whipped cream as finger paint. She was oblivious, but I still worried about what would sink in.

"So, has Owen asked you to be his girlfriend yet?"

"Do kids have those conversations these days?" Walker interrupted, as if I was closer to Zoe's age than his wife's.

"Yes! We do. I don't know. I mean, I don't know how it works. I thought I already was his girlfriend." I felt like I was going to cry. They both looked up at the tone of my voice, which had raised several octaves higher than I'd intended. Even Zoe looked clued-in, for once.

"Awe you okay, Annie?" she wanted to know.

"Yes, sweetie," I said. "Just having a sad morning."

"Oh," she said, looking troubled. "I having sad mowning, too," she decided.

"Nope," I said. "You're the happiest little girl. You don't have a say in the matter."

"All right," said Walker. "I think that's my cue. I'm sensing that this is going to be a lady talk." He walked his plate over to the sink, swatting Libby on the butt with his newspaper as he went. I had never seen a man be so unabashed about his manliness. I thought maybe it had something to do with him being from Texas. Then it occurred to me that I was probably stereotyping.

Libby brought her coffee mug over to the kitchen table and scooted her chair over by me. She reached out and placed her palm gently on my forearm. "Did he break up with you?" she asked softly. I felt myself responding physically to her concern: relaxing a little, leaning toward her.

"No," I said. "Not yet, at least. He's moving."

"Moving? Moving where?"

"Durham. What I can't figure out," I said, sniffling, "is why he would have started a relationship with me if this was a possibility all along."

"Well," Libby said in a maternal tone, "I know you'll be okay. You had to have known he wasn't going to live with his parents forever." Maybe I should have known it, but it honestly hadn't occurred to me. I hadn't quite gotten there yet. I had just been enjoying the feeling, hoping it lasted. "It's obvious what you have to do, of course," Libby said then.

"What?"

She raised her eyebrows, like she was shocked I'd even have to ask. "Break up with him. It's a no-brainer."

"I don't know," I said. "Maybe we could make it work." I'd been holding out hope; after all, isn't that what people were supposed to do when they found someone special? Make it work against all odds?

Libby leaned back in her chair, looking irritated. "Nanny," she said. "You absolutely have to break up with him. There are a myriad of reasons. First of all, you'll never be able to see him. Not with work and school. There's just no way. And long-distance relationships flat out don't work, unless there's a light at the end of the tunnel. But what are the odds that he'll move back onto Belvedere Island? None. Zero. Not unless he becomes insanely wealthy." I nodded in agreement, though I was a little surprised by the reference to her own wealth.

What she was saying, though, was what I'd already been thinking anyway. Although it would have been nice to hear her say she'd support me taking time off once in a while. *But you came out here to work*, the voice in my head said. *You can't blame her. Weekend visits to the boyfriend weren't in the job description.*

"But also," Libby continued, "you need to take control of the situation. You need to take a stand, to take the reins. It's the only thing that really works. Trust me. I've dated my fair share of men. I learned how to do it well. How do you think I wound up with Walker? I know how to manage men, and I know how to manage my own feelings. If he breaks up with you, it will take you months to get over it. Maybe longer. Because you'll feel like you weren't ready. But if you break up with him, you'll feel as though you had a say in what was happening. The end result is breaking up; it's going to happen anyway. Why wouldn't you want to do it on your own terms?"

I nodded. It all made sense. But the thought of actually *doing* it—ending things with him—made me sick to my stomach. I wasn't sure I could. Not without trying first.

"Annie, you have to," Libby said. "It's the right thing to do.

And you need to get it over with right away. The longer you wait, the more it'll hurt."

"Okay," I said. "I just want to take a day to process it, think it over a little."

Libby pushed her chair out from the table abruptly. "Do it how you want," she snapped. "It's not my business, just as long as you don't cry in bed all day when you're supposed to be watching my children."

"I didn't mean—"

"Never mind," she interrupted. "Really. I shouldn't have spoken up." It was obvious from her tone that I'd offended her by rejecting her advice. But I just didn't know if I was ready to do what she was suggesting.

As the day dragged on and I didn't hear from him—not one word, not even a text—I thought that maybe she had a point. The feeling of waiting was terrible. It was worse than I'd imagined. I compulsively checked my phone; I couldn't think about anything else. At least if I told him not to talk to me, I'd know what to expect. I'd have an active role in everything. I just needed to forget about the way he looked at me; the way he said my name, his voice soft and deep; the way I felt wrapped in his arms, like the tiniest, most delicate thing. Until I met Owen, I'd never in my life felt like I'd been taken care of.

I decided to do it that night, after the kids were in bed. I sent him a text: "Meet by mailboxes 2nite @ 11? I have 2 talk 2 u." Less than a minute later, I got his response: "K." Just, "K." Nothing else.

I'd be brave, braver than I'd ever been. And then I would

tell Libby in the morning, and she would be happy. I owed everything to Libby, I really did. Breaking up with Owen would bring us closer. It would show her that I trusted her advice. It would help repair some of the damage I'd caused with the small mistakes I seemed to make every day. And ultimately, it would be the best thing for me. I really believed that.

# CHAPTER NINETEEN

**BY TEN FIFTY,** I was getting anxious. Everyone was in bed, but I really didn't want to wake up Libby and Walker. I didn't want them wondering what I was doing out there so late at night. I would have waited, except I didn't know how long it would be before I'd have a chance to talk to Owen again. Besides, I wanted to beat him to the punch, like Libby said.

His figure blended into the darkness so much that I could barely make him out against the backdrop of trees and garbage cans. He was wearing a gray hoodie, and his back was facing me. He turned as he heard me approach; I couldn't read his expression.

"Hey," he said.

"Hey." We stood there awkwardly for a minute, neither of us sure what to do with our hands. I folded mine across my chest, he shoved his deep in his pockets.

"There's something we need to talk about," I said finally.

"Yeah. I figured there was a reason for this late-night rendez-vous, but I was kind of hoping I was wrong."

"Listen," I started, fighting to keep my voice steady. "I really care about you. You know that. But I'm really hurt by what's happening."

"With my move, you mean."

"Yeah." I bit my lip, waiting.

"Truthfully," he told me, "I think you're overreacting. I think this shouldn't be such a big deal, I think we could work it out. And I think you're being a little self-involved for making it such an issue, when really it could be something to celebrate."

"*I'm* being self-involved?" His words were like multiple punches that left me breathless. I felt dizzy, like my body was no longer an adequate support system for my emotions.

"Yeah," he said. "I didn't want to say it, but you are. And you know what? I'm not sure how I feel about that."

"Well, let me save you the trouble of figuring it out," I hissed. "I can't do it. I don't want any part of it. So you can go on and have your awesome, charmed life, in Durham, without me. Since you clearly know exactly what you want, and I clearly don't factor into it enough for it to make a difference."

"What are you *talking* about?" He raised his voice to nearly a yell. "Do you understand how delusional you sound? And also, we've only known each other for, what, two months? Did it occur to you that me confiding in you about it the second I found out shows *exactly* how much I care?"

When he finished, we were both shaking in anger. The

words *delusional* and *only two months* played on a continuous, ever-more-rapid loop until it all blended together in an amalgamation of hurt and anger. I couldn't hear anything else he was saying, just that.

"It doesn't matter," I said finally, mainly to fill the silence. "It really doesn't matter anymore. Because I can't do this." And then I walked away.

I spent the rest of the night in my room, crying. But no amount of crying made it any better. The pain was deep and aching, worse than anything I'd ever felt. Worse than any amount of physical pain I could imagine. I felt sick inside, and incredibly alone. I wanted Libby's arms around me, hugging me, telling me it would be okay, that in a little while I'd have someone like Walker, and none of this would matter at all.

**IT WAS NEARLY FOUR O'CLOCK** in the morning when I woke up, my eyes caked with sleep and tears. The light was off, but I had no memory of turning it off. I was asleep on top of my covers with my clothes on. I sat up in bed, blinking the sleep from my eyes. I felt disoriented and confused. I could have sworn I'd shut down my laptop before I'd gone to meet Owen, but there it was, shedding a dim blue glow over the room. I felt my pulse begin to race; it was clear that someone had been on the computer recently enough for the monitor to have roused from standby.

"Hello?" I whispered, every hair on my spine rising in fear. I wrapped my arms around my waist, feeling chilled by my nerves and the air that seeped in through the crack in my window, pre-winter air that gusted around the room and wound its way up my ankles and thighs like it was trying to consume me.

The window. Had I left it open? Had I cracked it as I sometimes did on warm nights? Then all my senses were on high alert. I stood frozen, eyes darting across the room, conducting an investigation as if independent from the rest of me. There was my journal, resting atop my bedside table. There was the clock, ticking away. And all the drawers to my bureau were closed tightly.

But had that painting been on my wall yesterday? The yellow wallpaper whirled around, highlighting it, forming a sort of spotlight for it. For a second I saw faces in the wallpaper. Grinning, crying, mocking me. All of a sudden I couldn't remember at all about the painting. It was just a generic sketch of a fishing boat docked to a wooden pier, choppy waters cresting in the background. It was entirely possible it had been there the night before, and the day before that; it looked like a painting I'd seen a million times. But something about it felt unfamiliar in the changing light of early dawn. And was the cabinet holding my jewelry, books, and TV just slightly ajar?

The computer monitor fell asleep, casting the room back into a murky gray darkness. I walked to the window and looked outside. The sun was beginning to rise over the water in the distance, and as I stared at the oranges that reflected out over the water, I began to feel safer. Calmer. It began to seem possible that I'd left my computer on, that my footsteps had jolted the table and the computer atop it, which had flashed to life. Nothing, after all, was on the screen. I checked the history, and the last entry was my e-mail account at five after ten the previous night. I must have cracked the window in the half-asleep state I'd been experiencing regularly since I started the exhausting task of babysitting Zoe. I decided to do one thing, just one thing to confirm that my room hadn't been tampered with.

I padded down the stairs and gently opened the door to Walker and Libby's wing. They had their own long hallway with several rooms branching off. I'd only been back there twice: the time Libby had given me her old clothing and the first day I'd arrived. On that first day, Libby had shown me around quickly before closing the door and informing me that there'd be virtually no reason to return to this end of the house. Zoe wasn't allowed; it was her parents' private space, their oasis from their married-with-children lives.

The hallway was carpeted, so I was able to slip noiselessly in. I just had to confirm that Libby was sleeping, that she hadn't woken up and snooped in my room. I knew I was taking a risk. There was no reason for her to snoop. But I was forgetting so many things lately, and my nerves were beginning to fray. I'd begun to feel anxious and high-strung. I had to know the extent of what was happening to me.

Libby's door was ajar. I peered in, my eyes adjusting slowly to the darkness of her room, which was more extreme than that of the hallway. All of her blinds were drawn. A strange, vine-gary smell permeated my nostrils. I took a step toward the massive bed, a king-sized, sleigh-style bed that rested in the center of the room as if on stage. It wasn't backed up against the wall; but then, the room was big enough for such an extravagant use of space. I could hear Libby's breathing, deep and slow. I moved closer. I felt compelled to see her. To prove to my brain that it was her in the bed, her sound asleep, her in the way that it could be no one else.

I stumbled into a pile of clothing. The smell grew worse as it shifted around, as if it had been burying something foul. Slowly, as my eyes adjusted more and more, I noticed similar mounds all around the room. Piles of clothes, plastic and paper wrappers balled up and discarded, makeup spilled on the vanity. There was the sour odor mixed with something rank and musty, like body odor. She was slovenly here, in the privacy of her own quarters, a space she believed no one else could see. When there's privacy, that's when you let your true self emerge.

Through it all, Libby breathed deeply, reassuring me that she'd been asleep the whole time. She wouldn't have had the chance to be in my room and get back here and fall into such a deep sleep otherwise. And why would she? She was my ally. Libby was all I had. She was everything to me.

Nevertheless, the knowledge wasn't enough. I crept closer to her bed until I was standing right above her sleeping form. I could see everything: the curve of her lashes, the rise and fall of her chest. The curly quality of her hair, let loose from its normal bun and falling into unkempt waves around her shoulders. I felt a kind of reverence overcome me as I did it. I imagined myself there, in her bed—not with her, not like that—but me there instead of her. For a second I saw my own sleeping form in that bed. I saw myself as Libby. With her life. Her husband. Her children.

I stared at Libby. I wasn't sure what compelled me to do it. But I stared at her in the darkness for a very long time before I went back to my bed.

# CHAPTER TWENTY

**IT WAS SUNDAY.** My official day off. If ever I deserved a real day off, it was now. The sun shone through my delicate gauze draperies, casting a friendly pattern on the floor. The night—everything that had happened after Owen—seemed like something I'd imagined.

What happened with Owen was different. Owen was raw and red and gaping and swollen. He was a wound that looked dubious, one that maybe would heal with care and time, or maybe would fester and worsen. I knew that in order for the former to come true, I had to drag myself out of bed. I had to take care of my wound, make it better before it worsened.

I was surprised to find that my clock read eleven o'clock. It was the first time I'd slept that late without someone coming in to wake me up. I wondered why they'd left me alone, if Libby had somehow intuited what had happened with Owen.

Every time I thought of him, I had to steady myself.

I pushed back my curtains and gazed into the backyard. My room overlooked the pool, the grass, and, beyond that, the water and the city. It was lovely. The island spread out on either side of the house like an unexplored wilderness. And Zoe and Walker and Libby and Jackson were all playing in the pool, which was now heated bathtub-warm so they could use it even in these pre-winter months. I watched Walker push little Jackson around in his baby inner tube, Zoe splashing in floaties nearby. Libby pulled herself out of the water and lay down on a lounge chair atop a towel, apparently content to let the sun absorb the moisture on her body. From afar, they were ever the picture of happiness. I badly wanted to go down and talk to Libby about what had happened the previous night with Owen. I felt like she deserved some of the credit for encouraging me to take that leap. And now, of all times, I needed her support. But all together, they looked like a unit. I would be an intrusion.

Even so, I had all kinds of pent up energy and emotions to expel. What had I done before, when I was upset about something? I had run. I used to run all the time. Anywhere, everywhere, all around Detroit, even through the bad areas, which just pushed me to run faster. But I'd been so constantly exhausted since I'd come to California that I hadn't thought about running even once. It had been such a big part of my life in Detroit that I was shocked I hadn't thought of it again until now. I grabbed my phone and looked at my text messages out of habit. Then I clicked over to the Internet before I could feel sorry for myself. In the Google search engine, I typed, "Belvedere Island hiking trails," and a list of results popped up. It looked like the closest hike was in the Muir Woods, seven miles away. Looking at photos of the woods made me extra-excited. There were gorgeous flowers in San Francisco—the California poppy, bright orange and welcoming; the crimson columbine, which looked like an upside-down star with a tiny blossom in the middle; the star lily, which looked like a cluster of snowflakes from afar; dozens of others in bright orange and purple hues that I couldn't name. Lissa had loved flowers, and these exotic species would have thrilled her.

I threw on my Lycra jogging pants and a tank top and sweatshirt, residual from my Detroit wardrobe, and ran down the steps. The hike was four and a half miles. It should take me just a little over two hours, if I kept it brisk. I dashed out the sliding door to the pool terrace just as Libby was about to step into the kitchen; we nearly collided.

"Oh!" I said, startled. "I'm sorry!"

Libby pressed a hand to her chest. "My god, Nanny. Be more careful next time, will you? Where are you going in such a rush? I'm glad you've come down, though. I thought you probably needed a good rest, but I could use a little help preparing lunch. What?" she asked, noticing my disappointed look. "Don't tell me you're meeting Owen."

"No." I shook my head. "We broke up. I broke up with him," I clarified. "Last night after I put Zoe to bed." I swallowed hard; it was really difficult to acknowledge it as reality and to believe that I had made the right choice.

"Oh, Annie," Libby said. "I'm so proud of you." She hugged me, then pulled back, gripping my shoulders and staring into my eyes. Her fingers were tight and talon-like on my shoulders. Her fingernails pressed hard into my skin, hard enough to leave bruises. "This was the right decision," she told me. "You'll find someone else in no time. You know, there was something I didn't like about him from the start. He always seemed a little cagey, like he had something he was hiding. . . ." As she rambled on, I erected an invisible shield all around me so the words would flow above and beyond, but never penetrate. I just couldn't handle it right then.

"You know," I interrupted, "I was hoping to have some time on my own, just to think. Do you mind if I take one of the cars over to that hiking trail in Muir Woods? I really want to go on a walk, and I'd love to see it."

"Absolutely," Libby said. "But don't you want to go somewhere closer? Why don't you just walk down by the water? It's so lovely right here. Besides, I might need you close today in case something comes up. Walker's busy preparing for his trip to Shanghai, and I could use the extra set of hands."

"I guess . . . I don't know, I guess I wanted to go somewhere a little more private," I told her. I needed this day off, for my sanity. And the truth was, I had always loved the woods. I loved how the trees closed in a canopy above me, so I was completely protected from the outside world. I'd only been on a few camping trips—once with school friends in Michigan, and once with my mom and Lissa long ago—but I remember feeling like I could spend forever in the forest. There'd been so much to see, and so many ways to get lost, but for some reason it had inspired comfort and happiness rather than fear. I wanted to feel that way again. On the shore at Belvedere, though, I could be seen by anybody in one of these houses. I'd be exposed, vulnerable. I didn't want that. I wanted walls. I wanted to wrap myself up in the trees and nestle down into the woods where I could feel like the only person there, like no one in the world could find me. But I couldn't say any of this to Libby.

"Don't be silly!" she insisted. "The bay is perfect for reflection and solitude. And it's so lovely. Why on earth would you want to go into the woods? It's filthy out there, and there are all kinds of bugs. What if you come back with ticks? Are you a hippie? Only druggies and hippies hang out in the woods, Nanny. I don't approve of the whole philosophy behind that way of life." She rummaged around in the cupboards, pulling out ingredients for the kids' lunches.

"I just really want to go on a hike," I said. "To see some nature." Libby emerged from the pantry, a jar of peanut butter in hand.

"What is this?" she asked, her voice cold.

"Peanut butter," I replied dumbly. I wasn't sure where she was going with it.

"Nanny, *why* would you bring peanut butter into our home? You know very well that Zoe's allergic!"

"I just thought—I didn't want to rely on you for food so much, and there are the safety locks on the cupboard—"

"I'm afraid you won't be able to borrow one of our cars

today," she said in a chilly tone, cutting me off. "It just isn't possible. We may need them. I suggest that you visit the beach if you'd like to get outside." Libby opened the trash under the sink and dropped the peanut butter in with a thud.

**WALKING ALONG THE BAY** a half hour later, I had the eerie sensation of being in the focus lens of a telescope. Waves crashed into the rocks that rose all around me, sending sprays of wet foam into the air. And the craggy hillsides certainly obscured some of the houses from view. Yet it felt as though everyone in the palatial homes surrounding the coast had trained their eyes on me. But why would they? I was so insignificant in their world.

Why did Libby have her eyes trained on me? There was something odd about the way she took an interest in me, the way she vacillated from concerned and caring to cold and disapproving. And the way my happiness in Marin County hinged on her approval wasn't right. I knew it. I wouldn't go as far as to call it pathological, but I had to get a grip, to form a social life outside of the Cohen family.

But how could I, when Libby had turned away the only girl I'd tried to bring home? When she'd encouraged me to break off the only real relationship I'd formed thus far? When I'd moved to Marin County, I'd thought I could have it all. I thought it would be a breeze in comparison to the worry and stress I'd felt over my mother's fate and my inability to break free of the poverty-clad binds that kept me tied to Detroit. But the truth was, being in California was no different. I was equally enslaved to my fate. It just happened to be a different life without choices. And as long as there were no choices, what did it matter where the insular sphere happened to be?

I knew I'd been emotional, overwrought, strung out. But how much of that had been me and how much had been Libby putting pressure on me? The more I thought about it, the more I suspected that I'd handled the Owen situation the wrong way. I should have put more thought into it, or at least waited until I'd calmed down. And now I'd ruined everything.

I moved away from the water, as close to the hill line as I could, in an attempt to conceal myself from any prying eyes. I took off my flip-flops and felt the sand sift over my toes. I rubbed its granules between my fingers, mostly just to assure myself that all of this was real. I was a real, rational, thinking person. And I knew in my heart that I had made a mistake.

I stood and began to walk back, feeling a new resolve. I'd apologize to Owen. I'd tell him I wanted to make it work, and that I was ready to support his business endeavors, no matter where they might take him. I'd set boundaries with Libby. I'd tell her what I wanted. I'd tell her that the yellow wallpaper needed to come down. And my door needed to go back up. And that I needed more than one day off in order to get through school. If only I could handle everything differently, all of it would get better. I needed to talk to Owen right away, though. I couldn't let any more time slip by.

I walked up the coast, back toward the house. Cutting up toward our lawn, I began to cross over toward the Oswalds'. I heard Izzy barking outside in the front yard as I approached from the back. I smiled to myself; Izzy had a strange way of normalizing everything. When I rounded the side of the house, Izzy and Owen were already outside. There was a car in the driveway, a red vintage convertible. I couldn't make out the driver, but it was obviously someone Izzy knew well; she had her paws up on the driver's side and was tucking her head over into the seat, where someone was reaching out to pet her.

Then the person turned off the car and opened the door. Out emerged the most beautiful girl I'd ever seen. She had long, tan legs and a tiny, athletic figure. Her blonde hair tumbled down her back in the kind of waves I'd always assumed had come from stylists, not nature. She was wearing low wedge heels and tiny red shorts with a loose-fitting white blouse. Bangles covered her wrists and large, black-framed sunglasses perched on her nose. She was too pretty for real life. She was even prettier than Libby.

Owen walked up to her and she leaped into his arms. She laced her hands behind his neck and gave him a huge kiss on the cheek. I paid attention to the way his arms were wrapped around her little waist, drawing her body closer to his. I froze. I was already halfway toward the front of the yard, on his side of the fence. If I turned back, they might see me. They might see me either way.

And then they did. *She* did. She nudged Owen and he turned. His face morphed from a happy grin to something carefully void of expression. I walked forward, placing one foot in front of the other, willing myself to endure the mortification simply because I had to. Izzy barked twice and ran up to me, covering me with kisses.

"Iz, stop," said Owen, clearly annoyed.

"Hi," the girl called out in a confused tone. "I'm Alexis."

"Annie," I said woodenly. I kept going, walking past Owen. I couldn't even entertain the thought of explaining to them why I was in his yard. Then I heard his footsteps behind me, and his hand was on my wrist.

"Annie," he said. "Annie . . . look. Just wait. I need to talk to you about some things."

"Sure seems like it," I muttered, trying not to cry.

"What? I—Annie, about Libby. About the Cohens."

"Owen, stop," I said a little too loudly. I looked behind him and saw his new girlfriend staring at me with wide eyes. "You've only made things harder," I told him. And then I turned from him and walked away. Whatever he had to say, it just wasn't worth it. Instead, I put one foot in front of the other one until I reached the house. Only then did I let the torrents of tears shake my body. I knelt on the floor of the foyer and sobbed until Libby found me there. Walker took Zoe from the room, and Libby put her arm around me.

"Nanny," Libby told me. "You're all right. I'm going to help you get better. Don't worry, you're all right. He's a smart guy, that Owen. He's a smart guy, but he doesn't know a thing about women. He's too smart for his own good." Her jaw clenched, and I leaned into her. I cried into her shoulder and it was muffled but violent. I was embarrassed. I couldn't help but look forward to Walker leaving on his business trip to China the following day. It would give me a chance to be with Libby, who cared about me. Walker was just a thing, an accessory I wanted to decorate my life with someday. Libby was a kindred spirit. A soul sister. She understood me without me having to explain. I cried and cried and cried into Libby's shoulder, because the person I cared about most had clearly been lost forever, and because Libby had been right all along. I could no longer trust myself and my confused psyche and twisted standards of what was right and healthy. I had to depend on Libby, and from now on, I would listen to everything she had to say. Finally I let her lead me to my room. The first thing I noticed was that my door had been replaced while I was gone. My door was back and everything would be okay again. Even so, I couldn't rest as Libby had suggested. I stared at the door for hours. It was my only protection from all the things that could hurt me.

# CHAPTER TWENTY-ONE

*EVEN BEFORE I KNEW what had happened, a feeling of dread consumed me, filling me up until I knew there was no other truth than that impending moment of horror. I stepped up onto the cheap, rickety deck of the aboveground pool. The water was still, serene. The pool looked peaceful, like nothing bad could ever happen there. If I focused on one spot in front of me, I could believe it.*

*If I ignored the lumpy, sagging form anchored by the far drain, I could believe that everything would be okay. If I could rewind to two hours ago and stop there forever, everything would be okay. So many "ifs."*

*I stepped closer because I had to. Her little hand reached out to me. She was long dead and still asking for help. Anyone could see she was way past saving. If only she'd been facedown. But she lay on her back just below the surface of the water, her eyes wide open and gaping, her mouth frozen in an expression of fear that I'd never seen before. It broke my heart. I only wanted her to die without experiencing that kind of fear. If she had to die, I wanted her to die innocent, free of any sense of the horror that could exist in this world.*

*Her hair was knotted in a big mass and tangled in the drain. She had fallen in, and then it had sucked her deeper. I wondered if she'd died screaming for help, if she'd believed I could save her up until the very last second before she lost consciousness.*

It was a dream, but it was also a memory. It was the kind of memory I fought to escape during the day. I hadn't experienced it so vividly at night since I'd moved to the Bay Area. I'd thought I was getting better, moving past my sister's death.

A frantic need to scratch my left shoulder pulled me more fully awake. The itch traveled down my thigh, my calf. I looked at my body: it was covered in red welts and vestiges of blood and raw skin from where I'd apparently been scratching all night. I couldn't stop itching. My fingers moved of their own accord, anxiously, as if eager to release the feelings I'd kept underneath for so long. My eyelashes were glued together where my tears had rendered my mascara a gooey, sticky pulp. I didn't remember scratching myself, but my legs were covered in red streaks beneath the hem of my cotton jersey skirt and there were bloody scabs, freshly congealed, on my arms. I looked under my fingernails and there were little flecks of it, red and black grime from dirt and skin and blood.

As I emerged from my haze, I remembered two things:

First, that Owen and I had broken up. Second, that before I'd dreamed about Lissa, I'd dreamed a million tiny worms with hooks were burrowing their way under my skin, threatening to change me into one of them. The memory of my dream made me itch more. I felt a tingling under spots on my right thigh and calf, both of my forearms, my neck. It spread and spread, the itch overwhelming my body until I felt as though my skin were on fire. For a brief second I imagined the worms were real, that my dream hadn't been a dream at all. That they were there, wriggling under my skin with their miniscule hooks, taking the *me* of me away and replacing it with Nanny, only Nanny. I swallowed hard to prevent myself from vomiting. I begged my fingers not to move. I thought if I could control them, I could control the sensations on my skin, too. But my fingers were aching to do more than just itch: the hollow feeling in my chest where all my love for Owen used to reside made me want to claw at my face. And the vivid reminder of Lissa made me want to shred my eyes. Physical pain was so much easier to bear.

It was the first time I'd called my feelings for Owen love— but why not? I cared for him as much as I'd ever cared for anybody. But maybe I wasn't capable of actual love. The one thing I couldn't trust after all of this was my gut.

My phone read eight o'clock. I eased out of bed carefully and padded toward Zoe's room, my head throbbing. Zoe was still asleep, her eyelids puffy and her hair a tangled mess. I smoothed her hair gently from her forehead and headed downstairs. The house was empty; there was no note. I knew Walker was now in Shanghai for a conference, but I didn't know what

Libby could be doing so early. I peeked out the back window at the pool; the water was unbroken. I helped myself to a cappuccino and hoped Zoe would stay asleep a while longer. My brain throbbed.

The kitchen was a mess. Libby rarely cleaned anything, but she rarely cooked either, so we ordered in a lot or ate whatever gourmet snacks she'd purchased. I'd grown accustomed to foie gras and salmon roe in the past months—it had been a bizarre and varied education, varied because for every pâté there was a carton of Goldfish crackers and hot dogs. Some days, I let Zoe design our menu.

*Maybe Libby had a solo binge,* I thought to myself, though I knew better. (Libby didn't eat.) There were open cheeses with huge chunks taken out of them and a slab of tenderloin doused in mushroom sauce. There were chocolate-covered strawberries with the bottom halves bitten off. It looked like the meat had been left out all night. A cluster of ants congregated atop it, drunk and drowning in excess. I hadn't noticed the mess when I came in last night, but I'd been so caught up in my own anxiety that it wasn't altogether surprising.

I walked to the coat closet and pulled out one of Libby's many cashmere "dusters," which were basically just long, fancy sweaters. I picked the red one. I wrapped it around me, enjoying the way its soft fibers brushed against my skin. I picked up my coffee in one hand and padded out to the front yard barefoot. It was a beautiful day. I wanted to sit in the sun awhile before I cleaned up the mess.

I wanted to sit in the sun forever. It warmed away the chill that had covered my skin since the night before, easing the intensity of the itchy rash that had wound its way over my arms and legs. There were welts now; I could see them. They'd popped up in mere moments. It was getting worse. I'd have to see a doctor once Libby came home. Sitting cross-legged on the lawn wasn't helping. I ran my fingers lightly over the spots the blades of grass had antagonized and prayed I'd have the strength to resist clawing at my skin. It was already looking so awful. Nothing was uglier than broken, diseased skin. Nothing was uglier than I was right then.

# CHAPTER TWENTY-TWO

**NEXT DOOR,** a curtain in Owen's room fluttered gently. I kept my eyes trained on his window, all aloof pretenses gone. I wanted him to see me. I imagined he'd come save me again. From what, I didn't know. I waited for his message in the window. I remembered the day he formed a heart with his hands and hoped for that all over again.

But it wasn't Owen's familiar face I saw outlined against the shadows of the window; it was a decidedly feminine bone structure with long, flowing hair. *Alexis.* It darted through my head, *Alexis*, just like that. *Alexis* so fast and so painful I couldn't keep it away. It wasn't her, it couldn't be her. *It wasn't Alexis.* He wouldn't do that, not so soon.

A truck pulled up, a mail truck. It stopped in the driveway. A man got out of the truck. He moved toward me on the grass like he wasn't sure what he was supposed to do. There was a mailbox right in front of him, but he looked at me like it was supposed to be my decision whether he dropped the mail there or not.

"It's okay," I told him from the grass. "You can drop the mail in the mailbox." He nodded and smiled just a little, and I smiled back at him reassuringly to let him know it really was okay, I hadn't just been saying that. He dropped the mail and got in his truck and drove away. And then I stood up and tried not to look at that face in the window. I looked anyway. But it was gone. I would call Owen when I got inside. I grabbed a handful of mail. One of the pieces of mail was addressed to Ms. Annie Phillips. It was from SFSU. I walked inside and put that letter in the trash without opening it and without really knowing why I didn't want to.

I picked up my cell phone and dialed Owen. It rang once, twice, three times . . . seven times . . . voicemail. *"You've reached Owen, leave a message at the beep. Beeeeep."* I called him again. I needed to know who Alexis was. I needed to know how he could do this to me. Seven rings and voicemail again.

I tried again.

Again.

Again.

I walked outside and his car was gone. They went away. I pictured them looking at his phone and laughing at my calls. Getting creeped out when I kept it up and then calling me a freak, a weirdo. *I don't know what I saw in her*, he'd say. And she'd say, *Yeah, and didn't she smell like the Goodwill bin?* I didn't feel jealous, exactly. What I felt was something more

complicated than that. I felt inferior. I felt like the little kid playing at having a boyfriend. And I felt like an idiot—how could
I have ever thought he'd be capable of falling for me when he
could have someone like her?

I couldn't turn off the sounds in my head, so I turned on
the iDock from where it was connected to Walk's iPod. The
sounds of Pearl Jam came through. I nodded along absently to
Pearl Jam and started to clean up. But I was ravenous. There
was a knife still on the counter, covered in steak juice and
mushroom sauce. I cut myself a long slab from the tenderloin
and picked it up with my fingers. I took a big bite out of it like
it was a slice of meat pizza, and I chewed. It was tender and
only a little dry on the outside from being out all night. It was
cooked medium rare, the way Libby always ordered steak. I
waved away a fly as the warm red juice trickled down my chin
and through my fingers. It was so, so good.

I reached for one of the cheeses. I didn't bother with a knife
because I was already so messy anyway. The cheese wrapper
was still there, crumpled next to the wedge. It read "taleggio." I
picked up the quarter-pound wedge and took a bite. Its flavors
blended with the steak in an unfavorable way. I picked up one
of the half-eaten chocolate-covered strawberries and ate that to
erase the bad tastes in my mouth.

When I finished my lunch, there wasn't a whole lot left to
clean except my own hands. I gave a quick wipe to the coun-
ters and gathered the trash into a neat pile on the counter to
push into the garbage bin. Finally, when I was done, I called
Owen again. He didn't answer.

Zoe still hadn't gotten out of bed, so I decided to take advantage of a good thing and get some more sleep myself. I walked upstairs and took off all my clothes but my underwear and tank top and crawled into bed. I knew I was falling asleep when the worms reappeared and began digging into my skin and I could no longer control my hands. They were their own species and could do as they pleased.

## "DO YOU CARE TO EXPLAIN THIS?"

Libby was standing over my bed, waving around a piece of paper, and for a minute I was sure I was still asleep and dreaming. Her face was beet red. I yawned and stretched and pulled myself up into a sitting position.

"Why are you yelling?" I didn't mean for it to sound whiny and petulant, but it did anyway.

"It's four in the afternoon, Nanny," said Libby. "Four in the afternoon on a work day, and my daughter is running about the house doing whatever she damn well pleases, because her nanny can't be bothered to wake her drunk self up to check on her!"

"I'm not drunk," I protested, still trying to work out the details of the scene in front of me.

"What you are is a failure," Libby said coldly.

"I got up to clean," I said, hating the sound of my trembling voice. "I cleaned the whole kitchen. I was only lying down for a nap."

"Wow," Libby said with an edge of sarcasm. "Thank you *so*

*much* for cleaning the disgusting mess you made in the first place!"

"What do you mean?" I was genuinely perplexed.

"Your mess. You must have ruined two hundred dollars worth of food last night. Easily. A bite here, a chunk there. Like you tore everything apart with your hands. It's disgusting."

"It wasn't me. I went to sleep early."

"It wasn't there when I went to bed at eleven."

"It wasn't me."

"Then tell me—who?"

"Stop it," I said, trying desperately to keep my voice even. "Stop trying to make me crazy." I put my hands over my ears. "La la la la la la la," I sang over and over.

"What is *wrong* with you?" shouted Libby, gripping my wrists and prying my hands away from my ears. But I kept on singing, just louder. Finally she slapped me.

The sting of the slap burned across my face. My face was on fire. I couldn't think of anything but the pain. I could think of only the heat I was sure was permanent, as though her hand had been tattooed across my face. The only thing I could hear was the panting sound of each of us coming down from our rage.

"I found this in the wastebasket," Libby finally said. "I think it couldn't have come at a better time. You need help, Nanny. Real help." She handed me the envelope from SFSU. She'd ripped it open, her nails tearing a jagged line down its center. It wasn't like her. Libby's mail was always opened straight, precisely, then stacked in neat piles. Her letter opener was sterling.

"Why did you open this?" My hands trembled. The shock of it spread down my spine to my entire body.

"Oh, don't act all sanctimonious," Libby snapped. "You went through our private belongings in the garage, for god's sake. I opened one measly letter. And thank goodness I did."

"What do you mean?" I was afraid. I didn't want to know what was in the letter.

"Open it. See for yourself." Libby crossed her arms over her chest and stared at me until I unfolded the letter and read its contents.

*Dear Ms. Phillips,* it started.

*Our records show that your attendance has been unsatisfactory for more than one of your courses. Your course administrators have corroborated as much. Your academic average, too, is just barely over passing. With only a few weeks left in the semester, you risk failure.*

*As it is our job to ensure that our students' financial and academic well-beings are in order, we are reaching out to you with your options. The dean of the School of Design has offered to defer you to next year's incoming freshman class. Your student record will be erased (though you will be reimbursed proportionate to your unfinished credits alone).*

*Your second option is to continue on with a strong risk of failure. Professor Meyers and Professor Malone have on separate occasions expressed concern. Each has now reported that*

*you would have to score 97 percent and 99 percent respectively
on your final exams in order to pass their courses. These high
scores, as I'm sure you know, are seldom achieved consistently
at a university level.*

*We are writing as your advisors and friends. We care about
each one of our students, and we trust that you will make the best
choice for you. Please do write us at studentadvisorboard@sfsu.com
if you have any questions. Call our front desk at 415-273-1192
to set up an appointment with an advisor, if necessary.*

*All best,*

*Dean Graham*

I leaned back on my pillow, not exactly breathless, because
I'd seen this coming. It was why I'd been afraid to open the letter in the first place. How could I possibly have passed when I'd
skipped over half my classes to babysit or because I was recov-
ering from something or other? I'd never had any real time to
study, either. I'd been a diligent and responsible student in high
school, but now I was overworked, overwrought, high-strung.

"So?" Libby wanted to know. "What are you going to do?
Walker appealed, you know. We got notice first."

"You got notice? Why?"

"Because we're writing tuition checks from here," she
snapped. "We registered as your emergency contacts, and this
is where the money comes from. Or did you forget that?"

I shook my head. It was true that they paid chunks of my
salary over to the school. I saw only a small portion of payment
for the work I was doing. But it was better that way. It allowed

me to manage my money instead of spending it before I could get around to paying tuition.

"How about a thank you," she said then. "I doubt they'd have been as lenient if Walker hadn't done something."

"Thank you," I whispered, and she walked over to sit next to me on the bed.

"Thank you, what?" she wanted to know.

"Thank you, Libby," I said in reply. Sure enough, she smiled wide and clasped my hands in hers.

"Just think, Nanny! You can put school on hold and act as an apprentice at my company! You can work more hours and put money aside in savings. It's going to be fabulous."

"You hate Zoe, don't you?" I cut in.

"What?"

"You hate your own daughter. You never ask about her. It's four P.M. right now and of course she's awake, but you probably don't even know where she is." Libby looked around nervously.

"Of course I don't hate her," she said firmly. "Why would you say such a terrible thing?" Libby's face went white. "You have no idea what you're talking about. You're even sicker than I thought. It is *your job* to watch Zoe, not mine. I have my hands full with the baby and my job. You know that."

"You don't love her," I whispered, my eyes welling with tears. "You don't care about her at all." Libby leaned close to me, gripping my jaw with one hand. I struggled to move away from her grasp, but she held me firmly. She forced me to look into her eyes.

"Stop transferring your own life onto hers," she hissed. Then she stood back up abruptly and strode toward the door. "Nanny," she said, turning back toward me, "I'm going to figure out what to do with you. We can't continue on like this. For now I want you to stay here. You're not well enough to be around the children." The threat hung in the space between us until she shut me in, imprisoning me in my yellow tomb. Just before the door swung shut, though, I saw little Zoe's frame hovering in the hallway behind Libby. She was sucking her thumb and staring sadly into my eyes. I couldn't tell how much she'd heard.

# CHAPTER TWENTY-THREE

**I HEARD A CLICK** after she left the room, but it was ten minutes before I could bring myself to check the door. She'd locked it from the outside, using the "mistake" lock that had accidentally been installed backward. I pounded on the door with my fist. It had to be a mistake. She couldn't—she wouldn't—keep me locked up here like a prisoner. It wasn't right. It was evil.

I pounded on the door until my fist ached. When that didn't work, I shouted her name over and over. I could no longer tell how much time had passed. She never came. Eventually I sank down to the floor with my back resting against the heavy wooden slab. The room was quiet; I could feel its walls closing in on me. I could hear the sound of my own breathing. I could feel a presence there with me, just outside the door.

"Zoe?" I whispered, shifting around to press my ear against the door. "Zoe, sweetie, are you there?" I heard a shuffling sound in response, and heaved a sigh of relief. My little girl had come to save me. "Zoe, honey? Can you open the door?" I waited five beats. Nothing. "Zo?" I tried again. "Sweetheart, don't be scared." I heard her moving again. I leaned my forehead against the doorframe and began to cry. "Please, sweetie. Please let Nanny out." I heard the doorknob turn. Looking up, I saw it trying to move and hitting something solid. "Zoe," I said. "It's the lock. Can you reach it? If you can reach it, Nanny will turn the knob." My question was met with silence again. I felt my blood course harder and my hands grow sweaty. I was beginning to panic. All she had to do was unlatch the lock. It was so simple.

"Zoe, please."

Then I heard the sound of footsteps in the corridor—the confident, quick footsteps of an adult.

"Zoe!" Libby's voice rang out high and horrified, as though she were appalled by Zoe's behavior. "What are you doing by Nanny's door? Get over here." Zoe's little footsteps pattered away as Libby hustled her downstairs. Then I heard her voice again.

"Don't try to get out, Nanny. I won't allow it. You'll stay in your room for as long as it takes for you to calm down."

"I am calm," I insisted, tears streaming down my face.

"You don't sound calm," Libby replied. "You sound rather upset. Almost like you're crying."

"I'm calm," I said again. "Please, Libby. Please let me out of here."

"Not until I feel you're no longer a danger to the children."

I burst into tears. "I would never hurt them," I insisted through my sobs. "Never."

"I know you would never hurt them *on purpose*, Nanny," Libby said softly. "But I can't trust you alone with them anymore. And I can't be everywhere at once. You'll stay there until we find someone who can help you."

"You're doing this on purpose," I said. It was a thought that had been simmering in the back of my mind for a long time, a thought I'd assumed was paranoid. Something I'd never allowed myself to acknowledge. But now I was giving it a voice.

"Keeping my family safe?" she said. "Of course I am."

"Trying to turn me crazy," I said. "But why, Libby? Why would you do that? What could you possibly gain?"

"You're being irrational," said Libby. "Just lie back down and go to sleep."

"Why would you paper my walls yellow? Because you saw my book," I said, answering my own question. "You knew it got into my head. You wanted to drive me insane."

"I'm not going to indulge this kind of talk," she said. I heard her footsteps recede down the hallway, and then I lost it.

I screamed, kicking the door with all my strength. I sobbed openly. I screamed harder, hoping it would get her attention. When it didn't, I pulled my hair so hard that it hurt. I liked the pain, because it was different from my heartbreak pain. I pulled hard and heard a ripping sound from my scalp. I looked down and saw a chunk of hair resting in my palm. I put my hand to my scalp and blood worked its way onto my fingertips, and the skin under my hair burned.

I wanted Owen so badly that I didn't know what to do. I wanted him back and I refused to believe that there wasn't a solution. I banged my fists against the door, and then I banged my head. I wanted him. I needed him back. The animal fury I felt made me want to press myself on his body one more time. It filled me with lust and rage and made me feel frenzied.

"Let me out!" I screamed. "Let me out of here!" I kicked and kicked and screamed until my throat was raw. Then I curled up on my bed, drawing my knees to my chest, and sucked on my thumb. The old nervous habit brought me comfort. I felt my eyelids drooping from the exhaustion of my emotional energy. Maybe Libby was right. Maybe I needed to fall asleep.

A VOICE WOKE ME UP; it was babbling nonsensically. It took me a minute to realize it was mine, and when I did I laughed aloud. The room was encased in yellow. I thought about the woman in my story, the story I had to read for Lit Sem, and I laughed some more. Libby had made me into that woman! She'd imprisoned me in the room of yellow. But in the story, the woman imprisons herself. She locks herself in. Had I actually done this to myself? No. I needed to get out. Libby couldn't get away with her lock and her yellow wallpaper and her calm voice that may as well have been made of knives, it was so lethal. I picked up my cell phone. I was surprised Libby had left it in here. I racked my brain for people who could help me.

*Owen. Morgan.* That was it. I had strained relations with both of them, but they were my only options. My cell phone showed no missed calls; Owen still hadn't called me back. But I didn't have a choice. I had no one. I was more alone now than I had been in Detroit.

*Ring, ring*, I thought, dialing his number with my right hand. I traced patterns on the wallpaper with my left. *Please ring.* Once again I had the eerie feeling that I'd been saying the words aloud without issuing the command to my brain. It was like there were two Nannies. *Nanny and Annie? Or Nanny and Nanny?* I'd started calling myself Nanny, I realized. How wonderful. Libby would be thrilled that I'd come around. There was no Annie, not really. She'd disappeared the day she agreed to be Nanny. Now Nanny was all she was. All I was. Now I was the Nanny who thought things and the Nanny who said things out loud. The Nanny who did things and the Nanny who forgot all about it the next day. The Nanny Libby loved and the one she loathed and locked up like a pet that had misbehaved.

I looked down at the phone in my hand. I had been listening to it ring for two minutes and fifty-five seconds. How many rings was that? Was it a ring every three seconds? Lots and lots of rings. It made me laugh. Owen wasn't going to pick up the phone. I tried Morgan. She didn't pick up either. I pictured Owen and Alexis sitting in his backyard, sipping Coronas by the pool, laughing together at how desperate I seemed. They didn't know I was locked in a yellow room. They wouldn't understand even if they knew. Owen was my only hope, and he wasn't picking up.

I tried Walker. I prayed his phone still worked in Shanghai. It rang once, twice . . .

"Annie?" His voice sounded distant, harried.

"Walker! Walker, thank god." The words tumbled out of my mouth, rolling into and over themselves. "Walker, you need to come back. You need to help me."

"Nanny, what is it? What's happened?" I was comforted by the surge of panic that decorated his otherwise groggy-sounding voice. "Is it the kids? Is someone hurt?"

"No, no!" I laughed. His concern was so comforting. Finally, someone who cared. "You need to come home and let me out of this *room,* Walk. Libby locked me in and—"

"She what?" His voice had gone flat.

"She locked me in the yellow wallpaper room. She won't let me out until I calm down. But I am calm. I need to get out! I need to get out of the yellow room right away! Come back, come let me out," I pleaded, my voice bordering on hysteria.

"The yellow room? Do you mean your bedroom?"

"Yes, she won't let me out." Now I was sobbing into the phone.

"But no one's hurt."

"No! But she's trying to make me crazy. Libby, she—"

"Annie," Walker started, his voice cold, "do you have any idea how much it costs for me to answer a phone call from America in China? *Any idea at all?*"

"No, I—"

"And do you have a clue how busy I am over here? And how early it is here? It's four A.M.!"

"I'm sorry, Walk, I was just desperate."

"Fuck," he mumbled to himself. I heard him take two deep

breaths. "Desperate isn't all you are. And don't call me 'Walk.' You need to start respecting boundaries. God, Annie, why do you think I came out here for so long? I jumped at the chance to get away from the constant drama at home. There's so much tension between you and Libby. I couldn't stand it anymore. I don't want this for myself. I want my family. A normal family."

"Boundaries? What do you mean?"

"Stop," he ordered. "Just stop acting so innocent. You know *exactly* what you're doing. Look," he started, "whatever is going on between you and Libby is between the two of you. *It's between the two of you.* Do you understand me? Leave me out of it." His voice had risen to a yell. He was furious. He didn't understand. He wasn't going to come back to save me.

"Yes, I understand."

"Good."

And then the line went dead.

I knelt on the floor, tears streaming down my face. Outside my window, the sun was shining brightly as if nothing at all was wrong. But here, things were black. How could the sun go on shining when Nanny was falling apart? How could the rest of the world keep moving when everything in the yellow room was black and still? There was literally no one left to ask for help. It was a bad feeling, knowing no one cared about Nanny.

I picked up the phone and dialed the only other number I knew by heart.

"Mom?" I said when a smoke-congested voice picked up. "Mom, it's Nanny."

"Who is this?" the voice snarled back. It sounded like a

bunch of gravel scraping together. "Mom? It's Nanny. Your daughter."

"I don't know no Nanny," the voice said. Then the phone went muffled and I heard a voice in the background asking who it was. "Some girl named Nanny," the gravel-voice said. "Must be a wrong number. Sorry," the voice said. "No one by the name of 'Mom' here. Better check that number you callin'." Then the line went dead.

It was my mother's voice. I was sure of it. It was Dean's voice in the background. I was sure of it. But I was sure of so many things that had turned out wrong. Why would they pretend they didn't know me? Why would my own mother do that to me? I wrapped up in my comforter, shivering violently. The only thing to do in times like these was sleep.

**"NANNY, DARLING,"** said the voice. It was soothing and warm and disembodied. It felt like the way hot chocolate smells, foggy and sugary and warm. "Nanny, wake up. I brought you your dinner."

I opened my eyes to a dimly lit room. It look me a minute to be sure my eyes were even open because the light was so dim. I startled when I saw to whom the voice belonged. She held a tray filled with a bowl of soup and a sliced-up pear. There was a glass of orange juice on the tray, and a pill.

"I just brought you some things, darling. To make you feel better." I stared at her warily, uncertain whether to trust her kindness.

"Does this mean I'm allowed out?"

"Oh, Nanny," she said as if I were a child being particularly silly. "Come on, darling. We can't let one little fight spoil things. We're sisters, after all. You're family now. Families go through hard times, but we always stick together." I nodded. I so much wanted to be part of the family.

"Zoe?" Libby called behind her. "Zoe, come give Nanny a kiss." Zoe peeked out from behind the door and eased into the room. She looked a little bit shy, which wasn't normal for her.

"Hi, Zoes," I said. "Thanks for coming to see me."

"Zoe, give Nanny a kiss," said Libby. Zoe shook her head vehemently. I couldn't help it; I let one tear slide down my cheek. "Look, Zoe, look how sad Nanny is. If you give her a kiss, she'll be all better." Zoe moved forward and climbed onto my bed, crawling toward me slowly. She was humming, as always, humming "Rockabye Baby" over and over. The closer she got to me, the louder she hummed it, until Libby began to wince.

"Just give her a kiss," she said through gritted teeth. "Quit that humming. You're giving Mommy a headache." But Zoe kept humming until she came right up next to my cheek. Then she did something unexpected. She sang the words to the song.

"Wockabye baby on the twee top, when the wind blows, the cwadle will wock." Then she kissed me on the cheek.

"Thank you, Zo-zo," I told her. "Thank you very much." She stared at me and, her eyes unwavering, climbed back down and wandered out of the room, still humming.

"I'm sorry," Libby said with a pained look. "I think she was a little frightened by your . . . outburst." I nodded, my eyelids already feeling heavy again. There was a ringing in my ears, and Nanny was saying *be wary of the soup*, but my stomach was growling and so I tuned out her voice.

"Nanny," Libby said gently, "I'm sorry I lost control earlier. I'm the grownup here, and I shouldn't have let my temper get the best of me. I want you to know that I've thought it over, and I know the best way to get you the help you need."

"What?" I asked. "What do I need?"

"Remember how I asked you to trust me, way back when you first started?" I nodded in response. She'd asked me always to trust her—said she would never lie to me no matter who else did. "Well, now is one of those times you'll need to put your faith in me, Nanny. Can you do that?" She reached out with one hand and stroked my hair, pushing the matted pieces back from my forehead. Her touch felt so cool and comforting on my hot, feverish face.

"Yes," I said. And I really believed it. "Take care of me. I just want someone to care for me."

"That's why I've made a decision," she said in that maple-butter voice. "You need more help than I can give you here, Nanny. You need to go to a place where there are loads of people who can help you. You will be safe, I promise. And we will all visit you until you're well again."

"Where are you taking me?" I asked. But inside, I had already said yes. It didn't matter where I went, so long as I wouldn't have to fight anymore.

"A very nice hospital called Richmond-Fost. You will have the best care there. We'll pay for it, Walker and I. And it doesn't even need to come out of your wages. You're lucky you have us, Nanny. We have enough money to get you the proper care."

"Will I come back to work someday?"

"Of course, darling. Someday when you're well." If there was a lie behind her words, I couldn't find it. She kept stroking my hair soothingly.

"I'm not sick," I protested feebly.

"You are, Nanny. But it's not your fault. All the things that happened to you in your life . . . they would make anyone fragile." She lingered on that last word, *fragile*, like she wanted me to really feel its implications.

"I don't think I'm fragile," I whispered weakly.

"But, darling, you are," she said sweetly. "You've been having such a hard time, haven't you?" Something in her voice made me want to agree with everything she said. I nodded in the direction of her voice, though I'd already leaned back against my pillows and closed my eyes again. Maybe she was right. Maybe I just needed someone to take care of me for a while.

"Eat this soup," Libby told me, "and take that Valium. It'll relax you. Tomorrow, we'll take care of everything." She rested the tray on the table next to my bedside and left the room. The door clicked behind her. I was too tired to check whether it was locked, and it didn't matter anymore anyway. Even if I left, I had nowhere to go. *It would be much easier*, I thought, *for Nanny to take the Valium.*

# CHAPTER TWENTY-FOUR

**ZOE AND JACKSON WERE STRAPPED** into their car seats, and my overnight bag was packed with the essentials. To hide the scratches on my body, I'd chosen to wear a long-sleeved black T-shirt. At the last minute, I'd grabbed the gorgeous sea-green-and-blue scarf I'd found in the garage and wound it around my neck. I figured Libby wouldn't notice; she had so many clothes and accessories that it would be impossible to remember them all. The Valium still hadn't worn off, so I was foggy and shaky as Libby led me from the yellow room out to the car. I felt a brief sense of ecstasy when I left the yellow room, followed immediately by a gaping emptiness. Once you've gotten past the thing that's plaguing you, then what? It occurred to me that I'd gotten so used to being unhappy that I didn't know how to be happy anymore. Or how not to be alone.

As I climbed into the car, I looked up toward Owen's room. Owen had briefly made me happy. He had infused me with hope. I thought I saw a shadow dart behind the window, and then the curtain drew back slightly. I turned away; I didn't want to see the girl's mocking profile again. I slid all the way into the back seat next to Zoe and shut the door behind me, refusing to look back. I wanted to be as close to Zoe as possible before I had to give her up.

"Everybody ready?" Libby asked cheerfully. I looked at Zoe, and she stared at me with eyes pensive as she hummed around her pruny thumb. I put my own thumb in my mouth and stared back in solidarity. Out of the corner of my eye, I saw Libby wince, so I laid my hand on my lap and clasped it in my other.

Zoe popped her thumb out of her mouth and appraised me seriously. "Thas Mommy's," she said with her baby lisp, reaching over to tug at the scarf I'd draped around my neck.

"I know, sweetie," I said, glancing at Libby for her reaction. "It was for throwaway, so I borrowed it. I hope you don't mind," I said. "It was in all those old boxes, and I forgot to ask."

"It's fine," Libby replied, frowning.

Zoe screwed her face up and began to cry—long, gasping sobs similar to the ones that accompanied her nightmares.

"*Quiet*, Zoe," Libby snapped. "She's just upset that you're leaving," she explained. "It's making her fussy."

"*No*," Zoe cried out. "No, NO!"

"Zoe, darling, be quiet." Libby smiled through gritted teeth, looking back at us through the rearview mirror and offering Nanny a reassuring smile.

But Nanny wasn't reassured. Nanny was afraid of going to the hospital and staying there forever. What if Libby never picked her up? *She will pick me up*, I reassured myself. *She loves me. She said we were like sisters.* That is what people said when they felt love and care. Nanny had to learn it, the actions that are associated with love—but Libby was teaching her. But what about the scariest thing? What if Nanny never got better?

I shook my head violently to clear my thoughts. I was increasingly thinking of the two voices in my head, more and more unable to merge them into one again, one whole person who was me. It was getting harder and harder to remember who was Annie and who was Nanny and which one spoke the loudest.

We reached the big hospital and I climbed out of the car, gripping my bag tightly. The gray cement building was large and imposing. Libby had explained on the way there that Richmond-Fost, the ward where I would be staying, was only part of a bigger hospital. I saw a patient being wheeled into the hospital in a wheelchair. He was gnarled and filthy-looking with scabs on his scalp. I hadn't thought about that—the kinds of people I would meet. I felt terror reach its hungry claws into me, burrowing deep.

"Wait," I said as Libby pulled Jackson from his car seat and locked the car behind her. "What about Zoe?"

"She'll be fine there," she said dismissively. "We'll only be gone a few minutes. I left the windows in the back cracked, if you're worried about that."

"No," I said, though I was. "I only want to say goodbye."

"I'm not sure a mental hospital is the best place for a little girl," Libby told me. It felt like a punch in the gut. The words "mental hospital" threatened to rip me apart. Before, I'd pictured it as a happy place to convalesce. Nanny thought it was like a meditation retreat, where the focus would be on clearing our mind. If it was a mental hospital, that meant . . .

"There will be a lot of very troubled people here, won't there?" I asked. I felt my body begin to shudder.

"Don't worry, darling," Libby said, popping her sunglasses on and striding toward the building. "You'll fit right in, I'm sure."

"Please," I called out after her. "Please just let me say goodbye to Zoes."

"Of course," she said finally. She strode over to where I was leaning up against the car and pressed the unlock button. "But make it fast."

"Sweetheart," I said, looking in at my girl. "I'm going to miss you very much." Zoe's face was tear-stained. She turned away from me, putting her thumb in her mouth and humming loudly.

"Nanny, we need to go," called Libby. "They're expecting us. And afterward I have a four o'clock meeting with a client that I can't be late for."

"Okay, Zo, we've gotta make this quick," I said. "This is the deal. You're going to give me a kiss and cut out that humming for a second, and we'll promise to see each other soon."

"*Cwadle will fall, down will come baby!*" She yelled the last part angrily, her faced flushed. "You'we going to leave me," she accused. "You won't come back."

"No," I said softly. "No, sweetheart. I'll be back, I promise." But I wasn't sure. It was starting to feel like it might take me a long time to get well again.

I felt a hand on my shoulder, nails digging into my shoulder blades.

"Nanny," Libby said. "I thought I made myself clear. You've had plenty of time for goodbyes. Come with me *now*." She pulled me away from the car with more strength than I realized she possessed in her thin body. I looked back at the car as we walked away. Zoe's eyes barely peeked out over the side where the titanium stopped and the glass of the windows began. She looked so small, so vulnerable.

**"YOU NEED TO SIGN HERE,** miss," said a tired-looking receptionist in the lobby of the fourth floor, which was where I'd be staying.

"Can't I have a look around first?" Beyond reception was a locked steel door with a narrow window. Through the window I saw an old woman walking slowly down the hall with the help of a metal walker, a trail of something wet oozing from beneath her left foot.

"I'm afraid we don't have time for that, Annie." Libby smiled broadly at the receptionist. "Just sign on the dotted line, and this will all be over."

"It'll all be over," I repeated faintly. I accepted the pen and watched its tip hover above the line I was about to sign. Phrases leaped out at me from the page: "legal recourse," "self-harm." I couldn't make sense of any of it; the Valium had rendered my brain useless. It was something thick and cloudy. It felt more like matter and less like neural impulses. I tried to read the first few lines in a systematic way, but I could feel Libby's impatient gaze bearing down on me, and so I signed.

"I can leave whenever I want, right?" I asked the nurse. She just smiled back as if she felt sorry for me.

"Can you please let Dr. Clarkson know we're here?" asked Libby with a broad smile. "He's expecting us."

"You know him?" I asked. "You know one of the doctors?"

"Only a little," Libby said. "I decorated his home. I knew enough to contact him to ask about the quality of this hospital. He was very kind. He's offered to keep an eye on you."

"First door on your left," the receptionist called out, hitting a button next to her glass-encased desk. "But drop your overnight bag in the tray next to the door. We'll need your scarf, jacket, shoes, and anything in your pockets, too, please. I did as she asked, unwinding the scarf from my neck with regret. It was the one thing that was making me feel normal and beautiful. As I lay it in the tray, carefully folding it next to my other belongings, I heard Libby sigh behind me.

"Hurry, Annie," she said with a note of barely concealed impatience in her voice. "What is it with you and that thing? It's not even that pretty." As I tucked it next to my overnight bag, I noticed a delicate purple embroidery near the hem of one end: ACE. Adele *something—maybe Elizabeth*—Cohen. The scarf wasn't Libby's at all. That explained a lot. I ran my thumb over the embroidery, feeling more unwilling than ever to part with it, until Libby snatched it from my hands and placed it in the tray.

"For god's sake," she said. "Come on, Annie." And then the metal doors swung open in front of us. Libby ushered me to the room the receptionist had indicated.

Dr. Clarkson was a short, slight man with pale skin, only a little older-looking than Libby but already starting to go bald. He looked like the kind of man whose ambitions had never been connected to this reality he now lived. He had a permanent frown-face that lit up only slightly at the sight of Libby. Libby gave him a tense hug.

"So this is the girl," he said, appraising me. "Did you give her the Valium?"

"I did," she told him, nodding quickly. Dr. Clarkson opened his mouth as if about to say something further, but Libby cut him off. "I should really be going now," she said. "I have an appointment."

"Won't you stay to talk a moment once she gets settled?" he asked plaintively. "To discuss her case, I mean."

"I really can't," Libby told him. "But feel free to call Walker if you have any questions."

Dr. Clarkson's face fell. "Very good," he said, clearing his throat. He finally turned to me and pressed a button on a panel to his left in one smooth motion. "Your name is Nanny, is it?" I looked at Libby, who nodded slightly toward me.

"Annie," I said, confused. "My name is Annie."

"Very good," he said again. "Miranda will escort you to your room." He nodded toward the door, where a woman in pink scrubs was waiting.

"Well, come on," she said without smiling.

"Goodbye, Nanny," Libby said, giving my shoulder a quick squeeze as I passed. "Everything will be fine, I promise."

"But I can leave when I'm better, right? And then I can come back?"

"We can talk about it when you're better," Libby said. "But that won't be for a long while. You're in a safe place now. As long as you stay here, everything will be okay."

"Yes," I agreed. "Everything will be okay." I was so tired. Maybe it wouldn't be bad to be taken care of for a while.

**"WHATCHOO STARING AT?"** my roommate, Millie, asked for the dozenth time. "Whatchoo staring at?" I'd tried looking away, facing the opposite wall, but I'd learned quickly that it didn't matter where I was really looking. Millie thought I was staring at her all the time. "Don't tell me you ain't staring," she insisted. "I see you stare. I see you stare, girl. You lookin' like you want something, I don't have somethin' for *you*."

The first day, I tried to talk to Dr. Clarkson about it. Libby hadn't mentioned a roommate, I'd explained. I didn't think I should have a roommate. I valued my privacy. I liked to be alone. I didn't like having people in my room at night. When Dr. Clarkson asked me why, I'd told him. I'd told him about Dean and how Dean almost came in my room a few times when I was a teenager, and how now it was hard to sleep if I thought I wasn't alone. And then Dr. Clarkson said, "I know all about your fears, Nanny." And, "Don't you think, Nanny, that it's better to confront your fears?"

But I wasn't like the rest of the patients at Richmond-Fost. Some of them didn't know where they were, couldn't tell the difference between the dog they used to love and the dirty hand towel in the washroom. I started thinking I didn't belong with these people. I was tired, sick, confused. But I wasn't crazy. All of it—Libby, the long hours, the lack of sleep—had switched around my brain so everything overlapped and nothing was clear and in its right drawers. I just had to have some time to rest, and I would sort it out.

I'd asked for my belongings, and they told me they were being held until I was released. In the meantime, they said, I'd be fine in the standard cotton uniform. There were only women on this ward. But a man snuck into the room the first night, maybe a male orderly, and I could hear him and Millie giggling and kissing and panting all night. I ran out of the room and told the night nurse and she sent me back in, said, "Stop causing trouble. Just go to sleep." But she did check to make sure both our doors were locked. The man was gone by the time she came to check. The next day, Millie scratched me so hard with her fingernails that I bled. I was sent to Dr. Clarkson. I told Dr. Clarkson the whole thing and he suggested that I hurt myself, that I'd made up the story of the night visitor as a manifestation of Dean and I'd scratched myself out of self-loathing. Because the hospital would never allow men in the ladies' rooms at night. He said I had a long way to go and I'd be better off making friends with Millie than alienating her. He gave me some medicine and told me I'd had enough settling in and I'd have to go to group classes the next day. I told him I was feeling better, asked him if I could leave, and Dr. Clarkson asked where I'd like to go. Would I go back with Libby? Would she take me back without me giving the program a real try? I realized then that I had to do it, to make myself stay. I had no other choice. And I was still so tired.

The medicine made me sick to my stomach and hazy in my head. Worse than the Valium. That just mostly made me sleepy, but the other medicine, the cluster of yellow and white pills, it made me somebody else. It made my tongue swell up like cotton balls and made me jittery. I started having thoughts I didn't normally have. I started wanting to smack Millie when she pointed and laughed, even though I knew she couldn't help herself and she would point and laugh at a blank wall if that's what happened to be in front of her. But all I felt was foggy with these bursts of violence. I wanted to tape Millie's mouth closed so she'd quit her hacking laughter. It was the medicine. The medicine was changing me, rewiring my brain. But what if I couldn't get back to normal? What if I stopped taking it and I stayed in an angry fog always?

I wanted to eat a lot, too. I wound up chewing on my fingernails a lot. That's what I did, sat and chewed on my fingernails and tried not to listen to Millie accuse me of looking at her and hearing her thoughts.

I wasn't sure anymore how much time had passed. I kept track of time for the first three days, and then I lost track. One

day I took my pills and fell asleep and woke up and wasn't
sure if it was still that same day or the next day.

**I HAD JUST COME BACK** from group therapy. Justin had
told us about his relationship with his brother. Cara had told us
about her relationship with her pocket knife. I'd been invited
to speak, but I'd refused. I had nothing to say. Millie was acting
as though she had something to say, though.

"You too skinny to know what it's like," she informed me.
"You don't even know. People think fat people, we hungry
all the time. Like we have some choice in the matter. Like we
choose to be fat. Like it's some sort of immature *decision-
making* process."

"You're not fat, Millie," I said. I immediately wished I hadn't.
Millie bared her teeth at me.

"You don't know I'm not fat," she snapped. "You can't see
into my head. You lookin' in my head again?" She eyed me
suspiciously from where I sat on the twin bed opposite hers. I
shook my head. I didn't have the strength. I didn't know how
Millie kept her energy up. My medicine made me want to sleep
all the time. But sometimes, like now, I couldn't. Zoe's face
mixed with Lissa's would flash in my head just as I was about to
nod off, or my inner voice would think anxious thoughts about
needing to keep myself locked up here forever.

Kayla, the day nurse, knocked on the door, interrupting
Millie's monologue. "Visitor, Nanny," she said. "Waiting in the
rec room." I felt a rush of adrenaline. Maybe it was Libby. I so
badly wanted to see her that I nearly cried. I'd tell her to bring

me home. I padded out of the room, forcing my eyes open as wide as I could make them go. They had been prone to drooping at half-mast. It was the medicine. But I didn't mind so much. I liked the rest. I liked passing my days in a haze of sleep. It all felt imaginary, and that was good.

"Jesus."

It took me a minute to register the shocked voice as Owen's. He was sitting in a plastic chair next to one of the tables. He'd unfolded a chess board and was playing with no partner. Playing against himself, it looked like. Owen was so healthy-looking. I almost cried seeing him there like that. He stood out like a splash of energy in the cold, listless room. He looked strong and alert; his eyes were open all the way and he wore a backward baseball cap, jeans, and a T-shirt. He looked normal the way none of us did at the hospital. I wondered if he would look as normal when he left. How long would it take him to turn into everyone else? That's what this hospital did. It made us all walking, talking, sluggish clones.

"I had no idea." His eyes looked watery, like he was trying not to cry. But maybe that was just my eyes. They were filmy. Every day when I woke up, I felt like I was looking through a shower curtain. "You don't belong here, Annie," he said quietly but intensely. "Why didn't you ask me for help?"

"I called you," I said. "But you didn't answer. And then I saw you with her. . . ."

"Who? Saw me with who?"

I thought hard. I couldn't remember. Then I felt a flash of pain.

"Alexis. You were laughing at me." Owen looked sick to his stomach. He gestured for me to take the chair across from him.

"Annie," he said, taking my hand, "Alexis is my cousin. She was staying with us that week. She'd come in from Rhode Island."

"Wow." I let it sink in, afraid of showing how happy I was. But he still hadn't explained a few things. "But what about the calls?" I asked. "You never called me back. I called you a million times."

"I swear I don't have any missed calls from you."

"That's crazy. I called you more times than I'm comfortable admitting. Everything just kind of fell apart, Owen. I didn't know what to do." I swallowed back my tears, but I couldn't control the shaking of my hands. And the temporary lucidity I felt in Owen's presence was starting to give way to the fog that had encompassed my days since I'd arrived and started taking medicine. "Just check my phone," I insisted. "We'll see your calls. They'll be on my phone." But as soon as I said it, I realized I didn't have my phone anymore. It had been confiscated.

"That's why I came, Annie," Owen said gently. "I think something really weird is going on with the Cohens."

"What do you mean?" I asked. "They've been so kind to me. Are they okay? I hope they're okay."

"Annie, listen to me." Owen's voice was low and urgent. "You don't belong here. I think they brought you here on purpose. *To keep you away.* Or at the very least to damage your credibility."

"No," I told him, pulling away from his grasp. "No, I need

to be here. I want to be here. They are very kind to be paying for my treatment. I couldn't afford it otherwise. Now I just need to get better so Libby will let me come back."

"Annie, look around you!" Owen said, gesturing to the patients who sat in various states around the room. Only a few looked alert. Several were dozing or staring blankly into space. One had a large spot of blood on the back of her gown.

"I'm not even sure they're paying for this place at all," Owen told me. "It's state-run. And if you came here willingly . . ."

"Libby knows Dr. Clarkson," I said faintly. "He's high up here."

"Annie, I went to the house looking for you. I saw you drive off with the overnight bag last week, and I got worried. So I went over there the next day, and Libby said you'd gone back home to be with your family. Why would she say that if she was planning to take you back? And then the next day I was walking Izzy, and Zoe was out in the front yard playing all by herself. I asked her if she knew where you were, and she just said 'hospital.' She wouldn't say anything else. She probably doesn't understand. So I called all the hospitals in the city until I found you. But when they told me what ward you were in . . . I couldn't believe it."

I'd started crying by then, silent sobs that I could barely feel. My tears traced patterns on my cheeks, forming little rivers and inlets that separated and met up again. They made me feel alive.

"Shhh," Owen said. "You've been through so much, baby. I

wish I'd known." I leaned into his shoulder for a blessed minute, enjoying the warmth of his body. I believed him.

"Ms. Phillips," Dr. Clarkson's voice connected with my ears at the same time as I registered his palm on my shoulder. "Visiting hours are over."

"But they end an hour from now," I protested.

"Sir," Dr. Clarkson said to Owen, "I need to ask you to leave now. You're causing a disturbance to the other patients."

"But—" I began again, quieting when Owen shot me a look.

"We understand," Owen said. "I'm sorry, sir."

Dr. Clarkson gave Owen a long look before nodding. "Just hurry and say your goodbyes," he said, shuffling off to another patient.

"We're not doing *anything*," I said to Owen. "What's his problem?"

"He's probably supposed to be watching out for you," Owen said. "Didn't you say he's the one who knows Libby? I'm serious, Annie, you need to trust me. I'm going to do some digging, figure out what the hell is going on in that house. Just stay strong. I'm going to figure everything out."

I nodded, feeling the weight of my anxieties lift a little.

He bent to kiss me one last time, and then he was gone.

# CHAPTER TWENTY-FIVE

**I WAITED FOR OWEN,** but he didn't come. I checked the visitors' registers so many times that Dr. Clarkson upped my anxiety medication, leaving me feeling even more lightheaded than before. Two or three days later, I woke with the kind of headache that felt like an axe splitting my skull. I thought maybe it was one of the migraines my mother got, the kind she promised me I'd one day inherit. I made an appointment with Dr. Clarkson.

"Tell me," he said in a benign tone, "when did your mother experience these headaches?" He was fiddling with a pen and jotting down some notes on his tablet. His legs were crossed at the knee like a woman's.

"I don't remember exactly." I reached back into my memories of my old life but came up empty-handed. "I think maybe after she'd been drinking, or when she was in a slump."

"Tell me what you mean by 'in a slump.'"

"Depressed. Feeling low, I guess."

Dr. Clarkson tapped the pen against his chin thoughtfully. "Would you say you're in a slump right now?" he asked.

"I don't know," I told him. "Maybe? Yes." I was confused. He was confusing me.

"What was your relationship with your mother like?" the doctor wanted to know.

"It was good at first. But then Lissa died, and she married Dean and started drinking a lot. So we didn't talk much anymore."

"You say Lissa died. Can you tell me more about Lissa?"

"She was my little sister," I told him.

"When and how did your sister die, Nanny?"

I took a deep breath. It was hard, saying all of this. I wasn't prepared for it. "She drowned in a swimming pool when she was six and I was fourteen," I told him. "So about four years ago."

"Uh-huh. And do you think that maybe being around a small child again triggered latent feelings about Lissa's death?"

"Maybe," I nodded. I felt the tears deep inside my chest, long before they made their way to my eyes. "Dr. Clarkson?" I asked. "Do you think we could talk about something else?"

"Okay, Annie. We can talk about this another time." I nodded, grateful.

"You know," I said, when I'd regained my composure. "I think . . . I think some of my recent . . . stress . . . I think it has to do with Libby. She puts a lot of pressure on me."

"I see," the doctor said. "Why do you think that is?"

"I don't know." I shrugged. "She has her own problems, I guess."

"Nothing to do with you? Could you have done anything to contribute to the relationship dynamic?"

I shook my head. But then I thought hard. I thought back to that day in the garage, and how Libby had stood up for me to Walker. But after that, her behavior had become erratic, not as kind and compassionate as before.

"There was a day," I mentioned. "I accidentally knocked over a box in their garage, and Walker thought I was snooping."

"And Mrs. Cohen? How did she react?"

"She seemed fine. She believed me when I said it was an accident. She defended me to Walker, actually. But after that, I think, is when things started getting weird."

"What were the contents of the box?" Dr. Clarkson asked. "Was it material of a sensitive nature?"

"I guess so," I agreed. "But I didn't really see anything."

"Nevertheless, I think this moment is something to keep in mind. Why don't we revisit it next time. But for now, let's take a moment for a relaxation exercise that might help you manage your nerves." He gestured toward my trembling hands. I hadn't even noticed them myself. "Think of a place that makes you feel happy and calm. Focus on it, and let the air drain out of your fingertips, until they feel limp and heavy. . . ."

I thought of the woods in Michigan where I'd gone with Lissa and my mom. I focused on that, but I couldn't keep the other thoughts from pushing their way into my consciousness. Something about what Dr. Clarkson had said was bothering me. I thought back to the will, to that day in the garage. I felt around in my brain for whatever it was that was fighting to emerge.

I shook my head. There was some connection I was fighting to make, but I couldn't do it. I couldn't get there. Dr. Clarkson's eyes met mine. He looked alarmed by my reaction.

I was starting to shake.

"Calm down, Annie," he said. "Try to focus on the meditation."

"I came in here for a headache, Doctor," I told him rudely. All I wanted was to get out of there, to be alone, to think. "Can you just give me some Excedrin and we'll call it a day?"

"I'd urge you to speak to me with more respect," he said coolly. "Your headache is a manifestation of larger problems. I think there are some serious truths you need to confront."

"What do you mean?" I felt light-headed, nauseated. I knew I wasn't going to like what he was about to say.

"Mrs. Cohen was kind enough to disclose everything about your recent behavior."

"Everything?" I asked. There was a rushing in my ears like an ocean, and the walls and the floors began to close in on me. I felt stifled, hot. "I'm fine," I insisted. "I'm just a little tired, that's all. I just need to rest a little and then I'll be fine." Dr. Clarkson peered down at me from over his glasses. He glanced back down at the chart in his hand. "What did she tell you?" I asked, my voice laced with horror.

"According to Mrs. Cohen, you were born in Detroit eighteen years ago. You lived in a low-income housing development."

He looked at me for confirmation, and I nodded. "Your father left when you were nine years old," he continued, "and Dean moved in when you were twelve. Your mother developed an alcohol addiction a year or two after your father left."

"Yes, that's right," I said. "And Lissa died when I was fourteen. She drowned in the swimming pool. I should have been watching her more closely."

"Yes," Dr. Clarkson said. "And when you came to California, your behavior was dangerous and erratic. You had violent outbursts and hallucinations. Probably PTSD."

"No," I whispered. "That isn't true. None of that is true."

"I'm afraid it is," the doctor told me. "I have no reason to doubt Mrs. Cohen, Annie. And quite frankly, your reaction now only corroborates her story."

**ELECTROSHOCK THERAPY** wasn't as bad as I thought. I thought it was this awful, painful thing, like being in a medieval torture chamber. I thought every minute of it would be seared into my memory, that I would relive it in seconds-long segments every night in my dreams. But when it was over, I didn't remember any of it. I remembered the anesthesia, the rubber stick they made me bite on, the gas they made me inhale . . . and then it was done, and I was being wheeled into the recovery area.

Dr. Clarkson said it would help my depression. He said it would help me remember things, and that I wouldn't have to do it very often. But then he gave me more medicine and all I felt was floppy, and I didn't care what they did with my body anymore. They could shock it or sedate it or drug it up and it wouldn't matter because I'd still be in the hospital, wrecked.

I sort of liked therapy. It made me feel like I was taking steps toward getting better. It also pushed me outside my brain a little. I was spending too much time in there, Dr. Clarkson said, and he said the migraines were like an invisible wall in my brain blocking me from seeing the memories I didn't want.

Sometimes I thought about leaving—checking myself out, just like that. But the thought of having nowhere to go was crippling. So I just kept taking one more day to rest, until all the days began to add up. All I wanted to do was see Owen again, or at least see Libby and ask her if she thought I was well enough to come back. But Libby never came to see me. Sometimes I wondered if I dreamed her and Zoe and Walker up. Sometimes I thought maybe Owen was just my fantasy. It was so hard to tell. It was like the world was condensed to this one long corridor, so anything that existed outside that corridor was probably fake, or at least couldn't be proven.

I could tick off the things I knew were real.

Dr. Clarkson was real. My ugly cotton drawstring pants and matching cotton tunic were real. Millie was real, and the way that creeper came in to see her at night was real, even if Dr. Clarkson said it wasn't. The mashed potatoes and fruit cup from lunch every day were real. The pills I placed on my tongue might have been magical because they were there, and then they weren't. They disappeared down inside me every day.

But everything else . . . I could no longer be sure. And I was starting to wonder why it mattered. The only one that mattered anymore was Owen. And there was Zoe. If something strange was going on at the Cohens', was Zoe safe? I couldn't think and I couldn't do anything about it without Owen, but he never came.

**"THERE, THERE,"** said Miranda, the weekend nurse. Miranda liked me, I could tell. She wiped a bit of something off the corner of my mouth with her napkin. "We'll braid your hair after lunch, won't that be nice?" I nodded, even though it hurt sometimes when she pulled the braids too tight. But it was nice to feel her fingers through my hair. No one touched me anymore. Only Miranda. She was nice. It was funny how nice it was to feel her hands in my hair. It made me think maybe human touch was really important.

Millie finally left last weekend. She told me she was going to go. She went out through the shower, with a razorblade. I didn't see it, but Miranda told me, and then my room was empty, which was a thing Miranda said should be celebrated. Miranda told me a lot of things she probably shouldn't have. She was like my undercover spy. That was why she offered to braid my hair that day—because she knew from the guest register that I was going to have a visitor. She didn't know who, but I thought maybe Owen. I thought Owen, but I secretly hoped for Libby.

I'd always wanted to be like Libby. I wanted her to come back and tell me she admired me, that I did something good. That I did a good job when I was her children's nanny. If she did that, I could be happy. Sometimes at night I got really,

really worried. I worried that since I no longer took care of Zoe, I wasn't Nanny anymore. If I wasn't Nanny, who was I? My thoughts were confused all the time. I thought it was mostly the medicine, but lots of times I couldn't be so sure.

Two hours were left until visiting time. There were so many things I wanted to do when I got out of the hospital. I wanted to finish school and marry Owen and have a huge beautiful corner office and five children just like Lissa and Zoe. I would take excellent care of them and they would love me and weave my hair into plaits.

Miranda helped me finish lunch and then sponged my face and body and helped me into a new set of ward scrubs. My muscles were weak because I was getting so much ECT and they gave me muscle relaxants almost every day. It got so I could barely walk around without leaning on the wall or a nurse. On weekends we got Nutella and pita chips for dessert after dinner. I loved that.

"Will she love me?" I asked Miranda. "Once she called me her sister. Do you think she'll want me to come back?"

"Maybe," said Miranda. "She'd be crazy not to." I could tell she was being nice, mostly. I laughed when she said "crazy."

Besides group therapy, I mostly slept. I slept a lot more than ever before. Maybe fifteen hours every day. Now that I didn't have a roommate, I could sleep without thinking someone was going to come bother my privacy.

There was a knock on my door. Miranda said, "Come in." It was Dr. Clarkson and he said, "Your visitor is waiting."

"You look pretty, love," Miranda said. "I hope it's your

283

Owen." I smiled and walked out after Dr. Clarkson, but he told me to quit smiling, I looked like an idiot, so I turned the corners of my mouth back down. I was crossing every finger I could that it was Libby come to take me home.

I was very surprised to find that it wasn't Libby and it wasn't Owen. It was Walker. Dr. Clarkson told me to sit down, and he told one of the other nurses, Caitlin, to bring me a blanket so I wouldn't shiver so much. It was very considerate. Walker was looking surprised to see me, even though he knew he would—after all, he was the one visiting *me*. But there was shock all over his face. It made him look like a puffer fish, and so I laughed. He smiled back, but it was only his lips, not his eyes. Miranda was showing me how to tell when a smile was real or not.

"Annie," he said. "Good god. But you've only been here six weeks." I laughed again, mostly because I didn't know what to say. Now I knew how long it had been, and I could start keeping track of time again! "What are they doing to you?" he whispered. Instead of answering, I reached out and touched his face. He jerked away. But I'd only wanted to touch his beard. He didn't have a beard when I saw him last. Now he had prickly hairs in all different colors all over his cheeks and chin and neck and upper lip. There were gray and brown and black hairs. He waved over the nurse, and he leaned toward her.

"How long has she been like this?" he asked her.

"About ten days. Some days are better," she said.

"Isn't there anything you can do so I can . . . get through to her?"

The nurse said she'd be right back. She came back with water and told Walker it was all she could give me.

"Annie," Walker said. "Can you hear me?"

I nodded. I could hear him fine, but I was getting really sleepy.

"Just try to focus. I need to tell you something."

"Okay," I said, nodding.

"I know this hasn't been easy for you," he said, running his hands over his face. "I just didn't realize when you called . . ." He trailed off, as if choosing his words carefully. "I didn't know how bad Libby had gotten. See, Annie, Libby's had it hard. She puts up a good front, but she's more fragile than you'd think. The thing is . . ." He took a deep breath, working up the courage to say this thing that was obviously a burden of some sort. "Libby used to work for me."

"Okay," I said again.

"She worked for me and Adele, my first wife. You might have noticed that Zoe and Libby have a somewhat strained relationship. That's because Zoe is Libby's adopted child. Adele was her mother. Zoe doesn't remember her mother—Libby and I have been raising her as if she is Libby's, for Zoe's own good. Later, of course, we'll explain everything. But there's always been a lot of tension between them."

"Tension," I repeated. "But Zoe's only a little girl."

"Zoe looks just like Adele did," he told me. "Adele was

beautiful." He paused, sniffing hard and wiping at his eyes roughly with the back of his hand. "But I had an affair with Libby, who was our nanny at the time. Zoe's nanny. I'm not proud of it, but Adele and I had hit a rough spot and . . . don't get me wrong, I shouldn't have done it. But I wasn't thinking clearly. Then Adele passed away—she never knew about the affair—and Libby stayed on to help with Zoe, and, well . . . we fell in love. We got married, had Jackson, and moved to San Francisco to start fresh. But Libby was very affected by the accident. She still feels very guilty about the affair. She thinks Adele suspected. She loved Adele; Adele was her mentor. It wasn't Libby's fault our marriage was crumbling. . . ."

"I didn't know Libby was your nanny."

"How could you know?"

I winced as a sharp ribbon of pain wound its way through my skull.

"In any case," Walker continued, "it all may have happened too quickly. I think Libby never quite got over Adele's death, or her part in our failing marriage. And she's paranoid. That's what happens when you have an affair. You stop trusting anyone. And she's very young. She has a lot of responsibility for someone so young—running a home and a business, raising two children, one of whom is a constant reminder of her old mentor.

"I thought if she chose you, if she managed you herself and I had no involvement, that it might restore some of her faith. But I can see that it hasn't done anything at all. She was pushing you hard, preying on your weaknesses. And I think she started to see you as some sort of threat." Walker looked down at his hands awkwardly. "But the fact is, Annie, you wouldn't be here if there weren't something to push. And you signed those papers yourself. Now that you're here, what happens next is up to you."

"Why are you telling me all of this?" I felt curiously empty. The story made sense, and really it wasn't much different from what I already suspected. But my mind was so unreliable now from all the medication that even as I comprehended what he was telling me, I realized I would probably forget again by the end of the day.

"I guess part of me wants you to know the truth," he said, "so you can realize that all of this hasn't been your fault. And the other part of me doesn't want to carry around the guilt of lying anymore."

"Okay," I said.

"Okay." He stood up to leave. "Take care of yourself, Annie."

"Walker?"

"Yeah?"

"Do you think I'll ever come back? To be your nanny, I mean?"

"I don't think so, Annie." I nodded, my eyes filling with tears. I couldn't be angry as I watched Walker walk out of the hospital and out of my life. That was the way things worked. But Libby had told me to trust her. I still wanted to, somehow. I felt bad for her. It would have been awful, what she'd gone through. Walker, too. Falling in love. Seeing everything crumble apart. Feeling they were to blame.

After Walker left, it was time for medicine and dinner. After dinner, we were allowed to watch a half hour of TV in the community rec room. *I Love Lucy* was on, and we all laughed and laughed when Lucy stomped around in the tub full of grapes. It made me think I wanted to feel grapes squish beneath my toes. I liked these good times at the hospital. Sometimes I felt close to other people here. Sometimes it got harder and harder to figure out if I didn't belong here with all the rest.

# CHAPTER TWENTY-SIX

**THE PROBLEM WAS,** at the hospital we all spent too much time in our heads. I had a new roommate for two days before she would talk. She was fifteen, committed by her parents. I thought it would be a relief from Millie, but it was worse. She stared with wide, silent eyes. Then when she finally said something—to ask for my hairbrush—she looked afraid. And she chewed on the handle of my hairbrush. She said she didn't, but when she gave it back the handle had bite marks. She was a nervous type, so I didn't press the issue.

I worried about this. I thought about that time a few months ago when I was a college student and thought I could have it all. But now I thought maybe this was who I was, and I shouldn't fight it.

The phone rang in the hallway, and it was Owen. All the girls hooted like it was some big deal that a guy called our communal phone. I said I didn't think it was any big deal, but then my palms got sweaty like they do, so maybe it really was.

"Hey," I said, waving away the women who clustered around me. Some of them didn't care, they were smoking cigarettes out the window and watching the TV. They didn't care about my love life.

"Hey," Owen said back. "How are you?"

"Okay," I said. "Tired mostly."

"I'm going to come by today to see you."

"Oh yeah?" I fingered my oily strands and wondered if I wanted him to see me. "I don't know," I told him. "I'm not sure I want you here."

"Why?"

"I can't have you see me like this."

"I saw you already, Annie. And it's not you. It's that place. As soon as you leave there—"

"But what happens then? I'll be alone. What will I do?"

"I found something out. Something that I need to tell you right away. And Annie, why would you be alone?"

"You're moving," I told him. It was so obvious. I was surprised he wasn't gone already.

"Oh god," he said, sounding tired. "You don't know yet."

"Don't know what?"

"I went to Durham," Owen told me. "And it was great, and they're willing to invest. But then I got back to San Francisco and had a call from another guy, someone who'd seen my work and heard about the Durham investment from my dad.

He offered to top it. As long as he can hold stock in the company. I'm staying in San Francisco, Annie."

"Staying . . ." It took me several moments to process what he was saying.

"Yes," he said. "It's perfect, don't you see? We can be together. I can be here for you, I can help you get better. But I thought you knew already. I texted you the second I found out."

"Oh god," I said, starting to weep from shock and happiness. "They took my cell phone. I don't have it anymore. Owen, I thought we were done. I thought I'd lost you." Owen burst into laughter. But it wasn't mocking. Instead, it was happy, relieved.

"Wow," he breathed. "Just . . . wow. No, Annie, I'm staying right here in San Francisco. You can come stay with me until you get things figured out. If you want to, that is," he said, suddenly shy.

"Want to?" I breathed. "Are you kidding? Owen, it's my *dream*. But maybe I do need help. They take care of me here. Do you really want to take responsibility for me? Until I can do it myself?"

"Annie, don't you realize what Libby wants? She wants you to become dependent on that place. She'd like you to stay there forever so you don't find out and expose the truth. So even if you do suspect, you won't be believed."

"What truth? Just tell me." I wound the cord around my wrist nervously. I wasn't sure what to expect from him. What he'd found out.

"I'm coming over there," he said. "It'll be easier in person. I'll see you soon."

I started worrying that he wouldn't come. I worried that his car would find a tree, or he would find another girl. I sat on my bed and tried to wait patiently, but it was too hard. I could tell that Aurora—that was my roommate's name, a name as fragile as she was—was getting scared. That was one thing I was learning about the hospital. I always had to worry about people's feelings. I had to worry about people noticing and reacting to the things I did.

"He'll come," Aurora said. "I know he will."

"What do you know?" I asked.

"You're telling me. You keep whispering, *Please let him come*. He'll be here, I feel it."

"Maybe." But I felt something else. I felt something very close to hope again, and that was something that reminded me of the life I'd had before I'd come to the hospital. And I felt everything balancing tenuously on a tightrope. If Owen didn't get here to tell me what he needed to tell me before someone stopped him, I'd fall. And there would be no more hope. Was it so crazy to think something might happen to him? The word *crazy* meant nothing to me anymore. Anything could happen, no one could be trusted, except maybe Owen. That's what I'd learned. When your definition of reality is fluid, the world expands in front of you. Was it crazy to think that if one thing fell in Owen's path on the way to the hospital, my future would be sealed? Maybe it was. That's why I was so afraid.

• • •

"**WHERE IS HE?**" I asked. "It's visiting hours and he was supposed to be here."

"I think Dr. Clarkson got him," Miranda said. "He pulled him into his office."

I strode out of my room and down the hallway. Miranda chased after me, making feeble overtures as if to stop me. I reached Dr. Clarkson's ever-locked office and pounded on the door. I knocked five, six times before he poked his head out. "Annie," he said. "You shouldn't be here. You know that."

"Where's Owen?"

"I'm not sure who you mean," he said. "I have a patient inside, filling out an intake form."

"I know he's in there," I said. "I know it's him."

"You know I don't entertain visitors," Dr. Clarkson said, his irritation palpable. "If you're expecting a visitor, I suggest you go to the recreation area." He shut the door in my face, and I heard it lock behind him with a click.

"Miranda," I said, "are you sure it was Owen?"

"Positive," she told me. "I saw him the last time he visited. I wouldn't mistake anyone for him."

"Why, Miranda?" I looked at her shrewdly, and she blushed in response.

My senses were on high alert. I hadn't gotten a good look into Dr. Clarkson's office, so I didn't know for sure whether he'd been telling the truth. I jogged the last few steps to the recreation area. There was Owen. Waiting for me, like he'd promised.

"Miranda, go away," I yelled. "Just go away. You're no help.

You're making me insane. You made my heart stop just now."
Miranda looked confused, even wounded, but she turned and
left the room.

"Owen," I said. "I'm so thankful. I thought you wouldn't
make it."

"Of course I'm here," he told me. "Now stay strong, Annie.
I'm going to tell you what I found out very quickly, because
it's awful. I need you to commit it to memory no matter what.
I need you to focus very carefully on everything I'm about
to say."

I struggled to do as he said, to center my mind. I looked
into his green orbs and let them hold me steady. "I'm listening,"
I told him.

"I did some research. I went to the library and dug up
what I could. And when I started finding stuff that didn't seem
right . . . I hacked into some police files and the Cohens' home
computer. I dug up some really serious stuff, Annie. The Cohens
lived in Pennsylvania before they moved to Marin County. But
Walker was married to a woman named Adele first. Zoe was his
daughter with Adele. And Libby was their nanny."

"Yeah, I already know all that. Walker had an affair with
Libby. And his wife died, and he and Libby got married and
had Jackson. Walker stopped by and explained everything. To
clear his guilty conscience, I guess."

Owen didn't bother to hide his surprise. "If you know all
this, why were you keeping it to yourself?" he asked.

"How will any of this help me? What does it matter?"

"Annie," Owen said. "You don't know everything. When I

was looking up birth and death records, I realized that Libby had Jackson just about six months after Adele died. Libby was pregnant *when Adele died*." I still wasn't seeing a point here.

"Okay," I said. "So they didn't exactly fall in love after the fact, like Walker said. But he didn't deny having the affair. He didn't seem to mind my knowing that. I still don't see what you're trying to say?"

"They lived in a house in the country, by a river," Owen told me. "Did Walker tell you how his first wife died?"

"No." I found myself dreading what Owen was about to say. I still felt squeamish about implicating Libby. I still cared about her, despite my efforts to hate her.

"Well, she drowned," Owen said. "Libby was there."

"That's awful. Poor Libby." I couldn't imagine how traumatic it would have been for Libby to see her employer drown and not be able to do anything about it. It explained why she was so fragile from time to time, why she always worried about being second-best to Adele.

"Annie, set your feelings for Libby aside for a second, okay? She's not who you think she is."

"Owen," I said, getting impatient. "I have no idea what you're getting at. Just say it."

"Don't you get it? Adele's death was not an accident."

I was getting angry and impatient. "Owen, what are you talking about? Stop accusing and just say something I can actually understand!" I'd started biting my fingernails, trying to make sense of it all.

"I'm sorry," he said. "It's just that I put it all together just yesterday, and I've gone over and over it, and I'm pretty sure it's foolproof. I'm just really excited, I guess. I just want you to get out of here." I glared at him silently, willing him to continue.

"So Libby told the police that Adele had been behaving strangely, that they'd just had a disagreement over laundry or something silly: Libby had accidentally ruined Adele's favorite silk dress. Libby didn't want Adele driving in such a state of anger, but she couldn't convince her to stay, or to leave Zoe behind. She was watching from the door as they drove away. Halfway down the driveway, a squirrel darted in front of the car. Adele swerved, lost control of the vehicle, and drove straight into the river. Libby ran after them, but she only managed to save Zoe, who wasn't fully strapped into her car seat. Libby was able to grab her easily, but Adele was trapped. In the end, Libby had to swim back to shore with Zoe, and by the time she got Zoe to safety, Adele had drowned."

"Oh god," I said, shocked. "That's so horrible. Thank god Zoe survived. But to see her mom die like that . . . poor baby. No wonder all the nightmares. I still don't get what this has to do with Libby being responsible, though. It seems like she was trying to help, if anything."

"Yeah, and that's basically how the papers painted it. One of the articles I read cast Adele as a totally neglectful mother, not properly strapping Zoe into the car seat and all. But Adele's cause of death wasn't drowning. Her heart gave out almost instantly from panic, even before she drowned, according to the coroner's report. Libby was regarded as a hero for dashing into the river to get Zoe. There were pictures of Walker embracing Libby and Zoe, almost like they were a family. He was so happy that his little girl was saved."

"So Libby saved Zoe, and Zoe watched her mom die. How awful." Suddenly Zoe's moody spells were making a lot of sense. Everything was falling into place.

"But, Annie, think," said Owen. "The will that you stumbled across. Walker stood to inherit a lot of money, and if Libby could get Walker to marry her, then so did she. I thought about that, and then I dug a little further. Apparently Adele left a note. The 'accident' was supposedly purposeful."

"Oh god. You're telling me it was suicide? But how did you get all of this information? The police reports and all?"

"You're forgetting that I'm an expert when it comes to computers," Owen said. "I can hack into almost any system. But, Annie, seriously. *Think hard.* You found the will. Libby started treating you differently. She convinced you to come to this hellhole to get you out of the way. *Libby killed Adele.* I'm sure of it. And she saved Zoe to secure Walker's loyalty. She was pregnant with his child. She wanted Adele out of the picture. And she had a motive. We *know* that. You discovered her motive! That's why you're here, Annie. It all makes sense."

"Owen!" I gasped. "It was an accident!"

"It's too weird," he said. "It doesn't add up. Unless Adele was suicidal, there's no way she'd have swerved all the way into the river. It was twenty yards from the road. I would've been willing to buy that maybe she *was* suicidal—her medical condition and all—if she hadn't brought Zoe with her. She wasn't a killer, and everything I found points to the fact that she adored Zoe. I thought it seemed a little too convenient, so I poked around on Libby's work computer. I was able to hack into her e-mail account. And I found something I'm pretty sure proves everything."

"What is it?" I whispered.

"Libby saved every piece of correspondence Walker ever sent her via e-mail. One of the letters said he wished things could be different—that if he had met Libby sooner, he would have married her instead of Adele. He thought Libby was his soul mate, but he didn't think he could break apart his family. And then Libby replied by saying she'd do whatever it took to be with him."

"But that isn't proof," I said. "What do you think she did?"

"I think she cut the brakes. That's my gut instinct. You're right, the letter isn't proof. But it's enough to spur an investigation. And even better"—he leaned forward, resting his arms on his thighs—"I found the car."

"What do you mean, you found it? This was ages ago! Where was it?"

"It's at a parts shop in Pennsylvania," he said. "Untouched. The investigation originally stalled, apparently because of the note—they found it the following day in her jewelry box. But the car was initially held as evidence. And as long as there's a chance for the case to open back up, the car has to be left alone."

"Oh my god," I said, putting my face in my hands. "Oh my

god, Owen. How could I have missed this? It makes so much sense—the will, the inheritance—but how could I have trusted her so much? I *loved* her, Owen! I thought she cared about me." I was shaking and crying then, and he wrapped his arms around me, holding me close.

"I know, baby. But it's not your fault. She's obviously a very, very messed up person. Maybe even a sociopath. She betrayed you. She lied." He spit the last words in disgust. "You couldn't have known, because you're not like that. You're a good person."

"She's a murderer," I whispered. "I've been living with a murderer all this time! What am I supposed to do, Owen? And, oh my god, the kids! What about Zoe and Jackson? They aren't safe in that house! We need to tell someone what's going on. What do we do?"

"Go to Clarkson, I guess. Is he the only option?"

"He's the one who runs the place. Do you think Walker knows?"

"I don't know," said Owen. "Nothing in the correspondence suggested he does. I think she's so twisted she played him as easily as she played you. Think about how far she's gone to drive you crazy, Annie. The door, the wallpaper, our breakup—for all we know, she's had a hand in everything that's come between us."

"I'm so sorry, Owen," I said, my eyes welling up. "I didn't mean to bring you into this. You're always saving me." My heart thudded madly at the implication of what he'd done for me: he'd uncovered a murderer on his own. He'd *wanted* to do it for me. He'd exposed the truth, and in doing so, he'd given me my future back.

"Annie?" Owen said, taking my hand. "Do you know how I feel about you?"

"I do now," I told him, bringing his fingers to my lips. "And I feel the same way. I've loved you all along."

# CHAPTER TWENTY-SEVEN

**"ANNIE, I'D LIKE TO SEE YOU** in my office." Dr. Clarkson's authoritative voice rang out across the hallway. Nine heads turned toward me, their eyes appraising me curiously. It was rare that Dr. Clarkson wanted to see patients outside of scheduled appointments. He disappeared again before I had a chance to stand. My heart thudded with expectation; he'd heard Owen's and my theory and had promised to check it out. That was more than a whole day ago. Twenty-seven hours with no word.

"Sit down." He gestured to the leather-backed chair, an unexpected luxury in the hospital, and waited until I got settled. I still felt nervous around Dr. Clarkson, even after our sessions. He had never put me at ease. "I had a private investigator look into your theory," he began, "and I have to admit I was skeptical. I've known Mrs. Cohen for a while and had believed her to be an exemplary individual." He crossed and uncrossed his legs and gritted his jaw as though he were about to say something distasteful. "However, even I can be a poor judge of character at times. Especially when it comes to master manipulators of Mrs. Cohen's variety."

"So you found something." I leaned forward in my chair, eager.

"Yes. It's almost as if she wanted to be caught. She wasn't very careful at all. The police opened up the case, and sure enough, the brakes in the former Mrs. Cohen's vehicle had been slashed. The police determined justified cause to search the house, and they seized both her computer and Mr. Cohen's. Libby's hard drive was riddled with allusions to the late Mrs. Cohen's murder. It seems she was fairly obsessed with Adele Cohen. Libby is in custody now, and there will be a trial. Naturally Mr. Cohen is devastated. The family is ruined. Those poor children." The news seemed distasteful to Dr. Clarkson. Rather than reacting as if a murderer was about to be put behind bars, he seemed to think Libby's arrest was somehow regrettable.

"As you know, you are able to leave the facility at any time. However, it is my recommendation that you remain here under my care. Frankly, Annie, I believe you must."

"No," I said, trying to prevent the smile from spreading across my face too quickly. The thought of freedom was dazzling. And terrifying. "No, I would like to leave."

"I thought as much. You may leave tomorrow at noon unless you inform me otherwise. You and I will meet tomorrow morning at nine o'clock as usual to discuss your medication and outpatient options. For now, you are free to take advantage of group therapy and say your goodbyes as you see fit."

I tried not to let his voice haunt me all the way back to my room, where I unearthed the outfit I'd arrived in from my cubby. I tried not to let it mirror the tiny seed of doubt that wondered if I was truly ready for the real world.

"Why are you pulling that out?" Aurora asked timidly. She was lying on her back, reading. Books were the only form of entertainment allowed from the outside. Aurora let me borrow from her stack of novels sometimes. She was eager to please. Her mother brought new ones every time she visited, and she was happy to share.

"I'm leaving tomorrow," I told her, trying to keep my voice even and quiet. "Don't tell anyone, okay?" I didn't want the others to know.

"Okay," she said dreamily.

"I'm not meant to be in here. I was never meant to be here in the first place."

"I know," she responded seriously. "Neither am I. Bring me McVittie's from the outside, okay? If we're not playing pretend, I mean."

"We're not playing anything," I snapped.

"We'll never forget you, you know."

I sighed, taking her hand in mine. It was frail and criss-crossed with scars. "I know," I told her. "I'm sorry I snapped. I'll bring you entire cartons of McVittie's, okay?" Aurora leaned over and gave me a kiss on the cheek so light, it could have been the brush of a feather.

**IT WAS EIGHT FIFTY-FOUR.** Just over three hours until I could leave. I only had to get through my appointment with Dr. Clarkson and bide my time until Owen arrived. It was only then, as I lay on my bed killing time, that I realized something so terrifying it made me turn on my side and gag, a series of painful dry heaves that felt endless. All the times Libby had told me she was behind me *despite my history* ran through my mind. I thought of the times she'd told me she'd checked out my background in advance and that we were two of a kind, she and I. And then I thought of the times she'd turned from Zoe's embraces, carelessly disregarding even her most pitiful needs. And how Zoe's bedroom was the only room in the house that was practically bare, completely free from Libby's designer touch.

*Why had Libby hired me? Why had she hired someone who had been indirectly responsible for a child's death?* The only plausible truth was so cold that I reeled from it, hardly able to believe it despite everything I knew now.

*Libby had wanted Zoe dead.* She'd wanted a perfect life with Walker and *her* baby, all traces of Adele eliminated. She'd wanted me to be held liable if an "accident" happened. It was the only thing that made sense. No one else would have hired me to watch their kids. No matter how much they believed I deserved a second chance.

I walked into Dr. Clarkson's office confidently. I hadn't

bothered to take my medication the night before. I wanted to be alert and ready to leave. But now I felt strange, like the whole world shifted when I moved my head too much. Like my brain was sloshing around in there and trying hard to keep up. But it was also like a sheet had been lifted from my eyes, erasing some of the fog.

"You're looking well today," he said dryly as I entered.

"I feel well," I said. He squinted at my eyes.

"Are you taking your proper dosage of medicine?" he wanted to know.

"I cut back a little," I admitted, glossing over the fact that I hadn't taken any the night before. "I figured I'd need to taper off."

"I see," he said. "Though I wish you'd have consulted me first. Stopping psychotropic drugs abruptly can often cause dangerous withdrawal symptoms. I'm going to go ahead and prescribe you a lower dose right now. I want you to take this dose once per day for another two weeks, just to make sure you do this safely. Can you promise me you'll do that?"

"Yes," I promised him. "I will."

"And Annie," he said, handing me a folded piece of paper. "Here are some numbers for fantastic psychologists in the area. If you return to school, you should be covered under a good insurance plan. I strongly urge you to contact one of these doctors. I think you should continue seeing someone after you leave Richmond-Fost."

"Why?" I asked, my voice guarded.

"You experienced a great tragedy at a young age," he said.

"That sort of event doesn't just disappear from someone's psyche once it's done its damage. You need to work through those feelings so you can heal properly. And, Annie, can I be frank?"

"Of course," I told him. I would have given him anything just then.

"Libby is clearly a master manipulator, and a very dangerous one. There's no question that she toyed with you, exploiting your weaknesses. But the fact remains, Annie, that you were able to be targeted. If you had been stronger, things may never have reached this point."

"Are you saying this could happen again?" I asked warily.

"Theoretically, yes. But is there a likelihood that you'll encounter another person as pathological as Libby in your life? I'd say the odds are slim. Nevertheless, you need to get well. These kinds of people are eerily adept at targeting victims. They recognize psychological vulnerability a mile away. So I need you to be careful. I need you to get well."

"Okay," I told him. "I'll make sure to see a doctor."

"At least once per week," he said firmly. I nodded in response. For the first time, I felt something like affection for Dr. Clarkson. Maybe he did care how I turned out. Maybe he wasn't so awful after all. Or maybe Libby was just that good: she'd been able to manipulate both of us.

"Tell me about your friend Owen," Dr. Clarkson prompted, just as I was about to dismiss myself.

"Well," I began, a question in my voice. "I trust him. I really do, and I don't think I've ever said that about anybody. I think he genuinely cares about me and wants to help me get my life together."

"I only ask because he hasn't really come up previously," Dr. Clarkson said. "And I want to make sure you're protecting yourself. That you're going to be with someone who can support you."

"I know," I said.

It had occurred to me that with Owen's support, I could reconnect with my mother. Maybe when I was well enough.

"Does Owen resemble anyone you know?" Dr. Clarkson persisted. "Your father, maybe? Try to remember back."

"No," I said, shifting around in my chair impatiently. "Why would he remind me of my father? I barely remember my father."

"I'm just suggesting that maybe Owen serves an important place in your life. Maybe he's your way of filling some sort of male void. You've been betrayed by men before, after all; maybe Owen is your subconscious's way of seeking out something you crave."

"Or the universe's way, I guess," I said skeptically. "But really, Owen is the most genuinely caring person I've ever met. You don't have to worry about him."

"Annie, I have to say, I'm pleased with your positive outlook. I think it bodes well for your recovery."

"Thanks, Dr. Clarkson," I said, standing up. It was time for me to get my things together. I felt strangely reluctant to leave, in a way. A little dose of fear had wended its way through my extremities. But I could do it. I was stronger now, I was sure of it. I knew to trust my instincts when I felt something wasn't entirely right.

"Be well," he said. "And keep in touch, if you'd like."

**I WALKED DOWN THE HALL** after signing my discharge papers, and I couldn't help noticing the faces that peered from their rooms as I passed through the stark hospital corridor. I was careful to take measured steps, not to seem too desperate. It was odd how now I had to focus on appearing especially normal, because what I'd become accustomed to, and where my instincts had led me for the past few months, were on the opposite end of the spectrum from that. I'd have to retrain myself. I realized then that the human brain is endlessly changing, its inner workings restructuring and recalibrating to form new systems of thought and feeling. Now I needed to realign myself with what was considered normal.

I never wanted to be one of those gaping faces again, myself. The problem was, I felt perilously close to crazy. Like I was just one of the many walking the tightrope between normal and not. How long could I continue walking the rope without tumbling down?

# CHAPTER TWENTY-EIGHT

**IT'S SUNDAY MORNING.** I wake up to Owen's sleep-face next to mine, his arm draped around my waist. He likes me to face him, even though I fit better the other way. Even asleep, he holds me like he'll never let me go. I trace his cheek stubble gently with my fingers. I love tracing his jaw, and I love when he feels it in his sleep and smiles just a little. His smile is my favorite thing. Waking up next to him will probably always feel like a miracle. Being safe will always feel like a gift, like something I don't really deserve but am incredibly lucky to have.

It's taken me a long time to feel comfortable with Owen, to stop waiting for the other shoe to drop. To know that I deserve happiness.

He stirs under my fingertips. His eyelashes flutter open to reveal the depth of his startling green eyes as they look into mine. I run my hands through his hair softly, and he smiles his adorably crooked grin. He has one tooth that's a little longer than the rest. He has a little bit of hair on his left shoulder. His earlobes are shaped slightly differently from each other. I take in all of these details because I can, because discovering the things about him that no one else sees is my favorite thing.

"Hey gorgeous," he says sleepily, leaning toward me for a kiss. He presses his lips against mine and pulls me close until I feel my naked skin pressing against the length of his. It's been months and months and my heart has never stopped speeding up at the touch of him. He teases me a little, touching my bottom lip lightly with his, then moving away again, playing a game that leaves me hungry.

We lie there for a while, kissing and talking, like we usually do on Sundays. It's my favorite time with him: when the afternoon stretches ahead and we have nothing to do but touch each other's bodies and look into each other's eyes and laugh and talk about things that only matter to the two of us.

Eventually we'll go out to brunch, because that's what we always do when our growling stomachs are painful enough to make us want to move from bed. We like to pick a different place each time. San Francisco has so many good places to eat. And today, I want Mexican food. I don't want breakfast at all. I want a carne asada burrito from El Tonayense. I know if I ask him, Owen will laugh and say it's okay with him. Everything that happened with Libby seems impossibly bleak now, and, contrasted with those six months, my new reality is heaven. I need to find my own place soon, but neither of us is in any particular rush.

I like to wander outside Owen's apartment without asking anyone's permission. I like to go to the hiking trails that stretch through the outskirts of town. Sometimes Owen comes with me, but sometimes I wander the trails by myself, wade through the creeks and cross the fallen trees that serve as bridges, just like I did with Lissa when we were little kids.

Once I finish getting dressed, we hop into his car, a sleek black convertible. Owen's business has taken off in the past year. "After burritos, let's go to Cups and Cakes," Owen suggests. "After all, this is a celebration." He reaches over and clasps my hand in his bigger, stronger one. I tense up despite myself at the word *celebration*. This morning, Libby was sentenced to life in prison for the murder of Adele Cohen. I guess it's something to celebrate, but I don't want to think about it at all.

"I really want to see Zoe," I tell Owen. All this time, he's urged me to wait until Libby's trial was wrapped up and things died down for Walker. But I've missed my little buddy. I hope she and Jackson are doing okay. She must be just about ready for preschool by now. Owen takes a left out of our neighborhood, and I realize we're going the long way. I can't help but smile slightly, despite my worry over the kids. I love driving past the townhouses that decorate the hills in little rows, and Owen knows it.

"Soon," he said. "Don't worry. We'll go visit. Let's just give them a little time to get over the shock of the news, okay?"

"Okay," I agree. "Owen," I add, "we have another thing to celebrate."

"What's that?" He grins over at me, his green eyes sparkling as we speed down the highway, the San Francisco Bay flashing on our left, just the way I always imagined it would.

"My course catalogs came today. I'm almost ready to register." I'd taken the rest of the year off as I sought intensive therapy with a doctor Owen helped me find. I'm excited to go back to school. It will complete my transition to "normal." And then I'll visit Dr. Clarkson in person, let him see what a success story I am, how far I've come. How I'm not a victim anymore.

"That's great, babe," he says, although I can see his brow creasing with worry. I know he's concerned about what the pressures of school might do to me, now that I've just gotten back to a place that feels really safe. "Let's look at it together later, okay?" I nod, a little annoyed, and he senses it.

"I'm sorry, Annie," he tells me, bringing my fingertips to his lips. "I'm just worried about you. But you're right, we have so much to look forward to." He turns and smiles at me, and I settle back into my seat, leaning my head against the headrest. He understands why it's important for me to start over, why I need an entirely new life. He worries, but he knows. We'll look through the courses together, he said, and I know we will. Owen never makes empty promises. But for now, I'll just enjoy the drive until we get our burritos. Besides, I'm feeling a little tired, and I could stand to rest my eyes.

I gaze at the sky, my head leaning against the warm leather of the seat cushion. I think about my second chance, the future I have to make for myself. I'm determined to have it this time. I know I can have the life I want, as long as I am strong. I think about this as I let Owen's hand caress mine, let my eyelids droop closed. I am so profoundly exhausted that I miss my favorite part of the drive: watching the California coastline zip by. *I always wanted to see the California coastline*, I think dreamily. But I can't seem to find the strength within myself to open my eyes just now. It doesn't matter, I decide, giving in to the weight of my eyes. The California coastline can wait. It'll be here, and I'll be here too, no matter what.

# ACKNOWLEDGMENTS:

**THANK YOU TO MY FRIENDS,** family, and colleagues. As I started writing these thank-yous, I realized exactly how lucky I've been to have all of you in my life.

Caroline Donofrio: My editor, confidante, friend, and fellow troublemaker. You have been a gift whom I couldn't do without. I have so much respect for you as an editor and human being. I'm so glad you came to Razorbill to guide me through this process as well as the process of daily life. You are another person who understands the value of living a good story.

Jocelyn Davies: I didn't know, when I received that first e-mail you sent me in India with all its clever quips, that it would be the first of thousands of such e-mails, phone calls, texts, and conversations that define the sort of friendship that lasts forever. You are responsible for the initial conception of this novel, and for so many other nuggets of brilliance (and melodrama) that have inspired me. I love you!

Laura Bernier: I hope one day I can show you the friendship you've shown me. The year of writing *The Ruining* has been a turning point. Your constant support and guidance have been invaluable. You are a rare person whom I respect and value more than I can express.

Ben Schrank: Thank you for choosing to publish this oft-weird novel, bearing with me during difficult times, and being generally hilarious and inspiring. I have learned a great deal from you.

Josh and Tracey Adams: For caring about managing my career, but also for believing in me as a person.

Louis Berger: For Z(Izzy) and canned sardines, and for being a wonderful first reader and friend. Happy Birthday!

Jess Rothenberg: For letting me camp out on your sofa for (almost) forty-eight straight hours and providing me with a plethora of delicious treats while we both raced to meet deadlines. And for giving me the courage to be braver than I'd ever been (you know what I'm talking about) when I most needed it.

Mom and Dad: Thanks for offering suggestions, tiny and large. I'm sorry for rejecting most of them in a huff. I lucked out in the parent department, and although I don't often say it, I hope you intuit my gratitude from my very vague and subtle actions. You have surprised me (unfairly—I should never have been surprised) with your unwavering support. You never surprised me with your love, but I will no longer take it for granted.

Mandi Dillinger: Indirectly, you inspired this novel. That's because you're the craziest lady I know. Just kidding. You're one friend I'm certain of, because you rented a Zipcar and welcomed me and all my belongings and my dog into your home when I was homeless. And because you laugh at the stuff other people raise eyebrows at. And you've dealt with my mood swings, and you've poured low-budget wine into me when I lost my kitten, and you sat in the veterinarian's office when it looked like my dog might need major surgery, and you met me in that sketchy park on Christopher Street and sold me drugs (for those who don't know: this is grossly exaggerated). And you've sent me dozens of cards with your adorable backward *y*'s. You've been a better friend to me than I to you—and you've tolerated my months of absences due to writing deadlines—and I swear I'll make every effort to make up for it. Knowing you, I'll be constantly in your debt. You are most certainly my partner in crime (literal crime—Grey Goose incident of '06).

Kourtney Bitterly: I've canceled on you to hit writing deadlines, I missed L.A. because I was waiting on my next book check, I stopped contributing regularly to our blog because I couldn't fit it in, I generally have been a pathetic, stick-in-the-mud friend—and yet you've stuck by me. Not only that, you're one of the most adventuresome, creative, fun, and inspiring individuals I know. I think it was fate that brought us together in New York. Here's to our California trip and many more.

Jackie Resnick: I look forward to our writing dates at Building on Bond, and our writing dates in your backyard, and our wine-fueled confessionals, and everything else. Here's to SMEF and margarita pong and staying in Brooklyn forever, preferably always within a short walk of one another.

Margot, Samantha, Madeleine, Alexander, Sydney, and Reagan: I love you cutie-pies so much. You are brilliant delights. You were all inspiration for Zoe in one way or another (I did my very best), and you're my favorite little readers. I'm the luckiest aunt. I can't wait to continue to watch you grow up.

Chris, David, and Alex: Because I want you to feel obligated to read my book, and I'm in a generous mood. Also: I love having brothers, and I love that they wound up being the three of you.

Wendy, Adelaide, and Amy: The most supportive room-mates I could have had while getting back on my feet in NYC. I will miss you so much! I will miss splitting wine and talking about men, I will miss swapping clothes, and I will miss shielding Amy from small children, old ladies, and delivery boys. This will be a sad parting, but not a permanent one. (Ad, I will come see you compete in the Olympics one day soon!)

Mochi/Pumpkin-Butt/Cheeser: For chewing sticks like a good dog, and for loving me unconditionally despite my myriad of dog-mom, negligent faults. For snuggling after I return from bad dates, allowing me to style your toupee with hair gel, tripping over your own ears, and fighting other dogs when they threaten my personal space. And for grabbing that dishrag every morning.

Pam McElroy: For agreeing to read/fact-check this novel upon seeing me for the first time in three years, then agreeing for the second time and doing such a good job of it. You were responsible for putting my mind completely at ease.

Mike O'Reilley and Andrew Bartlett: For an accurate or semi-accurate description of San Francisco as you saw it. Thank you for providing me with essential world-building information the night before my draft was due, at Loki Lounge in Brooklyn, completely by surprise. The best developments are usually those that are unexpected.